"I have often wondered how a man of your notoriety seduced women."

Addie waved a hand in front of her face as if to cool off. "You are indeed very good at it." She was very careful not to let her gaze drift downward. The top half of his body was devastating enough.

Guy chuckled, quite enjoying the hunt. "But not good enough to draw you to my bed?"

"Precisely. I hope you are now convinced of that. Why I am here has nothing to do with...promiscuity. I came to give you a warning. Never again ignore my request. When I want your presence at the house, you will come immediately. Also, you are never again to say one uncomplimentary thing about me."

Guy stared at her in disbelief. "You're threatening me?"

"I most certainly am. And last, but certainly not least, you are never to touch me again!"

Dear Reader,

Since her first book, *Bittersweet,* was published by Harlequin Historicals in 1987, DeLoras Scott's popularity has been growing with every entertaining story. With *Addie's Lament,* Ms. Scott returns to her tried-and-true combination of a feisty heroine and a hero who is a little full of himself in this engaging tale of a young woman who has always dreamed of bettering herself and the man who somehow always seems to manage to get in her way. Don't miss this delightful story featured as this month's Women of the West title.

And from Nina Beaumont comes her fifth historical, *Tapestry of Dreams,* set against the rich backdrop of nineteenth-century Europe. In this dramatic sequel to her previous work, a gifted nurse joins a former soldier on a dangerous journey to right the wrongs of his past. Be sure to keep an eye out for this passionate tale of danger and desire.

Also this month are *Once a Maverick,* the first in an exciting Western trilogy from Theresa Michaels featuring the Kincaid brothers, and a medieval tale from Merline Lovelace, *His Lady's Ransom,* the story of a nobleman who tries to discourage his brother's infatuation with a notorious widow. And don't miss either Theresa Michaels or Merline Lovelace in our August short-story collection, RENEGADES, featuring *New York Times* bestselling author Heather Graham Pozzessere.

Whatever your taste in historical reading, we hope you'll enjoy all four titles, available wherever Harlequin Historicals are sold.

Sincerely,

Tracy Farrell
Senior Editor

Please address questions and book requests to:
Harlequin Reader Service
U.S.: 3010 Walden Ave., P.O. Box 1325, Buffalo, NY 14269
Canadian: P.O. Box 609, Fort Erie, Ont. L2A 5X3

DeLORAS SCOTT

Addie's Lament

Harlequin Books

TORONTO • NEW YORK • LONDON
AMSTERDAM • PARIS • SYDNEY • HAMBURG
STOCKHOLM • ATHENS • TOKYO • MILAN
MADRID • WARSAW • BUDAPEST • AUCKLAND

ISBN 0-373-28877-8

ADDIE'S LAMENT

Books by DeLoras Scott

Harlequin Historicals

Bittersweet #12
Fire and Ice #42
The Miss and the Maverick #52
Rogue's Honor #123
Springtown #151
Garters and Spurs #179
Spitfire #204
Timeless #225
Addie's Lament #277

Historical Christmas Stories 1991
"Fortune's Gift"

DELORAS SCOTT

was raised in Sutter's Mill, California—an area steeped in history. At one time it was gold country, and the legacy of wagon trains, cowboys and miners has remained. It's no wonder she enjoys writing about a chapter of history referred to as the Old West.

Chapter One

San Francisco—1853

The young men's laughter drifted in though the open window, giving Adelaide Thompkins cause to grin. Guymour and William were on the back lawn playing something they called baseball. Though they claimed it was a real game, Adelaide suspected it was just something they'd made up between them. If all went as usual, soon the cousins' merriment would turn to quarreling, then fisticuffs, and finally their grandfather would march out of his study and put an end to the squabbling.

Though fifty-five years into his prime, Mr. Gordon Bently Stockman was still quite capable of handling both his young grandsons when they came to visit. Adelaide had overheard the butler tell Miss Carpenter, the housekeeper, that the boys' fathers had been exactly the same when they were that age.

Adelaide finished making the master's bed, then went to the window. Two stories below, the tall, lank cousins were concentrating on their sport. Except for their dark brown eyes and a certain set to their jaw, they looked nothing alike. Guy had thick black hair and wonderful eyes that always seemed to be daring her, and could catch and hold a girl's heart forever. Will was the shorter of the two,

though not by much. His hair was curly and light brown
and he could be equally charming.

Adelaide leaned her elbows on the windowsill and
watched Will pitch the ball. Guy swung and missed. Even
though she considered it a senseless game, she would like to
have joined in. Anything was better than constant cleaning. And after all, she was only two years younger than
their fourteen. Miss Carpenter had commented that girls
matured faster than boys. If that was so, why couldn't she
consider herself fourteen instead of twelve?

Adelaide sighed and straightened herself. Here she was
daydreaming again. Of course she couldn't play games with
them, nor did she care to. According to Beth, the cook's
helper, the young gentlemen's games now included taking
off clothes. "After all," Beth had said knowingly, "they've
reached an age where they need a woman to satisfy their
wants."

Adelaide wasn't about to remove anything for anyone.
Moreover, she knew her place. Miss Carpenter was always
reminding the maids that no matter what their age, servants did not socialize with the upper class. She giggled
when Guy hit the ball, which in turn hit Will's leg. Will
charged forward and tackled his cousin. Fists started flying, and yelled accusations began. She'd never seen either
of the young gentlemen back away from a fight.

As Mr. Stockman hurried out of the house, Adelaide
stepped away from the window. She didn't want anyone to
see her lolling about instead of attending to her duties. Lord
knows there were enough rooms in this place to keep a soul
busy. Thank the blessed Lord that all forty-three weren't
cleaned daily.

She grabbed the feather duster and returned to her
chores, her thoughts still on the boys. Even with the black
eyes the Stockman cousins usually sported, they were still
handsome enough to make any girl swoon. When Guymour and William were due for a visit, Miss Carpenter
would give the same speech. Adelaide knew it by heart.

"While the young gentlemen are here, avoid them as best you can. They are troublesome. Fortunately they never stay long, so you should be able to manage until their departure. And don't let their age deceive you. They are practically grown men." Then she would clasp her arms about her flat bosom and say, "And you would do well to remember that men of wealth look upon female servants as objects of pleasure!"

Adelaide dusted around the wag clock. Avoid the boys, indeed! Ever since Mr. Stockman had taken her out of the orphanage three years ago to be trained as a servant, the so-called young gentlemen had acted like hunters—she being the rabbit. Not that she was afraid of them. They had never harmed her and they treated her more like a buddy than a girl. Unfortunately, and for some unknown reason, teasing and playing pranks on her seemed to be an unending source of delight to them.

On their last visit, Guy had asked when was she going to get melons. The boys had laughed uproariously when she said they were out of season. Will had held his hands in front of his chest and puffed out his cheeks to indicate breasts. She had been quick to inform them that it wasn't any of their business.

Having finished the room, Adelaide ran her hands across the satin bedspread one more time to make sure it was smooth, then quickly glanced around the master's bedroom to see if she'd left anything unattended. Satisfied, she walked out into the hall, silently closing the heavy door behind her.

"Well, well, Cousin, look what I've found."

The sight of Will made Adelaide's heart turn to soft honey. Nevertheless, she wasn't about to let him, or Guy, get her in trouble again. "Both of you begone," she stated firmly. "Miss Carpenter still doesn't believe I didn't put your grandmother's ashes in the fireplace. I should never have let either of you talk me into keeping quiet."

"We wouldn't have been able to sit for a week," Will complained. "Grandfather would have taken a buggy whip to our backsides."

"What about me? I could have lost my employment!"

"But you didn't," Guy reminded her good-naturedly. "Besides, that happened a long time ago."

"A long time ago, bah! It's only been two months since your last visit."

Guy laughed. "I came to tell you goodbye."

"Goodbye. Now leave me be!" She was convinced that it was Guy who always talked Will into mischief.

"You don't mean that," Will cooed, an equally big smile spread across his handsome face. "I saw you watching us from the window."

"Are you going to miss me?" Guy crooned.

"No." While Will always made her feel tingly inside, Guy tended to make her feel...strange. She had never been able to figure out why.

Guy shoved back the tuft of raven black hair that had a habit of falling over his right eye. "Addie, we're going to sneak out tonight and play hide-and-seek. Want to join us? Beth will be there."

"I thought you were leaving."

Will chuckled. "But not until morning."

"Don't break my heart, Addie," Guy teased. "Say you'll miss me. There's no telling when I'll return."

Addie looked at Will. "What is he talking about?"

"Since Papa's death," Will replied, "Mama has made up her mind to return to England."

Adelaide was thunderstruck. She turned to Guy. "Are you going, too?"

"Of course he is," Will replied. "Mama has enrolled us in some boys' school."

A lump formed in Adelaide's throat. She couldn't imagine what it would be like never having them around. Why, she might not set eyes on William's handsome face for years.

"Will you wait for my return?" Guy asked dejectedly.

Adelaide was surprised by the question. "Your return?"

"Of course."

Adelaide wasn't fooled by his show of sadness. The corners of his mouth were already twitching with humor. "I shall miss you," she admitted.

"It's going to be a long time until we return," Guy reiterated. He raised a dark eyebrow. "Are you sure you don't want to enjoy a game of hide-and-seek?"

All three of them knew she didn't dare say yes. If Miss Carpenter discovered she wasn't in her bed, she'd be shoved out onto the street. Jobs weren't easy to come by without references. She shook her head.

"Then farewell, beautiful maiden," Guy announced.

To Adelaide's shock, he made a sweeping bow, then kissed her right on the lips. He moved aside and Will did the same. They walked away chatting and laughing as if nothing unusual had happened. Guy turned, looked back at Addie and winked. "Maybe you'll have some curves and lumps when we see you next time." He chuckled and continued on.

Her heart pounding, Adelaide gently ran a finger across her lips. She had just received her first kiss. Not just one, but two! And from such handsome, dashing gentlemen. Never again would she wash her face. This moment would live in her mind forever. She already missed the boys' teasing—and they hadn't even left yet.

That night in the dormitory, Adelaide lay awake, staring wide-eyed into the dark. Once again she was reliving that magical moment when the boys had kissed her. Would she ever realize her dream of marrying Will and being mistress of his house? Though she would miss both boys terribly, at least she'd be older when they returned. In her mind's eye, she could visualize them sweeping her off her feet, and Will declaring his love. Of course Guy would also realize he loved her. Maybe they would even end up fighting over her. She smothered her laughter in her blanket. Yes, she would grow and wait for them to come home. She heard Beth's bed squeak as the cook's assistant sneaked beneath the covers.

Beth leaned over and whispered, "Addie, guess what I just did with the cousins."

"Played hide-and-seek," Adelaide whispered back. She couldn't resist adding, "They asked me to join them, too, but I said no. Now leave me be. Morning's going to come too soon as is."

"Don't you want to hear how much fun I had? When the boys found me in the hayloft, the games really began."

It was apparent to Adelaide that Beth was bursting to share her secret with someone. The mattress complained when Adelaide turned her small body on its side. "You didn't..."

"I certainly did."

Adelaide's eyes widened. Beth was fifteen and knew a lot about men. "You...you only did it with Guy, huh?"

"I did it with both boys," Beth bragged. "Will liked what I gave him so much, he promised to come back for me as soon as he comes of age and gets his inheritance."

Adelaide's stomach suddenly felt hollow. Beth was wrong! Will couldn't have said that!

"He wants to marry me."

Adelaide could never remember feeling such pain. "But that's a long time off," she said more to herself than to Beth. "He'll forget about you. Miss Carpenter says gentlemen can't be trusted."

"He'll remember, and he'll come after me."

Adelaide didn't miss Beth's smug tone of voice. Hurt, and consumed with jealousy, Adelaide flopped onto her back. She didn't begrudge Beth stepping up in life, but why did it have to be with Will? He belonged to her! Silent, salty tears began to trickle from the corners of her eyes and into her hair. Angrily she brushed them away. Earlier today,

Guy had asked her to wait for him, but she hadn't believed he was serious. Perhaps Will had teased Beth in the same manner. Or what if Will didn't return? Or Guy, for that matter. Beth had to have misunderstood.

Adelaide closed her eyes and bit her bottom lip. If it hadn't been Beth who captured Will's heart, it would have been someone else. Though she didn't want to, Adelaide forced herself to admit that Will would never think of her as desirable. All her notions about marrying and being the mistress of Will's home were nothing more than daydreams. She was too skinny and . . . and she didn't have big melons like Beth. Another tear rolled down her cheek. If she could never have Will . . . she'd . . . become the mistress of this house! Yes. That was exactly what she would do. It was doubtful the boy's grandfather would ever marry again. She would learn everything necessary to become Gordon Stockman's housekeeper. Then she would be the one who gave the orders and reigned over his house. She didn't need Will, or anyone else for that matter!

As the months passed, Beth's stomach grew larger and larger, and Adelaide's romantic notions faded. Beth, of course, was fired from her job, but, fortunately, the man she claimed was the father of the child willingly married her. Adelaide was convinced Beth had no idea who sired the babe. It could have been Will, Guy, or several other men the girl had bragged about. But Adelaide tended to blame Will. Probably because, after saying he wanted to marry the cook's help, he didn't even write to see how she was faring. When it came to gentlemen, Miss Carpenter had been right all along. Never trust one.

Chapter Two

Thirteen years later

"Miss Thompkins."

The housekeeper stopped midway up the stairs, turned and stared down at Guymour Stockman. "What can I do for you, Mr. Stockman?"

Guymour stared up at the slender woman, wondering at her transformation from a pixy waif he'd known so many years ago to a woman of steel. "Someday you might try calling me by my first name again." Seeing Adelaide's stern look, he laughed. "On the other hand, it's doubtful. When are the guests arriving for Grandfather's birthday celebration?"

"Are you inquiring about the supper or the ball?"

"Both."

"The first guests will arrive at seven o'clock. Dining will commence promptly at eight. The ball will start at ten."

"I hope I didn't take up too much of your time," Guy stated with a strong hint of sarcasm.

"Was there anything else you wanted?"

Though he'd had his fill of her haughty, self-righteous, pragmatic attitude over the past six months, Guy smiled. The woman was always so stiff it was a wonder she didn't snap in two. "Oh, there are a lot of things I'd like to know, *Miss Thompkins*, but since my return, I haven't found you to be the least obliging." Had he seen a momentary look of sadness cross her face? No. Impossible.

His gaze remained on Adelaide's back as she continued up the stairs and disappeared from view. More than once he'd been tempted to try to melt away that frozen crust she flaunted like some damn flag, just to find out if there was any warmth behind that cold demeanor.

"That woman is beginning to give me a fixation."

Guy turned to his cousin, who had walked up behind him. "She certainly doesn't let her guard down. I still find it difficult to believe the skinny little strumpet we used to tease has changed so much."

"She may be a bit stiff, but the swan has definitely developed into a rare beauty."

Guy chuckled. "A beauty who has developed a mouth that spews acid, and can follow that with the sting of a wasp." He pointed at the glasses and dusty wine bottle Will was carrying. "I hope you plan on sharing that."

"But of course."

The two men strolled to the billiard room.

"Why do we bother trying to seduce Grandfather's housekeeper?" Will asked.

"You, not I." Guy strolled over to the fireplace and held his hands out to the warm flame. "Damn, this house is cold. I'll be glad when this unseasonable weather ends. I still can't get used to it. I had my fill of rain and fog during the war." Guy's thoughts flashed back to the mud and water he'd thrashed through, and the weeks, months, years he'd spent moving ahead of the Union troops; building the bridges needed to ford rivers, checking to see if the ones standing needed to be shored or if they would hold up long enough to let the troops and artillery cross over. It was a hard, filthy job, and more than once he'd come too damn close to getting his head blown off by some Confederate soldier.

"I know we've discussed this before, but I still find it uncanny that we managed to arrive back in San Francisco within a month of each other." Will removed the cork from the bottle and sniffed it. Satisfied, he poured their drinks. "Especially after being apart four years." He handed Guy one of the crystal wineglasses. "It couldn't have been better timing. These last months of frivolities brought to mind the old days. I think we both needed our time apart to lick our wounds."

"True." Guy knew the war had changed him, and the past months had helped him rediscover the pleasant side of life. He tasted his wine then nodded his approval. "Did you love her?"

"Who?"

"You know damn well who I'm talking about. Olivia. Your wife."

"I suppose so," Will admitted. He moved to the billiard table. "It hurt when she died. We'd actually become quite fond of each other. I'm sure I was even a nicer person when I was with her. But I have no desire to wed again. I like my life just as it is."

"The frivolities and idleness you spoke of are becoming tiresome. There seem to be few challenges left now that the war is over," Guy commented offhandedly. "I think tomorrow I'll do some serious dallying in the stock market."

Will set his glass down and took out a cue stick from the tall, wooden case standing against the wall. "You should consult with Grandfather." He placed the cue ball where he wanted it on the billiard table. "I didn't realize you had money left from your parents' inheritance. At least not enough to think about stock."

Guy removed his own cue. "You forget. I didn't remain in the social whirl of London, nor did I marry. I returned to America, and it was rather difficult to enjoy luxuries in the midst of a war."

After determining who went first, Guy stood back and let Will concentrate on knocking balls into the side pockets. As he perused his surroundings, he realized he'd always felt comfortable in this room. Unfortunately, most of the other rooms in the mansion lacked the same appeal. The parlor was a good example. Though well kept, the rugs and heavy furniture were dark, faded and worn. Everything his grandmother had transported from England had long since lost its usefulness. There was no telling how old it had been before they moved here.

Will missed pocketing the five ball. Guy stepped up to the table. "You know, I don't believe Grandfather has changed a thing in this house since it was built." He sank the ball into the side pocket. "Last night, Grandfather asked me to live here."

"What did you say?"

"I told him that, like you, I preferred my privacy." He made the next shot.

Will released a grunt. "He asked me to move in, also. I'm of the opinion that he wants us here so he can keep an eye on us." He wanted to discuss the degree of his cousin's wealth, not living accommodations. Just how much money did Guy have? The black-headed devil had always been closemouthed about such matters. He chose not to let Guy see just how interested he was. "I'm surprised Addie hasn't changed this place a bit," he commented as Guy made a perfect bank shot. "You know, I think I'd be willing to give my racing stallion for one night in bed with that woman."

"You're welcome to her. I can't even understand why the old man is so fond of her. True, she's been working here for years, but how could he abide to be around that washboard countenance? She's had the run of the house for so long she considers herself its mistress. She needs to be put in her place." Guy pocketed the last ball.

"That's one game for you. I'll rack," Will stated. He proceeded to remove the balls from the pockets. "Don't you think you're being a bit hard on her?"

"Perhaps."

"Maybe she'll sweeten up after I've had her in my bed."

"I'd wager that will never happen." Guy chalked his cue.

Will turned toward his cousin. "What will never happen? Her becoming sweet, or her in my bed?"

"Both."

"I believe you underestimate me. You've made me curious. Who do you think is the most capable of getting any woman he wants? You or I?"

"That's a strange question to ask. I'd say we're fairly even." Guy's mouth curved into a broad grin. "However, I do believe the teeter-totter tends to lean a bit in my direction."

Will sipped his wine. "I'm equally sure the teeter-totter leans in my direction. You mentioned a wager. If you truly believe your statement, surely you wouldn't be averse to putting up...say...five thousand to prove it?" He was curious as to how much money Guy could afford. "You just said there were few challenges left and that Addie needed to be put in her place. Why don't we see who can bed the priss first."

Guy's hardy laugh filled the room. "And people always think you're the nice one."

"It's the British accent," William said with a grin. "It works every time." He had dully noted that Guy didn't flick so much as a lash when the sum was mentioned. "Well, what do you say? Can you not afford the loss, or did the war emasculate you to the point of not being able to accept such a challenge?"

"Oh, I can afford it, but the real question is whether *you* have the finances to pay off such a debt. According to Grandfather, you and your wife spent all of your inheritance and you now live off his monthly allowance."

"W-well..." Will stuttered, "he gives you an allowance, too. Besides, the wager wasn't about me paying you."

Guy raised his dark eyebrows in disbelief. "Then do tell, what is to be my reward?"

"The pleasure of the lady's company."

"Pleasure? Let me make sure I understand what you're proposing. If I lose, I pay you five thousand dollars. If I win, my payment will be the questionable pleasure of fornicating with a woman who is probably as stiff and cold as a block of ice?''

Will picked up his glass. ''Well, I wouldn't put it exactly like that. However, to answer your question, yes. Besides, the woman has been a virgin entirely too long.''

''What makes you think she's a virgin?''

''She's very ill at ease around men. As for the ice, I would assume you're capable of melting it.''

''I admit the challenge piques my interest, but not under those terms. If I win, you give me that racing stallion you just spoke of. And there are to be no rules, except she can't be forced to do anything against her will.''

Will laughed with delight. He could already feel the winnings in the palm of his hand. ''Forcing her would take the sport out of it.''

They clinked their glasses together to seal the venture, then drank.

''Oh, there is one thing I forgot to mention,'' Will said gloatingly as he poured more wine. ''Our target has already stated she thinks I am far more the gentleman than you. I do believe that gives me a bit of an edge.''

''You know, when I was fighting for the North, one of my men was fond of saying, 'Don't count your chickens before they hatch.''' Guy raised a dark, meaningful eyebrow.

''Mr. Stockman.''

Both men turned and spotted the maid standing in the doorway.

When she realized they had the same name, the pretty woman's cheeks dimpled. ''Mr. William Stockman,'' Ivy clarified. ''The master would like to see you in his study.''

Will walked up to her, smiled and tweaked her chin. ''Listening at the door, sweet thing?'' he asked softly.

''I heard nothing, sir,'' the shocked maid quickly replied. ''I just walked in.''

Will searched her face for any hint of a lie. Seeing none, he handed her his glass and continued on his way. At last he was about to receive his monthly allowance. Creditors were already knocking on his door.

"Is there anything I can do for you, sir?" Ivy asked Guy.

He shook his head. A schoolboy couldn't have missed the seductive look she gave him, but he wasn't interested. He watched her shoulders slump with disappointment as she left. There were always available women to take care of his needs, but with maturity the desire to see how many he could bed had lost its appeal. Hard-won conquests had proven to be by far the most pleasurable.

After returning the cue sticks to the cabinet, Guymour strolled out into the marble reception area, which was one hundred and ten feet long and forty feet wide. He'd personally measured every foot of it. The carved ceiling had a beautiful fresco in the center, and the stained glass windows were perfectly placed so as to be seen at their best advantage. The entire house was a magnificent piece of architecture. But he had never realized how much he cared for the manor until the war. This was the only place he'd ever truly considered home, and his family roots had become important to him. When his grandfather passed away, he'd buy Will's share of the place and keep it as his own.

His gaze shifted to the wide staircase. Strange that on the very day he'd had his fill of Miss Thompkins's superior attitude, Will had suggested a wager.

Guy finished his wine. Will wasn't going to win the bet. The time had come for *Miss Thompkins* to learn a few of life's amenities, and he was going to enjoy every minute of being her teacher. She had a vulnerable spot somewhere, and he was going to find it. He wanted to see her desire ridden—that thick, blond hair loose and spread out on a pillow—and those amber eyes smoldering with passion. Maybe he'd even be able to teach her to join the human race! Not likely.

* * *

Guy glanced around the dining table at the thirty people who had been invited to the private birthday dinner. Later, others would arrive for the ball. He was well aware how mothers virtually vied for invitations for their daughters to attend such occasions. They had high hopes that the misses would catch the eye of one of the cousins. A situation he and Will had become accustomed to.

Though Guy gave proper attention to the ladies seated on either side of him, his mind was on the housekeeper. What would she look like wearing something other than that high-necked, long-sleeved black gown with the white collar and lapel watch? And why must she always wear her hair pulled tightly in a knot at the nape? Did she sleep in that same ramrod-straight posture? Until his return, he'd never met a woman who could keep her face devoid of expression no matter what the circumstance. She'd make a hell of a poker player.

Before the guests had been seated at the table, he had gone to the big kitchen to take a hard look at what he was going to be dealing with. He'd positioned himself where he could keep an eye on Addie yet remain out of the way of traffic. As he'd watched her moving about, competently tasting the food and making sure it would be ready at exactly the right time for the butlers to serve, he knew his biggest obstacle was going to be her restraint, the reserve that he was going to have to break through.

"Is something wrong, Mr. Stockman?" Adelaide had finally stopped and asked.

Guy smiled. "Not that I know of."

"Then why—"

"Am I standing here?"

Adelaide clasped her hands in front of her. "Exactly."

"To watch you. I find you to be a most interesting woman. For instance, until I took a good look at you, I'd never noticed what a long, graceful neck you have. And not until you turned to the side did I discover your dress tends

to hide your full bosom." When he'd seen her amber eye
darken with anger and she had glanced about to be sure n
one had heard his comment, he had been satisfied for th
time being. He'd left the kitchen without saying anothe
word, but thinking the game might just turn out to be mor
interesting than he had expected.

The nine-course meal was served flawlessly. The cra
bisque was without a doubt the best Guy had ever tasted
He had to give the housekeeper credit. Not only was th
food superb, the table had been set to absolute perfection
Colors from the freshly picked flowers decorating the ta
ble were reflected in the sparkling crystal stemware an
saltcellars, and the silver was devoid of blemish. He wa
sure that if he tried, he could see his face in the fine Min
ton china.

There was no doubt in Guy's mind that his grandfa
ther's housekeeper was a perfectionist. So why didn't h
just leave her alone? Because, whether she realized it or not
her aloofness had the quality of waving a red cape in fron
of a bull. Whether the wager with Will had been made o
not, he would have eventually gone into battle with Addie
The bet just served to speed it up.

Guy caught a glimpse of an older gentlemen sneakin
into the kitchen. Mr. West should be more careful. Befor
the door had properly closed, he had placed his hand o
Adelaide's fanny. He was only in there a moment befor
rushing back out. Guy found the action to be most inter
esting. He considered the possibilities. Either West wa
Addie's lover, one of several lovers, or just another gentle
man trying to get beneath her stiff skirts. That would com
as no surprise. The woman was quite attractive. Since tak
ing the time to examine her more closely, he'd discovere
some very appealing qualities. He raised his napkin to hid
a grin. Had Will given any thought to the possibility tha
she might prefer women?

At the ball, Guy noticed how Addie remained in th
background, seemingly blending in with the woodwork. O

more than one occasion, he'd seen Will already trying to corner the lady. Addie had made certain that none of the guests wanted for a thing. She had even provided plenty of cigars for the men when they departed to the outside to smoke and discuss politics. Something Guy found himself doing quite often.

Even when surrounded by women, Guy was bored. He was beginning to wonder if the evening would ever end. He'd seen Will follow Addie as she left the room. Will was definitely not letting any grass grow underfoot. Guy suddenly wondered what Addie would look like when she laughed. Assuming she was capable of it. When they were young, she had smiled a lot. He unconsciously grinned. He and Will knew she had had a crush on them—especially Will—and they had used it to coax her into not telling on them.

The night hadn't been a total waste, Guy decided as he rode home later that evening. Though Addie remained stoic and her eyes were cold and ungiving, she'd given up one of her secrets. She looked away too quickly when they discussed something, and she made a point of staying away from him. He made her nervous. Interesting reaction for a woman who supposedly didn't like a single thing about him.

Guy's good mood had returned. Bedding *Miss Thompkins* should prove most interesting.

It was two weeks before Guy was able to turn his full attention to Adelaide's seduction. Nevertheless, he had given it considerable thought. With Will's constant pursuit, as of late, Guy had decided he'd get quicker results by taking a different approach. Adelaide gave the impression of being a matter-of-fact-type woman, so why not just tell her flat out what he wanted?

It was after dining with his grandfather several evenings later that Guy had an opportunity to confront the housekeeper. He had seen her pass by the French doors and as-

sumed she was going for a walk in the garden. The timing
was perfect. His grandfather had just bid him good-night

The full moon offered plenty of light to see by, and Guy
had no trouble locating his prey. Addie was sitting on one
of the stone benches, situated a short distance from the
house. The sweet smell of jasmine permeated the night air
and under normal circumstances he would have consid
ered it a most inviting opportunity to woo a lady.

"Good evening," he said casually.

Adelaide jerked her head up to see who had intruded on
her privacy. Deep in thought, she had been caught of
guard.

"If I also sit on the bench, are you going to go running
back to the house?"

"No." Addie wasn't about to let him think he'd chased
her off.

Guy grinned. "Good. I've been wanting to have a tall
with you." He sat beside the striking beauty, making sure
there was adequate space between them. "Do you mind i
I continue smoking my cigar?"

"Not at all," she replied curtly. "What did you want to
say to me?"

Guy raised the cigar to his mouth, took a long puff, then
slowly let the smoke back out. "Try to not be offended, bu
I've made up my mind to bed you."

Addie scooted to the far side of the bench so fast tha
Guy was surprised she didn't fall off the end. He chuck
led. "Believe me, my dear, it isn't a fate worse than death
I assure you, you would learn pleasures your mind couldn'
even conceive."

"How dare you speak in such a manner to me!" Addie
carefully rose from the bench, alert should he attempt to
grab at her. "You have no right!"

"Have you been enjoying Will's attention?" Will had
told him that Addie savored his stolen kisses.

Addie glared at him. She knew she should leave, but she
was curious as to why he had asked such a question. "It'

not my place to enjoy or not to enjoy," she said angrily. "I'm here to serve your grandfather. I do not owe allegiance to either you or your cousin."

"Oh, really?"

"As for William, I will say that he isn't as crude as you."

"I can be equally charming when I want. You're only attracted to William because he's pampered you."

"That's a lie," Adelaide protested.

"And," Guy continued, "the reason you get upset with *me* is because I come right out and tell you what is on my mind. I make your emotions work overtime and you don't know how to handle that."

"The reason I get upset with you is because of your lack of gentlemanly behavior. I'm appalled that you would even have the nerve to speak to me in such a manner!"

Amused, Guy watched Adelaide run away. He took another puff of his cigar. Well, she wasn't exactly running, but damn close to it. There was no need to detain her further. He'd put a bee in her bonnet and now he'd let her stew on it. Besides, as skittish as she was, if he tried going after her, she'd probably accuse him of attempted rape.

Chapter Three

Watching over twenty-seven servants was a continuous task. But as Adelaide strolled about the parlor, checking to see that the lanterns had been properly trimmed and cleaned, her thoughts weren't on household chores. She was remembering William and Guymour's return after being gone for so many years.

Like their grandfather, Mr. Gordon Stockman, she had been beside herself with joy when he had informed her the boys were coming home. It had been over a decade since Will and Guy had set foot in San Francisco. A brief letter was all that had been received when Guy had returned to America to join the army to fight the South. But at last, they were coming to stay.

William had arrived first. Adelaide could never remember having laid eye on a finer looking gentleman. She had wanted to hug him and welcome him back, but of course she didn't. And a good thing, too. He had looked right through her, as if she weren't there. He didn't even have a smile for an old acquaintance.

With Guy's arrival a month later, she'd remained in the background. But she was still excited. Though it had been silly, she'd wondered if he would remember asking her to wait for him before he'd gone to England. It had been painful to see the red scar that followed his hairline from temple to the top of the ear. The wound had prevented him from returning to San Francisco after the war had ended. She wanted to take him in her arms, also, and ask if he was all right, but again she had been ignored.

A sign of friendship wouldn't have been too much to ask and would have been greatly appreciated. So once again she had withdrawn. She then categorized the cousins with the other so-called gentlemen who frequently attended parties at the house, or just stopped to visit with Mr. Stockman.

After the excitement, each grandson had taken up his own residence in a different part of town. A routine quickly developed. The cousins visited their grandfather once or twice a month and attended all social gatherings Mr. Stockman deemed important.

Other than Will making an occasional suggestion that she warm his bed—or a question here or there—Will and Guy ignored her, which she deemed proper. Beth's pregnancy had shown her the end result of becoming involved with such "gentlemen."

Addie walked across the hall to the opulent dining room. How well her comfortable routine had been until two weeks ago, when it had taken a sudden turn. Will had started showing up at the house nearly every other day, dogging her heels. He said foolish things about how he loved her. He even tried stealing kisses! His apology for turning his back on a childhood friend had fallen on deaf ears. He'd even gone so far as to excuse his bad manners by saying he hadn't realized the beautiful housekeeper and the little girl he used to tease were one and the same. Too much time had passed for the excuse to be plausible.

Last Monday William had had the brazen audacity to pull her into a corner and kiss her solidly on the lips. Mr. Stockman and Guy were even sitting in the adjoining room! She couldn't verbally protest because the others would hear, a situation that Will had obviously been quick to take advantage of.

Fortunately, though William tried to press himself on her, he wasn't difficult to handle. She had made it clear that she had no intention of putting up with his foolishness. She was no longer the naive little girl he'd known so many years ago. Nor was *he* the same person. His kiss had improved considerably since he was fourteen.

Realizing she was staring blankly at the long table, Adelaide glanced around to see if anyone had observed her idleness. Seeing no one, she pulled out the end chair and sat. There was no use in trying to think about other things. She had a problem that needed to be thought out.

Besides Will's ardent attention, she now had Guy to contend with, as well. She knew intuitively that he wasn't going to be as easy to handle as Will. And, also, unlike Will, Guy wasn't coming at her with kisses and sweet words. Instead he'd blatantly stated that he wanted her in his bed! Now he was making unexpected visits, too. Though he always kept his distance, he conducted his approach with words. "Addie, why do you fight your desires and curiosity?" Another time, "I can make all your dreams come true. Being shy will get you nowhere." Or, "You know you're curious." Three days ago he'd caught her in the kitchen preparing for another one of Mr. Stockman's parties. "You don't have to say a thing," he'd said. "Just nod your head and I'll do the rest." She had always thought of Will as being the one who would have the most effect on her. However, Guy's deep, seductive voice, that grin, those eyes that always seemed to be beckoning and daring, and his handsome features all culminated in a very persuasive gentleman.

Adelaide unthinkingly pulled a handkerchief from her pocket and wiped her nose. After so many years of tranquillity, she wasn't at all pleased that the orderliness of her life was being threatened. Would her apparent lack of interest eventually make them tire of their game? She had two of the handsomest...most eligible...most notorious bachelors in California focusing their attention on her. How could she not be affected by their charisma? Though she might disapprove of their antics and rigidly refused to be swayed by either man, she was, after all, a woman.

"Are you pretending you're entertaining?"

Addie jumped to her feet. Guy was standing not more than five feet away, his shoulder resting against the hand-painted wall. The scar on his face certainly didn't detract from his masculinity. Actually, it made him look even more the dangerous renegade. Nor was he as thin as when he'd first returned home. He now presented a most dashing figure. She shoved the chair back under the table. "How long have you been standing there?"

"Long enough to see you were deep in thought. Dare I hope you were thinking about me?"

"I'm sure you would dare just about anything if it caught your fancy. No, I was not thinking about you," she lied. "My thoughts were on other matters."

Guy's gaze took in her rigid stance and the belligerent tilt of her chin. "Do you act like this all the time, or is it just with me?"

Addie made no reply.

"*Miss Thompkins,* why can't you just admit that I tempt you?"

"Because you don't."

Guy smiled. "You remind me of a young man I knew in England. A bully who was always warning other boys in school that if they gave him any trouble—or didn't do what he said—they'd end up with a broken nose and ribs. Everyone believed him."

"Except you."

Guy moved away from the wall. "Except me."

"What is the purpose of this story?"

"The boy was a bully and a coward. He used threatening words and a tough appearance to hide his fears."

"Surely you're not comparing me to him?"

"That's exactly what I'm doing. So don't try using that superior act on me unless you want the consequence."

Addie marched toward the door, but Guy reached it first, effectively blocking her escape. She crossed her arms and glared at him. "Is there also a reason for this?"

"I have something to say that you'll find most interesting."

"Then say it so I can leave."

"Why don't we move to the morning room where we can sit in comfort? It has been a long day for me."

"It has been a long day for me, too, but I'll stand. It's not my place to sit with those of your class."

"Why can't you let go of that reserve for at least one damn minute?" Guy raked his fingers through his thick black hair and took a deep breath. The top of her head barely reached his shoulder, and he could crush her with one hand. Yet there she stood, defiant and refusing to give ground. "We'll make an exception." He stepped aside and waved her forward.

When they entered the other room, Addie had no choice but to settle herself in the white wicker chair.

"Have you been enjoying Will's company?"

Addie's eyes shifted to his. He'd asked her the same question the other night. Why? Did he think she was enticing Will? "I have told him that I do not appreciate being hounded by his . . . friendliness."

"How interesting." Guy leaned back in his chair. "Haven't you found his sudden attention to be a bit strange?"

"I haven't time to think about such things."

"You're going to have to make time, because I'm going to give you even more to think about. Haven't you stopped to wonder why I want to make love to you?"

"Well, I . . . I . . ."

"Let me help you. To begin with, you're an extremely beautiful woman, and at nearly twenty-five it's way past time to discover the pleasures to be shared between a man and a woman. But more importantly, darling, I'm going to break that suit of armor you wear, and it's not only going to be when I take your clothes off."

Addie caught herself squirming in her chair and stiffened. "Are you finished?"

"I haven't even told you the purpose of my being here. I've come to the conclusion that it is only fair that you know the reason for all the sudden attention you've been receiving from Will and me. It's a wager. Five thousand dollars to whoever can bed you first."

Addie jumped to her feet. "You're a liar! Will would never have anything to do with something so vile."

Guy smiled. He'd finally gotten an honest emotion out of the woman. "I'm not lying, and you know it."

"You're betting on me like I was a . . . horse? Oh!" Had there been something near, Addie would have thrown it at his smug face. "You're even more despicable than I gave you credit for. This was your idea, wasn't it?"

"Does it matter?" Guy rose to his feet and pulled on the fine leather riding gloves he'd been carrying.

"How many more know about this?" Addie asked bitterly.

"Only Will and I, and now you. I've told you this as a favor."

"Favor?"

"Now you'll have no misconceptions as to what is going on. The wager is now a three-way affair, with you holding the answers."

"I'll tell Mr. Stockman about this!"

Guy chuckled. "No, you won't. You never were a snitch."

"You can't be telling the truth. You wouldn't have let Will get a head start."

"You're too much of a fighter to allow anyone to bed you in two weeks, and I had other commitments."

Addie turned her back, trying to control the inferno blazing inside of her. Of all the rotten, despicable— She spun about to confront Guy, but he had silently left the

room. The realization that they had been playing a game
with her emotions caused bile to rise up into her throat. She
wanted to scream, yell...pound his back...but she
wouldn't. She took several deep breaths. One way or another, she'd get even with them for this.

Shoulders squared, Adelaide lifted the hem of her gown
and headed for the kitchen. She had to inform the cook that
Mr. Stockman had requested an apple pie for dessert.

The following morning, Adelaide stood in Lillian Stockman's old room. When she was young, she used to come
here a lot.

"Miss Thompkins?"

Addie spun around so quickly, she nearly dropped the
delicate music box she'd been listening to. "What is it?" she
asked irritably as she shut the lid. She felt guilty at being
caught in the private morning room. She wasn't even sure
why she'd come here.

"I'm sorry, Miss Thompkins," the dimple-cheeked
woman said worriedly. "I thought you heard me enter. I
didn't mean to scare you."

"Never mind, Ivy. It wasn't your fault and no harm has
been done. What was it you wanted?"

Ivy pulled a handkerchief from her apron pocket and
blew her nose. "I've a terrible cold, ma'am, and I was
wondering if I might go lay down a bit."

Addie went to her and felt her forehead. "You do have a
bit of a fever. Go have cook fix you a toddy first." She
smiled at the pretty, red-nosed woman. "I won't expect to
see you before tomorrow morning."

"Thank you, ma'am. I'll go see Della right away."

"And Ivy, you did a fine job attending to the guests last
night."

Grinning from ear to ear, Ivy scurried away.

Addie turned and stared at the painting hanging on the
wall. It used to hang in Mr. Stockman's study, but for some
unknown reason he'd placed his wife's picture in here about

a year ago. "You need to have a good talk with your grandsons, Miss Lillian," she told the empty room. She set the music box on a small table. "I'm a damn good mistress of this house, and proud of it. So why must they keep taunting me? Do they think that because I'm not married that I'm fair game? I could have married several times, but *I* chose not to jeopardize my position here!"

Spying a cobweb, Addie realized it had been some time since she'd given the place a thorough cleaning. She never permitted anyone else to do it, and kept the door locked so nothing would be disturbed.

She looked in the adjoining bedroom. The old mistress's lovely gowns still hung in the armoire, and her partially finished needlework lay on the bedside table, as if waiting for her return.

Did Mr. Stockman ever come in here anymore? she wondered. Addie had spent hours in these rooms when she was a child, especially when she had a problem to work out. She had always felt comfortable here. Maybe it had to do with being brought up in an orphanage until she was nine, and never knowing what it was like to have a mother. She used to pretend Lillian was her mother, which in turn made her a fine lady. Enough. She was no longer a child.

She left the room, closed the door, locked it and dropped the key into her pocket. Suddenly she felt better than she had in days. Why had she allowed herself to become so overwrought? Yes, she had every right to be angry about the wager, but nothing had happened, and nothing was going to happen.

As she walked down the long hall, Adelaide thought of Mr. Stockman's friends who over the years had tried to get beneath her skirts, patted her fanny, and had left black-and-blue marks from countless pinching. But none of those men had pulled anything to equal William and Guymour's stunt. A wager, indeed!

It was the sound of the floor squeaking that warned Addie she wasn't alone in the long hall. She managed to move to the side just in time to prevent Will from wrapping an arm around her waist.

"I've missed being with you."

If it hadn't been for Guy, Addie would have believed him. "Would you stop this? I'm not your prey!"

Will grinned. "Stop pretending you're upset with me."

"I am upset! Your cousin told me about the wager. How could you stoop so low? I've had enough of your pathetic attempts at seduction."

"Pathetic?" Will thought a moment. "Why would Guy tell you about the wager?"

Addie gasped. "You haven't heard a thing I said!"

"I heard, but I just can't believe the pathetic part, and I fail to see what you're upset about. We meant it in the greatest respect. Your beauty has been driving me wild with desire for months. The wager was simply a means of getting money out of Guy."

"I have never given you any reason to believe I would... Why didn't you select one of your wealthy ladies to play your game with?"

"They're too easy. It's your untouchable attitude that drew me to you."

"And so war was declared." She placed her hands on her hips. "I feel nothing but disgust and pity toward the both of you."

His curiosity getting the better of him, he asked, "Just what did Guy say when he told you about the wager?"

Addie groaned inwardly. Her scathing words had absolutely no effect on him. "He said he was letting me know exactly what was going on and what his intentions were because it made the game all the sweeter."

"That dog!" Will stated good-humoredly.

Addie was seething. Her feelings were of no importance to either of them! She continued down the hall.

Will took his time trailing after her. "That sounds like something he might say. Never trust him for a minute, my dear. He's wily."

Addie again stepped aside when Will moved too close. She realized her mistake when she felt the wall at her back and the handsome man was hovering over her.

Will cupped Addie's delicate chin in his palm. "My dear Adelaide, you'll soon be twenty-five and it's long past time for you to learn the joys—"

"You're only repeating what Guy has already said. It didn't work for him and it won't work for you. I'm tired of the two of you constantly being in pursuit. If this continues, I shall report your actions to your grandfather."

Will leaned down and gently kissed her full, inviting lips. He might as well have kissed a stone. Not even an eyelash twitched.

"If you are finished, then move aside so I can go downstairs."

"You must have felt something," Will said in disbelief. "Is this the same reaction Guy gets when he kisses you?"

"Guy has made no effort to kiss me." She gave Will a hard shove and continued on her way.

Will followed. "That's hard to believe. What does he do?"

"He talks."

Will stopped and stared at Addie's back. "He what?"

Addie slowly turned. "Will, there is something I've wanted to ask you ever since you returned. Why didn't you ever come back for Beth?"

"Beth? Who is Beth?"

"She was the cook's helper thirteen years ago," she reminded him with disgust. "Do you remember the last night before you moved to England? You and Guy played hide-and-seek and ended up with Beth in the hay. She told me about it. She also said you promised to come back for her once you received your inheritance. She truly believed you would make her your wife."

"Wife? Even if I had chosen a paramour, it certainly wouldn't have been her."

"I see. And what about the baby she was carrying? Never once did you send a message inquiring about her health, or telling her what you were about. How could you be so thoughtless and uncaring?" Addie felt the need to defend the girl. "Well, it didn't matter anyway. She never stopped enjoying men's pleasures and finally ended up marrying a fine one from the country."

Addie disappeared around the corner, but Will didn't follow this time. Though he hadn't admitted it, he remembered Beth very well. It had been the first time he'd been made love to so thoroughly. He'd been so young then and had actually believed he was in love. It was Guy who made him see the impossibility of the situation, and it had been Guy who proved to him that when it came to bedding, there were other women just as capable—and better. But no matter what the realities of life, Will still had a soft spot in his heart for the cook's helper. And she had been pregnant. There was no telling who the father was. Beth had lost her virginity way before he'd bedded her.

William closed his thoughts of the past. Memories served no purpose. Besides, he had to think about the racing stallion he could lose. Guy had made a smart move. By telling Adelaide what this was all about, he'd knocked Will back down to where he'd have to start over. He'd have to find another way to coax Addie to his bed. In all honesty, the chance of that happening seemed more and more unlikely. At least he had the satisfaction of knowing Guy wasn't doing any better.

He started down the stairs, still finding it hard to believe that his kisses had no effect on the twit. This had never happened before, but then he'd never been involved in such a situation. The women he knew were willing, if not anxious, to be in his arms. Pathetic? Ridiculous!

Chapter Four

Addie stood in the linen closet, trying to count napkins, a seemingly impossible task since her thoughts continued to drift to Will and Guy. She hadn't seen hide nor hair of either one for over a week. Not since she'd asked Will about Beth. She had known from the start that their attention wouldn't last forever. Admittedly it had put diversity into her life, but she was ready to return to her normal routine.

Hearing the door close, Addie glanced over her shoulder to see who had entered. Guy was standing just inside the room, his height and broad shoulders reducing the small space to nothing. A spark of fear was making its way up her spine. Not for a minute did she trust the grin toying at the corner of his mouth. Was he going to force himself on her and put an end to the wager? The closet was way to the back of the house, cutting her off from the servants. No one would hear her scream.

It was all Addie could do to stand her ground and not move to the back of the room. She didn't draw a clear breath until she suddenly realized Guy wasn't making any effort to come near her. She was disgusted at herself. Once again she had allowed her imagination to run amok. Of course he wasn't going to attack her. Any fool could tell he was perfectly content to remain leaning against the closed door.

Adelaide turned back to her work. Her fear had obviously stemmed from that dangerous side of him that he always seemed to display. Or maybe it was because he was too masculine—too everything. Much more than Will. Guy was also used to getting what he wanted.

"Come, come, Addie. Can't you at least say hello? What is it about me that disturbs you so?"

"You . . . you don't disturb me."

"No? Then why are your hands shaking?"

Addie clasped her hands together then immediately released them. She was acting like a young girl who had never been with a man. Needing to do something, she moved to a stack of sheets and started counting. She could feel Guy's eyes on her, and it was unnerving. Did he have any idea how disrupting his presence was?

"I mean you no harm."

Addie lost count and started over.

"Quite the contrary. I want to bring pleasure into your life."

"You need not inconvenience yourself. My life is as I want it." Addie refused to show her anger at his intrusion. "I believe I've made it quite clear that I want nothing to do with the likes of you," she snapped at him. "I don't even care to be in your company. Now leave me alone. As you can see, I'm busy." She tried to ignore his knowing chuckle.

"Your cheeks are flushed."

"It's warm in here with the door closed." Addie pulled a small piece of paper from her pocket and wrote the number of sheets in the second stack. She placed the marker on the shelf and started on the next pile.

"I've noticed your cheeks turning red on several occasions when we've been together."

"You make me angry."

"While sitting alone last night, I suddenly wondered if you'd ever lain naked beside a man."

Addie's mouth dropped open and it took a minute before she could speak. "How dare you ask such a question?

I'm not some wharf harlot. I'm a woman with morals, and don't you dare forget it!''

"Remember? I'm the one you said would dare just about anything if it hit my fancy. Believe me, there has never been any doubt that you are a woman of high morals. It is your other attributes I have a problem with. For instance, there have been several times when I've been tempted to cut your tongue out. Your statement about not wanting to be around the likes of me is a good example. Need I remind you who the employee is?''

"I know my place, *sir*, but I only give respect where it's due. Please remember that this is not your house and that I do not work for you. Your grandfather is the one I answer to, and the only one I hold in high esteem. And what about how *your* attitude grinds on me? How many times have you considered my side of all this?''

"Quite a bit. I'll make it up to you when you let me make love to you.''

"How magnanimous of you. You don't like me, do you?'' Addie asked.

"I haven't seen a lot to like.''

"Good. The feeling is mutual.''

"You think too highly of yourself.''

Adelaide placed her hands on her hips. "You of all people should certainly know about that!'' she accused. "When it comes to others, you and Will are as unfeeling as anyone I have ever come across. Especially you. Not once has either of you considered what you are putting me through. All you think about is your blasted bet. Since you dislike me so much, why don't you put a stop to this foolishness?''

"My reasons for wanting you have nothing to do with liking you.''

"Then why—''

"For now, it will suffice to call it plain lust.''

"I want this stopped. Now!''

"Do you? Very well, I know exactly how that can be accomplished."

Addie returned to her counting.

"Did you know that when a naked man and woman lie in front of each other without touching, blood rushes through their veins. And the longer they go without touching—"

"Where do you come up with these things?"

"Don't you think it's time to start learning some truths about life?"

"If I do, I'll let someone else be my teacher."

"Fine. Just make sure it's not Will and it doesn't cost me any money."

"Damn! You've made me lose count again."

Guy's grin broadened. He did so enjoy knocking *Miss Thompkins*'s feet out from under her, so to speak. He'd be willing to bet a mare that the woman hadn't even realized she'd uttered a curse word. "Out of curiosity, do you think you could lie naked with a man and not touch?"

Addie spun around, not even noticing she had knocked the marker to the floor. "Get out of here!" she said, seething.

"You're starting to repeat yourself, my dear. I must admit that when you flash those amber eyes at me . . . oh, but I mustn't offend your sensitive nature." He shifted his weight to his other foot. "I've been honest with you from the beginning. I told you my intentions. Why can't you be honest with me?"

"I don't know what you're talking about."

"Of course you do." Guy's gaze remained fixed on the enticing woman. What would she do if he mentioned that her increasing anger was causing her to breathe a bit heavily, thereby forcing her breasts against her bodice in a most pleasing manner? "I've done nothing out of the way and there's no harm in talking. Yet you can't even answer a simple question. Is that because you're afraid if you talk about such things you might become interested?"

"That's ridiculous." She wiped her damp palms on her skirt. "Are such things all you ever have on your mind?"

"You mean like bedding you? Not entirely, but it does take up a big part of the space. Addie, I'm quite willing to put a halt to all this, give Will his five thousand dollars and even put up with his bragging."

"If what?" Addie asked suspiciously.

"Lie with me naked for one hour. We'll just talk. I swear not to touch you without your permission."

"I'll do no such thing!" she gasped.

"Then apparently you're enjoying the attention Will and I have been giving you."

"That's a lie!"

"Yet you're not willing to put an end to it. Haven't you come to realize none of this is going to stop until there is a winner?"

"You'll not catch me in one of your traps, Guymour Stockman." Adelaide moved forward and tried reaching around Guy for the doorknob. When he put his hand down to prevent her from opening the door, she quickly stepped back.

"Tell me, sweet Addie, what is your worry?"

Addie clamped her mouth shut, refusing to say another word.

"You know, you not only lie to me, you lie to yourself." Guy reached out and gently ran the back of his hand down her smooth cheek. "For instance, you say I have no effect on you. Prove it."

Addie waited a moment too long to move away.

Guy took hold of her arm and pulled her to him, his deep, hardy laugh filling the small room. "You're such a coward, my dear."

Addie was unexpectedly lost the minute his lips came down on hers—warm, demanding lips that suddenly threatened to turn her into an erupting volcano as his kiss deepened. When her lips parted, his tongue caressed the inner sanctum of her mouth. She was being deliciously devoured. No one had ever warned her that a kiss could be so magnificent.

As soon as Guy felt Addie leaning into him, he slowly pulled his head back, then moved her away from him. Her eyes flew open, and he gave her a knowing smile. "My offer to put an end to this stands. Think about it. Nothing has to happen. Just two people lying naked on a bed."

Addie still hadn't recovered from the overpowering effect of his kiss. She had been right all along. The man was dangerous. "I will never consider your proposal. Why should I? If you and William wish to continue playing your little game, go right ahead. You'll discover that nothing is going to change," she bluffed. She thought of Beth. "Since you seem so intent, I'm surprised you haven't promised marriage to get what you want," she added sarcastically.

"It isn't necessary. You'd be surprised how quickly a person can be worn down by constant pressure. Should you change your mind and decide to take me up on my suggestion, you have but to nod your pretty head. I'll know what you mean." He opened the door, made a slight bow and left.

Addie lowered herself onto one of the small counting stools. She didn't have to look in any mirror to know her cheeks were scarlet. But that was the least of her problems. At this point in time she couldn't even make her mind function.

After the pictures Guy had painted in her head, Addie could think of little else. That night she closed her eyes and tried to envision Guy lying with her in the same bed. She repeated Guy's words that nothing would happen unless she wanted it to. Damn, she was tempted. Just an hour. Guy had promised not to touch her, and he always kept his promises.

Could she do it? She was curious. Guy made it sound so easy. But he reminded her of a man standing in the wings of the theater watching a play and patiently waiting for his cue to step into his role. No, she would be wise to stay away from Guymour Stockman. From now on she'd have to be more cautious. Never again could she give him the opportunity to kiss her. His kiss had created sensations she could ill afford.

Three nights later, Adelaide sat on the window seat. She couldn't sleep and had purposefully left her bedroom dark so she could look at the multitude of stars decorating the sky. The strange, wanton feelings Guy had created within her hadn't been as easily dismissed as she had originally thought. She'd never had such feelings before. And all because of one single kiss! Of course she would never do such a thing, but what if... just if... she agreed to succumb to Guy or Will? Which one would it be? They were so different. Will. It would be Will. She didn't feel intimidated by him. And though she would never admit it to a soul, she rather liked his kiss and the occasional feel of his hands gliding down her back. He was undoubtedly the handsomest of the pair. Just looking at his light brown curly hair, manicured mustache and strong, handsome features would make any woman's pulse race. Like Guy's, his clothes were always cut to perfection and rested easily on a trim, hard body. He had that ability to project a certain aura of innocence, even though a woman would be a fool to believe such. And his quick wit and British accent added to his appeal. She caught sight of a falling star streaking across the heavens and fading from view.

Feeling a bit chilled, Adelaide wrapped her shawl tighter about her shoulders. She sighed. Why was she even thinking about such things? Who was she fooling? Guy was the one making her heart beat twice as fast. He was taller than his cousin's and grandfather's six-foot-three frame, and every inch of him exuded raw masculinity. Even the war scar added to his rakish personality. His black hair, strong, molded features and hard body combined to present a most intimidating man. However, it was those dark brown eyes that gave her the most trouble. When Guy was of a cold and ungiving mood, his eyes turned black as his hair, then they could just as quickly become brown and dance with mischief.

Adelaide frowned as she scooted about to get more comfortable. She wasn't the only female who felt his appeal. Practically every maid in the house swooned when he did nothing more than talk to them. Most of the time when he stopped at the house to see his grandfather, there was some beautiful female hanging on to his arm as if she owned him. They were obviously mistaken, because Addie had yet to see Guy with the same woman twice. It wasn't decent that a man should have such an effect on a woman!

Addie leaned her head against the wall. Why was it that ever since she was a girl, she always tended to fantasize about Will or Guy? They were no different than the other men who had tried to bed her. They were worse! As far as she knew, none of the others had ever placed a wager on her back! If she continued to allowed such thoughts to play around in her head, she would be mentally succumbing to their desires. Actuality would follow. Then what? She'd get pregnant, lose her employment, there would be gossip, and she'd end up scratching for food because no one would hire a woman with a soiled reputation. And she could forget any notion that either gentleman would take care of her. For them, this was nothing more than entertainment. Them against her.

Addie thought about how tempted she'd been to accept Guy's invitation. She had to admit that the possibilities had temporarily excited her. Yes, the scale had leaned in his direction. But this fantasizing about being with either cousin had to stop. As of this moment, her mind was closed to all weaknesses. She had a strong backbone and it was time she used it. This had become a war of wills, and she was going to win.

* * *

It was still early morning as Will moved his gelding east on Taylor Street. He continued to hold his prancing steed to a walk because he wasn't particularly anxious to see Addie. He was still mulling over last night's drinking session with Guy, and his cousin's taunts of an approaching victory. Had Guy been telling the truth?

It was what Guy had said that made him decide to change his own strategy. Guy had been right. Will frowned. He was still nowhere nearer to getting Addie in his bed. Trying to steal kisses from Addie would now come to a halt, and henceforth he would only treat her as a lady. He would develop a friendship. He could even lead her to believe she was his confidant. He could confide his latest conquests and even ask for her advice about women. Surely that would titillate her own passion. Maybe she'd even get jealous. Too bad he couldn't be a fly on the wall and listen to what Guy had been telling her.

After having reviewed his plan once again, Will concluded it was an excellent bit of strategy. Addie couldn't help but wonder why his ardor had seemingly ceased, and eventually blame herself for being too aloof. Then she would give him the opening he'd been waiting for. And what did he have to lose? So far, nothing he'd tried had come out as he'd expected. Addie just didn't react like most women. He'd been stupid to make the wager with Guy. He'd never gone to so much trouble or planning for any woman!

He tipped his hat as he passed Mrs. Carson, walking down the street. An extremely versatile woman in bed.

Will found Addie in her small office at the back of the house, working on her household ledger. When she looked up, he smiled. She frowned. Were those dark circles under her lovely eyes, he wondered? "Are you not feeling well?"

Addie couldn't believe that she'd detected a note of concern in Will's voice. "I'm fine. I'd feel even better if I were left alone to do my work."

"Now don't go getting upset. I only wanted to talk." He sat on the wooden chair facing her. "I don't think you get out of the house enough. Have you looked out the window? It appears the fog has lifted. A perfect day for a stroll."

Addie looked at him suspiciously. "Surely you're not suggesting... why, good heavens, someone might see us together." She looked back down at her work.

"You misjudge me." Will stood and held out his elbow. "I think a stroll around the grounds would be quite pleasant."

"I have work to do."

With Addie doing nothing to further the conversation, Will was already at a loss for words. He sat back down. "Did you read in the paper that Lewis and Allardt won the best design for the new seawall?"

"No."

Will tried again. "What do you think about the journeymen plasterers going on strike for eight-hour workdays?"

"Whoever heard of such a thing? Eight-hour workdays indeed. They'll never get it."

"I'm not too sure about that."

For the life of her, Addie couldn't figure out why Will wasn't trying to steal kisses instead of wanting to chitchat. Was this some new type of trickery?

"Mr. Stockman," Roger said softly.

Neither Addie nor Will had heard the butler's approach.

"You have a female guest. Shall I escort her to the parlor?"

Addie watched a puzzled look cross Will's handsome features.

"Are you sure she didn't mean my grandfather?" Will asked.

"No, sir. She specifically asked for you."

"Very well. Show her into the parlor."

The concerned look on Roger's normally placid face strongly piqued Addie's curiosity. When the men left, she nearly knocked her ledger to the floor as she hurried out of the small room. She came down the long hall just in time to see the lady being escorted across the entry. Though her shiny brunette hair and clothes were clean, the style of gown she wore was long outdated and had seen better days. She was almost too thin, yet she had a strikingly attractive face. Addie was sure she had never seen the woman before. She couldn't be seeking employment or she would have entered by way of the back door.

Consumed with curiosity, Addie rushed back through the house, then bounded out the door. Minutes later, she had worked her way to the parlor French doors, and had positioned herself so as not to be seen from inside. She silently congratulated herself for having them opened earlier to air the musty parlor. While toying with a red rosebud so the gardener or anyone else wouldn't think she was eavesdropping, she strained her ears to hear what was being said.

"Where did you get the nerve to come here and accuse me of such a thing?" Addie was shocked at the anger in Will's voice. "I've never set eyes on you before, woman," he continued. "If I'm guilty as you stated, why didn't you come to my residence? Better yet, why didn't you confront me with this sooner?"

"I'm only two months along. If you didn't do anything about it, I thought your grandfather would."

Will released a cutting laugh. "Two months? I believe I can remember who I was with that long ago."

"You stayed with me for a week!" The woman began weeping. "What would Mr. Stockman say if he knew his grandson had stayed drunk, raped me, then said he loved me!"

"You discredit me, as well as the old gentleman. My grandfather probably knows more about this sort of thing than I do. Do you think he's been sitting quietly in this house for the last thirty years doing nothing? He enjoys women every bit as much as I do. I'll admit that I have done my share of drinking. There have even been weeks that I can't remember exactly what I did. Something you obviously found out about. Nevertheless, my dear, I know for a fact that we have never met. If I set my mind to it, I'm sure I could find at least a dozen other men with whom you've shared your pleasure.

"This time you picked the wrong one. You'll not get a penny from me, lady. If I were smart, I'd see you put in jail for what you're trying to pull, but I'll let you go and hope that you've learned a lesson from all this."

"You forced yourself on me!"

"I did no such thing! Now leave."

"The child is yours," the woman persisted, her voice cracking under the strain.

"Go find another to blackmail with your lies."

Addie could hear the pair struggling and there was no doubt the woman was being escorted out forcefully.

"I'll kill myself and the baby if you won't help," the woman threatened.

"You do that. At least one less crook will be on the streets."

Those were the last words Addie heard. She felt nauseous and angry at the uncaring way Will had treated the unfortunate woman. That could have been herself pleading for help. This was the response *she* would have received.

Addie cupped her hand over her mouth and ran toward the back of the house. She should have realized what Will was like. He had been just as insensitive when she'd asked him about Beth.

Chapter Five

The clicking sound of heels striking the hallway floor ceased when the slender woman came to a halt in front of the tall, heavy doors. After a quick check to be sure her blond hair was still smoothed back and the white starched collar properly situated, she raised her hand and knocked softly.

"Come in," called a deep voice from the other side.

Adelaide turned the knob and entered. The smell of cigar smoke still lingered in the study, and she wasn't surprised to see papers carelessly strewn across the top of the large mahogany desk. Some had even fallen to the floor. She looked fondly at the striking gray-headed gentleman seated behind the desk. She would always have the deepest respect for Gordon Stockman. "Hubert said you wanted to see me, sir."

"Yes, yes. Sit down, Addie."

"I would as soon stand."

Gordon Stockman looked up from his work and stared at his housekeeper. The picture of efficiency. "Had I wanted you to stand I would not have told you to sit," he stated softly.

Just like his grandson, Adelaide thought testily as she moved to one of the delicate upholstered chairs scattered about the room. She sat on the edge and properly rested her hands in her lap.

"Have you seen my will?"

Adelaide gasped. "Of course not!"

"Don't act so shocked. Since you know where everything else is in this house, I thought you might have seen it somewhere."

Gordon stood and walked around the desk. He was quite fond of Addie, and had been well aware that the transition from maid to housekeeper eight years ago hadn't been easy. She'd had to take over right after Estelle Carpenter had unexpectedly run off with that miner fellow. But Addie had never complained or failed in her duties. Surprisingly, she had proven to be even more efficient than her predecessor. "There is little that goes on in this household that you're not aware of, including my personal liaisons. Therefore, I assume you know of William's visitor yesterday. Most decidedly a woman of questionable birthright."

Adelaide nodded. Had someone seen her eavesdropping? She waited for the powerful man to continue. There was no doubt that the servants reported to him. How else could he stay so well-informed?

"And what else do you know?" Gordon questioned.

Not sure as to how much Mr. Stockman had been told, Adelaide had no choice but to tell the truth. "That she accused Mr. William of being the father to the child she carries, and that he sent her away, refusing to admit responsibility." She couldn't hide the bitterness in her voice. She was still deeply depressed over what Will had done. There was no doubt that he would have reacted the same had Beth confronted him.

Gordon frowned. "I had a footman follow the woman. I can see by your expression that you're wondering why." He leaned his hip against the edge of the desk. "I have seen too much of life to be taken in by a woman's trickery, still I can't help but wonder if the child really is William's. I've had plenty of reports as to his many affairs. At least Guy has the sense to keep his life more private," he said as an afterthought.

Adelaide watched Gordon rub the back of his neck. A sure sign that something important was on his mind.

"When William married in England, I had thought I would finally see great-grandchildren—male heirs to carry on the family name. His wife's untimely demise certainly prevented that from happening."

Adelaide couldn't understand why he would call her into his study just to discuss family matters. Had he heard about the wager, or that his grandsons had been paying her special attention?

"Neither Guymour nor William show any inclination to settle down. I love my grandsons, but I've come to realize they are nothing more than leeches. I've had enough of their arguing, womanizing, gambling, and heaven knows what else. And I know it isn't going to stop. As you're well aware, their fathers were the same way. Guymour's father went off to some island and met with a shark while diving for pearls! And what did William's father do? He got himself killed in a confounded buggy race! At least they had enough wisdom to marry and bear sons." Gordon looked toward the window to hide the hurt he still felt at having lost his sons so many years ago.

Addie had heard the stories many times. Guy's mother had also died, of malaria on the island. It was Will's mother who had taken over the responsibility of raising the boys. But death had continued to follow the Stockman cousins. Will's mother, Malenda Stockman, had died while the boys were away at school.

"I'm certain William and Guymour are waiting for me to pass to my grave so they can squander a family fortune that has been handed down from generation to generation. My forefathers, as well as myself, worked damn hard to amass such wealth. After we're married I shall have my will changed, making you the beneficiary."

"I'm sure you're falsely accusing them. The boys love you."

"How kind you are, but believe me, my dear, they do not deserve your banner. Even so, love has nothing to do with what I'm talking about. And why do you continually call them boys? They're older than you."

"I suppose because you do."

"Oh."

Adelaide couldn't stay her curiosity a minute longer. "Sir, why are you telling me all this?"

"Why not? You know as much about this family as I do. Possibly more. However, that is only part of why I wanted to see you. I was up most of the night thinking about my grandsons and that woman . . . the one with the child."

"Penelope."

"Yes. About Penelope. William is a lawyer, by damn, and yet he does nothing to advance a career. Instead, I give him an allowance that is quickly spent on pursuits of pleasure. Guymour's allowance . . . well, I'm not sure about Guymour. He also spends his time on pleasures, yet he never comes to collect his allowance. It's sent to his house. He hasn't asked for additional funds—so far—but it is simply a matter of time before he'll start showing up early like William. The boys are more like twins than cousins."

Addie realized that she had always thought the same until recently. She knew now that there was a big difference in how they handled their women.

Gordon began pacing in front of his housekeeper. "Guymour has a confounded engineering degree! He claimed he wanted to build ships. Do you see him building ships? So because of what they've become, or haven't become, and for their own benefit, I've decided not to leave my grandsons the whole of my estate."

Addie was dumbfounded. It took a moment for her to find her voice again. "But it belongs to them. It is their inheritance!"

"They're twenty-seven! It's time they learned how to handle money. Hands have to be soiled."

Adelaide could never remember a day that Mr. Stockman had soiled his hands doing any type of manual labor. He'd always played the stock market, used his mind on various business deals, and sold and bought land.

"There is, however, a problem. If I don't leave everything to my grandsons, who shall I leave it to? My old friends are dead and I'm too tight pocketed to give it to charity. Just the thought makes my stomach churn. And I certainly do not want to leave it to Hubert, my so-called manservant. We both know he's been stealing from me for years."

"Maybe I shouldn't listen to any more."

Gordon came to an abrupt halt. "I want the boy that woman is carrying, and I'll go to any extreme to get him."

"It could be a girl," Addie replied, still aggravated that Mr. Stockman would want to leave his money to nonfamily. Surely, given a little time, he'd come to realize the error in his thinking.

"It will be a boy. This family carries sons in their genes. And I'll know by his eyes if he's a Stockman." Gordon rubbed the back of his neck again. "Addie, I brought you in here because I've decided to make you a proposition."

Adelaide tensed. She instinctively knew that whatever Mr. Stockman said, it wasn't going to be in her best interest. No Stockman male had ever come up with a proposition that hadn't meant trouble. She stood. This time she was going to put her foot down and say no to whatever he had on his mind!

"I want you to be my wife."

"You what?" Adelaide collapsed back onto the chair, coughing. "Mr. Stockman," she blurted as soon as her coughing fit ended, "that wouldn't be proper!"

"What do you mean not proper?"

Adelaide looked up at the solid six-foot-three frame that was suddenly towering over her. Slowly she stood again, trying to feel less intimidated. "Mr. Stockman, are you into your cups?"

Even at sixty-eight, Gordon Stockman was still quite a charmer. But Adelaide refused to give in to that slow grin. It was the same intoxicating smile that his grandsons had inherited and that always seemed to get her into trouble. She wasn't about to let Mr. Stockman talk her into some foolish notion about marriage. To her shock, he reached out and took her hand.

"I've thought this over very carefully. Naturally I would want William's son to be raised as ours, but you need not worry. I do not expect you to share my bed."

"You're assuming too much. I would never consider—"

"Of course we'll have to make a convincing show of having consummated our marriage. I have known you too long to think of you as anything other than a daughter." He chuckled. "Besides, you would interfere with my other women."

Adelaide was beside herself. Mr. Stockman was acting as if she had already agreed to such a foolish notion. Age was undoubtedly getting the better of him. She snatched her hand from his. "I'm sorry, Mr. Stockman, but though I am indeed honored, I could never agree to be your wife."

"Surely you don't want to spend the rest of your years working as a housekeeper? You're young. You should be enjoying life."

"I am enjoying life."

"Nonsense. Look at you. Twenty-five, beautiful, and as stiff and ungiving a woman as I've ever met."

"That's not so. I chose—"

"Think of the possibilities. If you're like this now, what will you be like when you get my age? As my wife, you would have money to do anything you pleased, and your position would command the highest esteem."

"You seem to forget that I lack the qualifications of being a lady."

"What are you talking about? Being a housekeeper has given you the training and you've watched women come and go for years. I can assure you, you are far more a lady than most of them.

"I realize all of this comes as a shock and that you need time to think it over. Unfortunately, time is not our ally. If I am to successfully pull off what I have planned, it has to be done as soon as possible. I want you to go to your room and think very carefully about what I've said. We'll talk again tomorrow, after you've had a chance to absorb the benefits you're being offered."

Adelaide walked stiffly to the door. "You know the boys would never permit it to happen," she said over her shoulder.

"As my wife, you'd be my undisputed heir. But that is neither here nor there. When we return from our honeymoon, they'll quickly find out that no matter how they rant and rave, I have no intention of changing a thing. I shall also make it very clear that they are to treat you with the highest respect, or they will never show their faces in this house again."

With her back turned to Gordon, Adelaide allowed herself a smile. She could think of nothing she'd like more than to have the cousins put in their places. The offer was already starting to have possibilities.

Gordon's expression relaxed as he watched the rigid young woman close the door behind her. She had moved as if she were in a trance. But what had he expected?

He clapped his hands, quite pleased with himself. He had made the right decision. He'd always had a fond spot in his heart for her. She'd always been honest, hardworking and loyal to the core. She watched the household budget closely, and two years ago when he'd almost died, she had been the one to sit by his bed and nurse him back to health. Another big factor in her favor was that she was the only woman he knew who showed absolutely no signs of weakness toward his grandsons. He derived great pleasure in knowing they could talk her into nothing!

Still grinning, Gordon returned to his desk.

* * *

Deep in thought, Adelaide made her way up the second flight of stairs. Even though he hadn't admitted it, Mr. Stockman had to have imbibed too much liquor this afternoon. She was having a hard enough time sidestepping his grandsons without adding him to her problems.

Adelaide entered her room. Other than the new curtains and bedspread, it was exactly the same as when Miss Carpenter had been in residence. Sparse but comfortable.

A fire crackled in the fireplace, and Adelaide gratefully collapsed into the heavy armchair. The fire gave blessed warmth if she stayed right in front of it, but the rest of the room remained chilled and damp during the rainy season.

She picked up her shawl lying across the footstool, and draped it over her shoulders. January and February had been miserable months, and March wasn't showing any tendencies of being different. Rain and fog—then more rain and fog. The only bright day had been when the nitroglycerin had exploded at the Wells Fargo & Co. express office. "What San Francisco needs is a big drop of sun," she muttered.

Adelaide yawned. She was tempted to remove her high-topped shoes and warm her feet on the hearth. But as soon as she did, one of the servants, or Mr. Stockman, would need her help with some simple something. Even after all these years, it still amazed her how inept servants could be. Of course, Mr. Stockman's calls were understandable. He'd never known a life without being waited on.

She stared at the flames licking up the chimney. What if Mr. Stockman had been serious? No, the money rightfully belonged to the boys. On the other hand, why should she be concerned about them? They certainly hadn't given her any consideration when the wager was made. Wouldn't their faces turn blue upon discovering she would inherit everything?

No. It was an impossible situation. Ridiculous. She was daydreaming again. She was a housekeeper, nothing more.

Absolutely not a woman of quality. She had worked hard to keep her reputation spotless, and if she consented to marry, all of San Francisco would be saying she had been Mr. Stockman's mistress. On the other hand, Mr. Stockman had vowed to stand by her. It would certainly put an end to Guy and Will's pranks. And though she had always said she would never marry a man she didn't love, being rich could certainly fill in any missing gaps.

And what about the woman named Penelope? Will had no right to treat her in such a manner. Since his return, Addie had come to think of Will as...comfortable—an easygoing man with a big heart. He had been so convincing that she had actually decided he really wasn't the father of Beth's child. But this whole sordid affair with Penelope served to prove that her original accusations were valid. She'd as soon trust Guy as Will. That was ridiculous. Guy was even worse. Fortunately she wasn't the type of woman who would easily succumb to gentlemen's charms, she assured herself.

Mr. Stockman had been right. She would indeed be a fool not to jump at such an opportunity. It was time she started looking after herself. No one else was going to do it. She'd worked all her life and it would be wonderful to discover what it was like on the other side. And...she would be the *real* mistress of the house.

Addie stood, folded her shawl and placed it back on the footstool. Come tomorrow, if Mr. Stockman still wanted her as his wife, she would accept. Mr. Stockman wouldn't regret marrying her. She would be every bit as good a wife as she had been a housekeeper.

Her full lips curved into a rare, bright smile. She'd known there would come a day when she would be able to get even with Will and Guy for the way they had treated her. It would be worth everything just to see the looks on their faces when Mr. Stockman introduced her as their new grandmother.

* * *

The next afternoon, Adelaide returned to the study.

"Well, have you thought over my proposal?" Gordon asked nonchalantly.

"You haven't changed your mind?"

Gordon shook his head. "Nor do I intend to. Are there any questions?"

"Yes, one." Addie walked to the end of the room, stopped, then turned. "Since you've chosen not to leave your money to the boys because they would spend it, why would you permit me to go out and do the same thing?"

"Oh, but there is a big difference. You know what it is to work, and you know the value of money. You are very frugal with the household sum I give you. You could spend to your heart's content, but you'll always make sure the bulk of the estate stays intact. But I assure you, I don't intend to die anytime soon. When I do, the years would have already settled everything."

"Then I accept."

"Good. I know you're concerned about the boys, but look at it this way. Soon they will be thirty. When they reach forty, I'll probably be dead. I need to be sure there is an heir before that time comes. I can't turn my back on the chance that the woman is carrying my only great-grandchild."

Addie had forgotten all about the baby. She would delight in raising it, but would she make a good mother? She cleared her suddenly dry throat. "Because of your age . . . I mean since we are to raise the child as our own, is it possible—"

"Are you wondering if I could sire a child?"

Quite embarrassed, Addie nodded.

"I know of a woman, twenty, who just had her seventy-two-year-old husband's baby. Do not concern yourself about the boy being called a bastard. Not William or Guymour will ever know the truth. All I need is your consent of marriage and a promise to raise my great-grandson as your own." He lifted his gray bushy eyebrows. "Just think about how rich you are going to be."

How could anyone refuse such a devilishly handsome old man? Adelaide thought. "If you can think of a way to make this all appear proper, I promise the truth will never escape my lips," she said sincerely.

"Good. Stop looking so serious, Addie. I assure you, you're about to have a very pleasurable experience. I have already booked our passage to France and…what was that woman's name?"

"Penelope."

"Yes. That's right. Penelope White. She's been informed that in two weeks my coach will arrive to take her to the ship. The witch suspects she has me by the purse strings and has already demanded a personal maid of her choosing."

"You knew I would agree to this?"

"Of course. You've always been an intelligent girl. You couldn't afford to turn down such an offer."

Adelaide's head was swimming.

"Remember, Adelaide, you can't say a word about this to anyone." A hint of anger flashed in Gordon's dark eyes. "I have noticed Guymour and William paying a lot of attention to you lately."

Adelaide gulped.

"Be especially careful around them. Now be gone with you, and try to attend to your duties as normal."

"I should start packing."

"Do nothing, my dear. Everything will be taken care of." Gordon's expression softened. "And, Addie, thank you for being kind to an old man. You will never regret it."

A smile played on her lips. "Why, Mr. Stockman, I never thought I'd hear you allude to being old."

"My, my, Addie, I do believe there is still hope for you. You actually showed a bit of humor."

Addie's smile disappeared as soon as she left the room.

For the remainder of the afternoon, Adelaide moved about in a daze. She wasn't sure she was going to be able to hide her emotions, even if it did only require her to act normal.

By the following day Addie was convinced everyone knew she was going to marry Mr. Stockman. Of course she was being ridiculous, but she couldn't seem to help it. She'd never before carried such a secret.

As each day led into another, Addie became suspicious of everyone. Why did that butler smile, or, had those maids she'd caught giggling upstairs been talking about her? She would have sworn servants deliberately turned away to keep from staring. Had she inadvertently said or done anything that would alert them to the plan? At other times she felt guilty. Then there were the unexpected moments when the thought of going to France and being rich took her to the edge of giddiness. But not knowing what Mr. Stockman was planning invariably brought her back to her senses. At night, she even argued with herself as to what she would purchase first with her newfound wealth. She also worried about having to contend with Guy and Will. If anyone noticed something different about her, it would be one of them.

Each night she went to bed exhausted.

The hand suddenly placed on Addie's shoulder caused her to jump and spill coffee onto the kitchen table. She jerked around and saw Hubert standing behind her. "What do you want?" she snapped at the manservant as the cook's helper hurried over with a damp cloth.

Hubert smiled. That same sickening smile Addie had hated from the day they'd met.

"Now there's no need to be in such a huff," Hubert said.

As the lecherous old man's muddy blue eyes gazed wistfully at the maid's bottom, Addie used the moment to collect her nerves. As of late, she was as jumpy as a drop of cold water landing on a hot skillet. She could ill afford to get into an argument with Hubert. Should the dog get wind of the impending wedding, he'd go directly to the boys with his mouth running and his hand held out for money. It was no secret that Hubert had never accepted her position as housekeeper, or that he hated her for the way she constantly watched him.

"I asked what you wanted," Addie repeated when the servant had finished cleaning the spilled coffee.

Hubert sniffed, making his bulbous nose even redder than usual. "I thought we might make a trade."

"What kind of trade?"

The cook's helper handed her a fresh cup of black, aromatic coffee, and left.

"You tell me what the old man is up to, and I'll be quiet about how you flirt with his grandsons."

"You don't know what you're talking about."

"I'm not the only one who's noticed. You know how servants can talk."

"Then by all means, tell Mr. Stockman. It matters not to me." She would have fired the man years ago, but Mr. Stockman had insisted that Hubert had worked too long for him to be discharged. He might change his mind now that he was aware of Hubert's habit of removing things from the house and never returning them.

"You know what I'm talking about. The old man is up to something and I want to know what. I'm sure he tells you everything. You have him under your spell just like other men who come near you."

"I know nothing. It's all in your imagination. Now leave me be."

"You'll regret this," Hubert threatened before charging out of the kitchen.

The knock on Addie's bedroom door startled her. She glanced at the clock. What would anyone want with her this time of night? She set her plate of cookies on the floor and was about to rise from her chair when the door swung open. Guy Stockman filled the doorway. "What are you doing here?" she demanded, trying not to show her sudden, uncalled-for feeling of excitement. Realizing she had nothing on but her nightgown, she yanked the blanket she'd had laying over her legs up to her chin. "You leave my room immediately!"

"I just brought Grandfather home from a card game we had attended."

"That doesn't give you any excuse to be here." She could feel her heart pounding against her ribs. Why did she continue to allow him to have this effect on her?

Guy closed the door behind him.

"I asked why you're here!"

"My, what big eyes you have, my dear," Guy mocked as he walked toward her.

Addie tried reminding herself that it wasn't decent for a man to be in her room when all she had on were her nightclothes. Would he kiss her again? "Have you been drinking?"

"A brandy or two. Do you realize this is the first time I've seen you out of that damn black uniform?"

Addie knew the fireplace poker was within reach if she needed it. Whatever it took, she would defend her honor, but she couldn't seem to rid herself of the exhilaration she was experiencing. "There was no need for you to close the door."

Guy's laugh was clipped. "I closed it for your benefit, darling. I didn't think you'd want anyone to accidentally overhear us talking, or discover you're entertaining a male guest."

"Entertaining indeed. Get out of here."

"Am I imagining it or do you spend most of the time ordering me away from you? If you would feel safer, I'd be more than happy to open the door."

"No!" The word had rushed out of her mouth. How did he manage to get her in these situations?

"Contrary to what you apparently think, my purpose for being here is to tell I'm going to be away for a few days."

"What difference would that make to me?"

"When I return, I'll expect an answer to my solution for ending the wager."

"Answer? This may come as a surprise, but I don't feel the least bit threatened by you."

He slowly leaned down, his mouth only inches from hers. "Though you won't admit it yet, behind that facade of coldness is a passionate woman just waiting to be awakened."

His warm breath brushed across Adelaide's face. She should reach for the poker, but she couldn't take her eyes off his mouth. When his lips joined hers, it was as a soft promise of better things to come.

"If you take me up on my offer, what happens is up to you. If you don't, I can assure you . . . but perhaps that is what you really want."

"I want to be left alone," she whispered, still wallowing in the pleasurable feel of his lips on hers.

"That's a lie, and we both know it. You react too easily to my kisses. The only question left is how to resolve something we both want."

Again his mouth joined hers, and Adelaide's breast became taut, knots formed in her stomach, and she had to grab hold of the chair to keep from wrapping her arms around his neck.

"Tell me, Addie. Tell me what you want me to do, and I'll see that it happens."

It wasn't fair. It just wasn't fair that he could so easily make her feel like pudding. Unlike Will, Guy had only been toying with her so far. She had a strong suspicion that when he returned from his trip, he was going to pursue her in earnest. Her resolve was starting to slip, and at the rate things were going, Guy would have her deflowered before she reached the boat and her wedding.

"You're right." The words were barely more than a whisper. Adelaide had to clear her throat. "You're right," she repeated. Suddenly she had the answer to everything.

Suspicious, Guy straightened up and looked down at her. She wanted him? She would never admit such a thing, and her words were stilted. She was lying through her teeth. Something wasn't right, but he didn't have time to follow his gut feeling. He'd take care of that when he returned from his trip. He was due to meet Will in a half hour.

"You must also understand that bedding out of wedlock goes against my beliefs of what is right and what is wrong," Addie added for good measure. Though she might regret her words later, she was quite proud of her little act. "I have feelings for Will, also. I need time to make my decision."

Addie wondered if he would guess she was lying. Fortunately, the distance he'd now put between them allowed her mind to once again function. "Seven days. Is that too much to ask?"

"A week can be a long time."

"How can I think when you and Will are constantly hovering over me?"

"And Will?"

"I'll tell him the same thing. Neither of you have left me a choice." Addie waited for his reply.

"I believe I should be the first to know whom you decide on." *If it's Will, I'll just have to change your mind.*

"Very well, you'll be the first to know."

"I'm curious. How can you honestly judge between what is good and bad when you've never experienced pleasures? How can it be bad to want to feel my hands gliding across your silken body as I awaken your desire?"

Addie squared her shoulders, her determination growing by leaps and bounds. "Seven days," she repeated.

"Very well, I'll wait. I'll return at noon, a week from to-day."

Addie heard the door open and close. She leaned her head back and stared up at the fire shadows playing on the ceiling. Mr. Stockman, if you weren't telling me the truth about when we will leave, Adelaide thought, I'm going to have to do some very fast thinking. It's not the loss of my virginity that bothers me nearly as much as the reason for it! It seems each day brings more difficulties. When are you going to tell me about your plans?

Chapter Six

The thick fog licked up and around the two men's legs as they casually strolled along the Barbary Coast waterfront. At other times the fog covered them completely, giving them the appearance of having disappeared. The beaver top hats and expensive wool coats were a proclamation of the gentlemen's wealth. And though their footsteps were silent, the silver-handled walking sticks they carried could be heard tapping the wooden sidewalk. They paid little attention to the saloons they passed, or the music and bawdy noise that blared out at them from each doorway.

"You might as well start counting your money," Will bluffed. "You're going to lose, Cousin. In two more days, I'll be drowning in the pleasures our grandfather's housekeeper has to offer."

Guy had to jump aside to keep from being hit by a drunk who had just been thrown out of Blandon's Saloon.

"You know as well as I that with some women," Will continued, "you have to be masterful. I'm telling you, the woman is going to have to be led down the path of pleasure. She knows nothing of the joy of sex and it's against her nature to make advances. I'll change all that once I've bedded her."

Guy chuckled. "Tell the truth, Will. You're no closer to getting Addie in bed than I am. I'm beginning to admire her. She's putting up one hell of a fight. I know I've never had a lady hold out this long, and she's taking on the both of us. It's turning out to be a war.''

Ten feet away, four burly-looking men stepped onto the walk, blocking Guy and Will's path. The clubs in their hand left little doubt as to what they were up to.

Guy pointed his cane. ''You gentlemen would be wise to let us pass,'' he said calmly. ''You're asking for more than you can handle.''

The biggest of the four smiled, showing missing teeth. ''We ain't afraid of dandies like you. Now hand over all your coin, and be quick about it.''

''I can see I'm going to enjoy this night,'' Will said as he moved forward. ''I can't even remember the last time I had a good fight.''

Guy was right behind him.

Not expecting an attack, the robbers were taken by surprise. Before they could wield their weapons, Guy and Will were already upon them. Crunching blows were delivered. One of the culprits finally managed to swing his club, but Guy ducked and the club struck the thief's cohort, who immediately crumpled to the ground. A hard sock to the last man's jaw landed him beside the others. The fiasco was brief. Guy and Will straightened their coats and continued on.

Five doors down, the pair entered one of the quieter saloons, to partake of the entertainment and whiskey. Beautiful frescoes, arches and columns were only a part of the grandeur and richness of the place. However, there were few customers, and some of those appeared not to have bathed in years. It was easy to find a vacant table.

''I swear,'' Will commented, ''the Barbary Coast has to be the home of every criminal in San Francisco.'' He laughed. ''But what would we do without it? Where else could we find a place so infamous for its saloons, gambling houses and brothels?''

Guy nodded his agreement as he glanced at the assortment of scantily dressed women standing on the stage and making an honest effort to sing on key. None had any appeal, but it didn't matter. He had planned to keep an eye on Will tonight. Earlier, when his cousin had been talking about Adelaide, Guy had heard a glimmer of excitement in his voice. The curly-haired lover was up to something.

Instead of looking at the women, Will was trying to remember if there was a tree or anything else by Addie's window. Something he could climb. "Tell me, Guymour, why do you suppose we delight in being in rowdy places?"

"Because neither of us has learned the art of settling down, and it's far more entertaining than a boring party. Of course, the day will probably come when you'll want to marry again."

"I doubt it. It takes too much out of a man. It's you who has changed since your return. You seem more self-satisfied than I remember."

"War takes a lot out of a man. It wasn't just the carnage I saw. It was the determination and the sickening hatred between families that had been split in two because of their beliefs. Brother pitted against brother, each convinced they were on the right side . . . well, you would had to have been there. Let it suffice to say I have more admiration for the quieter things in life." He gave Will a devil-may-care smile. "But that doesn't mean I'm ready to give up life's pleasures. I'm just no longer willing to *make* it my life."

Will nodded. "The thought of death can play with a man's mind."

"Have you heard any more from that woman who claimed you were the father of her child?"

"No. She's probably still searching for someone to believe her. Let's be done with this serious talk. I thought we were out for a night's enjoyment."

They laughed.

When the men left the saloon several hours later, they were well into their drinks. After walking to their carriages each climbed into his own vehicle. The coachmen moved the horses forward. For no particular reason, Guy decided to follow Will a short distance. He realized he'd made a wise decision when Will's coachman headed the conveyance in the opposite direction of Will's house. Guy knew immediately that his dear cousin was going to the Stockman mansion.

A short time later, Guy stood in the shadows watching Will walk about the side of the house, looking up at the other floors. Was he trying to determine which room was Addie's?

Will jerked his coat off, flung it onto the ground, and proceeded to yank on the various gnarled vines going up the side of the house. After finding one that was apparently to his liking, he leaped up and started his climb.

Will was at least eight feet off the ground when Guy had seen enough. Just as he was about to put a stop to Will's escapade, there was a loud snap. The vine had broken. With a sickening look on his face, Will flew spread-eagled through the air and landed hard on the ground.

Laughing, Guy hurried forward. Will was passed out and snoring. He'd been too drunk to get hurt. Guy fetched Will's driver and gave instructions to take his cousin home and put him in bed.

Satisfied, Guy returned to his own coach. After all he'd had to drink tonight, he wasn't going to feel much like getting up in the morning.

The following afternoon, Addie took Will out to the herb garden where they couldn't be overheard, then requested a seven-day grace period. "At that time I'll have made up my mind as to whom I will share my favors with."

"Seven days of not seeing you? You're not acting like a friend," he accused. He glanced around at the plants until he had regained his composure. "How can I go that long without having someone to confide my problems to? Have you said anything to Guy about this?"

"Yes, and he's agreed to abide by my wishes."

"That bastard! He didn't say a thing about it to me last night."

"I'm sure he felt that it was my place to speak to you."

Will stepped up to Adelaide and took her face in his hands. "Forgive me for being so indelicate. Of course I'll abide by your wishes. I do hope that I will be the first to know of your decision."

"But of course."

Will leaned down and kissed Adelaide. "You have no idea how much I care for you," he whispered before making a grand exit.

Chapter Seven

Time was counting down, and the past few days had sorely tested Addie's nerves and endurance. She hadn't even been able to enjoy her reprieve from having Guy and Will underfoot. Hubert had taken their place and seemed to be constantly lurking about.

Why hadn't Mr. Stockman summoned her with more details of their journey? Had he changed his mind? She couldn't dredge up the courage to ask. She was well aware of the consequence hovering over her head should that happen. There wasn't any doubt as to whether the cousins would arrive on the given day.

Addie was in the wine cellar when Ivy came with the news that Mr. Stockman wanted to see her in his study. At last! She took off running. As she hastily started up the wooden stairs, she tripped but managed to regain her footing. She didn't care that Ivy was undoubtedly questioning the reason for her sudden haste.

When Addie reached the study, she stopped in front of the imposing door and tried to catch her breath. Her heart was pounding so hard it was a wonder it didn't leap from her chest. After giving the waist of her uniform a tug so the bodice didn't look mussed, she raised her hand and knocked.

"Come in."

She entered the room.

"Come in, Miss Thompkins," Gordon said. He waited until she had closed the door behind her. "I thought you would like to know that we will be leaving for the ship at four o'clock Tuesday morning."

Adelaide sat on the sofa and managed to suppress a sigh of relief. Tuesday. The very day William and Guymour were to arrive for her answer. Soon, all the secrecy would be ended. Everything was going to turn out just fine.

"Is something wrong?" Gordon asked worriedly. "Your face is flushed."

"I'm sure it is nothing more than excitement." Now that she could relax, she wondered why Mr. Stockman looked so stern this morning. "Have you considered how worried the boys will be when it's discovered you're missing?" It wasn't easy trying to sound intelligent when she felt more like celebrating.

Gordon's face softened. He'd had a horrendous argument with his lawyer this morning over making Addie the recipient of his fortune. Now he was taking it out on her. It was plain to see by the pinched look of her normally full lips that she was having second thoughts about everything. Perhaps he should have told her his plans sooner, but it was too late to worry about that now. He sat beside her and took her hands in his. "Don't worry. After our departure, the boys will be informed that I have left on a voyage. Now I don't want you to worry about a thing. All is in readiness."

"But I—"

"Shh. The day after tomorrow your entire life is going to change. You're starting on an exciting adventure. Now be on your way so I can tie up a few loose ends."

Adelaide nodded and left. As she entered the entrance hall, her gaze moved to the two beautiful Ming vases resting on pedestal tables, on to the freshly cut flowers and finally the stained glass windows. Soon this would all be hers. If someone could read her thoughts, she was sure they would consider her to be a greedy person. But she didn't feel that way at all. Maybe she was taking, but she was also giving. Mr. Stockman was going to be proud of her, and she'd become the best wife a man could possibly have.

Adelaide had a sudden surge of idleness. What in heaven's name was she going to do until Tuesday morning? It would seem like forever before she stepped foot on the ship.

An unaccustomed giggle escaped her lips. She had outsmarted Will and Guy. Knowing that she had finally beaten them at their own game completely brightened her day. She headed back to the wine cellar, humming a tune.

Adelaide was feeling like a sneak thief as she silently left the big house. At last the day of departure had arrived. Even though it was early morning, it would still be hours before the sun appeared. The darkness and thick fog added to the illusion of some impending disaster. Any minute she expected to see Will or Guy coming out of the mist.

The footman's strong hand took hold of her arm and guided her toward the shiny green carriage waiting at the back. She was quickly settled inside.

Mr. Stockman stepped in a few minutes later, and Hubert entered right behind. Judging by his anger at being inconvenienced at such an hour, Adelaide suspected that Hubert hadn't yet been informed of their destination. She would have preferred he didn't accompany them, but Mr. Stockman would need assistance with his dress during the long voyage. And, considering Hubert's inclination toward theft, it wouldn't have been wise to leave him behind for so long. Nothing would have been left upon their return.

When the buggy jerked forward, Adelaide was filled with a sense of excitement. This would probably be the greatest adventure of her entire life. She glanced at Hubert, and was unsuccessful at smothering her laughter. He was going to absolutely split his trousers when he found out she would soon be the mistress of the house.

Adelaide's laughter made Hubert livid. Why was she laughing at him? Nevertheless, he kept his thoughts to himself. If he confronted Mr. Stockman with her lack of respect, the old man would undoubtedly take Addie's side on the matter. To his consternation, Mr. Stockman also broke out laughing.

"Might I ask what is so amusing, sir?" Hubert inquired in the meek manner he exhibited when around his employer.

"I assure you, Hubert," Mr. Stockman replied, "you'll soon find out."

When the carriage came to a halt on the wharf, Adelaide was quickly assisted out the door. The smell of brine was especially strong. The cold, biting air seem to go straight through her wool coat, coming to rest in her bones. She pulled the coat tighter and stared up in awe at the steamship draped in fog. Out of the corner of her eye, she saw something move. A smile threatened to blossom when the fog momentarily cleared and she could make out a pelican perched on one of the wharf posts. Even the sea gulls were already making their presence known by squawking and flapping their wings overhead.

"Is Addie going somewhere?" Hubert asked with obvious glee.

"*We're* going on a sea voyage," Gordon informed his manservant.

"We? What do you mean, we?" Seeing Mr. Stockman smile at Adelaide, Hubert gasped. "You and Addie?"

"Of course, you'll be accompanying us. What would I ever do without you?"

"I'm not going anywhere!" Hubert declared. "I had my fill of ships years ago when I sailed around the Horn!" Hubert stared at Mr. Stockman. The stern look on the tall man's face was a warning that there would be no bickering over the matter. "I have no clothes. I'm not prepared. You should have told me," he persisted.

"Addie, my dear, you go ahead," Gordon instructed. "I want to have a private word with Hubert."

With considerable trepidation—and nothing more than the clothes on her back and a reticule with a few personal items—Adelaide started up the gangplank behind other travelers. She could feel the wood move beneath her feet. Was she the only one concerned about her falling into the water?

When the steward had departed, Adelaide stood in the middle of the large stateroom, staring at the opulence of her surroundings. It was a grand affair. Silk curtains surrounded the large four-poster bed, comfortable-looking burgundy tufted chairs and lounges were conveniently scattered about, two ornate armoires stood side by side, a round table and chairs stood away from the far wall, a commode, a bureau and even a secretary for correspondence completed the furnishings. She strolled to the nearest armoire to hang her coat. Her hands dropped from the handles as she swung open the doors. Without a thought, she stepped back and glared. Inside was a bevy of gowns, the likes of which she had never seen. She ogled the lovely colors, then reached forward and ran her fingers across the different materials, some of which she didn't recognize. They were so lovely, but obviously the steward had delivered her to the wrong quarters.

Hearing a light tap, Adelaide spun about, wondering if she had been caught snooping. Mr. Stockman entered through a door that apparently joined his room with hers. She was about to protest, but he spoke first.

"You need not look so shocked, my dear. Married couples do have adjoining rooms. If not, it would be rather inconvenient trying to consummate the marriage."

"But we're not married," she said, quick to remind him.

"Soon. Are your accommodations to your liking?"

"I suppose so...I mean, yes. Everything is fine." Adelaide's thoughts were still on the adjoining rooms and the consummation he'd mentioned. "If this is my room, then someone else's clothes have been mistakenly placed in it," she blurted, her nervousness beginning to show.

"On the contrary. I had everything made especially for you. I took an old uniform of yours to a seamstress to be sure of the correct size. Never again do I want to see you in one of those black abominations. When we are out to sea, have your maid throw it overboard."

"Maid?"

Gordon stepped forward. "Yes. From this day on, you will act and be treated as my wife. Come sit down, Addie. I realize it's way past time for us to have a talk, but I've been busy making sure everything has been properly arranged." Gordon crossed to a small table and pulled out a chair for her.

Addie hesitated only a moment before stiffly accepting the courtesy.

"Penelope White is also on board, in another part of the ship with her maid. She is being comfortably taken care of. Because of our social status, there will be no reason to meet during the voyage. I don't want to give Hubert a chance of finding out what we're up to."

Gordon steepled his fingers and touched them to his lips. "We are to be married later this afternoon by the ship's captain. A small party will follow. Besides Hubert, there will be plenty of passengers to attest to the marriage, should it prove necessary. Naturally I will leave instructions for Hubert that, henceforth, he is not to enter my room until he is called for."

"How are you going to keep Hubert from finding out about Penelope when we reach Europe?"

"I shall leave him in England with relatives and a very generous purse. I've had enough of his underhanded ways, and it's time he retired. Once we are rid of him, the rest will be easy. I've arranged for a villa on the outskirts of Paris where we shall remain until Penelope has her child. The infant will be immediately put into our care, making it appear you gave birth to the child. I'm afraid you will have to pad your stomach so no one will be suspicious. Penelope will be considerably wealthier for her efforts."

"What would keep Penelope from telling someone what took place?"

"The allotment she receives when this is finished. If she lets the cat out of the bag, her money ceases. I doubt that she would be foolish enough to allow that to happen."

Adelaide found herself becoming intrigued with the charade. "You've thought of everything!"

"Let's hope so." Gordon grinned. "Actually, I've rather enjoyed myself."

Adelaide laughed softly. "I can see that."

The aging gentleman's brown eyes sparkled with delight. He could already see a change taking place in Adelaide. The transition had actually started over a month ago, though he hadn't the slightest idea as to what had caused it. Right now, her eyes were bright and there was a sense of excitement about her. He thought of the joy he would receive watching her transformation from a stilted woman to a gracious, self-assured lady capable of having fun. By the time they returned to San Francisco, she would be an entirely different person.

"I'll send your maid in. Her name is Lucy. The ropes have already been dropped and the ship is free of her mooring. This afternoon, we will become husband and wife. I suggest the white grown for the occasion. Try to rest. It is going to be a long day."

It wasn't until the wedding vows had been spoken and the ship's captain had pronounced them man and wife that Adelaide truly believed what was happening to her. Seeing how red Hubert's face had become seemed to clinch the reality. She was glad Mr. Stockman had insisted he be a witness to the ceremony.

Mr. Stockman's kiss on the cheek brought Adelaide back to reality. The tall man looked most dashing in his gray suit and blue-and-red-striped silk cravat. He led her to the captain's table for a small celebration.

Adelaide wasn't sure she liked being the center of attention. She quickly tired of having to force a smile as strangers offered congratulations. But what was going to happen after the celebration? That was her biggest concern. Was Mr. Stockman still planning on a marriage of convenience? He'd only mentioned it that one time. Had he forgotten or changed his mind? As her husband, he had the right to insist she share his bed. Over the years he'd certainly had his share of lady friends, so bashfulness was not her ally. But they had made a bargain, and if necessary, she would remind him that sleeping privileges had not been included.

"Mr. Stockman, it was a lovely wedding," Addie managed to say.

"To my wife, the name is Gordon."

"Oh. I'm sorry."

"Addie, you are never again to apologize for anything you say or do."

"After calling you 'Mr. Stockman' for so many years, it's going to be very difficult to break the habit."

"I haven't had an opportunity to tell you how ravishing you look this afternoon."

Addie blushed. After the maid had finished dressing her, she'd turned to look in the full-length mirror. Even she couldn't believe the person staring back at her was one and the same.

Gordon chose not to add that until she had walked into the room wearing the lovely silk creation, he hadn't paid any attention to what a remarkable figure she possessed. Would it be too much to hope that after he passed away, one of the boys would have the sense to settle down and claim her as his wife? Yes. It was too much to ask. "Have a drink of wine, my dear. This is supposed to be a festive occasion, not a wake."

Adelaide gladly took the glass he handed her. After several quick sips, a waiter was there to refill her glass. She needed all the help she could get to prepare for later. But even after several refills, she still did not feel the needed calming effect. Her fear of having to battle Gordon continued to escalate.

When they left the party and headed for their staterooms, Adelaide's palms became moist. This was the moment she'd dreaded all afternoon. By the time they arrived at their stateroom, her knees had taken on the consistency of jam. Adelaide forced herself to enter. Gordon was right behind her. He placed his hand on her shoulders and turned her around so she was facing him. She was ready to go to war.

"When your maid arrives in the morning, try to act joyful and satiated, my dear. After all, we supposedly shared a night of delightful bliss."

Gordon leaned down, and Adelaide squeezed her eyes shut. His kiss was delivered to her forehead.

"Good night, my dear."

Nothing was going to happen! She swayed, then passed out cold.

The servant handed Guy the sheet of white paper and waited for any instructions. She watched him reread the scrawled message then wad it up in his big fist.

"The old fool has no business taking an extensive sea voyage," Guy muttered.

"I beg your pardon, sir, I didn't hear what you said."

Guy's gaze shifted to the charming little maid. "Who did Grandfather take with him?"

"Mr. Stockman took Miss Thompkins and Hubert with him."

"Miss Thompkins? Why would he take her?"

"I have no idea, sir."

"Who was left in charge?"

"Me."

"That will be all, Ivy."

Guy watched the girl deliberately sway her hips from side to side as she left the room, but she didn't draw his interest. His thoughts had already shifted to the acid-tongued Miss Thompkins. For the life of him, he couldn't understand what would prompt his grandfather to drag her along. It certainly couldn't be for pleasure. Perhaps he had taken a female companion. Guy hoped that when he reached his grandfather's age, he had the same fire left in him.

Guy suddenly broke out in a hardy laugh. As the laughter subsided, his eyes held the spark of humor. "Why that wily little witch. She knew all along about the trip!" She was definitely beginning to intrigue him. He removed one of his grandfather's cigars from a humidor, smelled it, then stuck it in the inside of his coat pocket. "That's all right, darling Adelaide. You're going to have to return eventually, and I'll be waiting. It serves to make the challenge all the sweeter."

Gordon sat on the bench watching his wife feed bread crumbs to the pigeons. She was virtually surrounded by the creatures. With all that padding, she really did look as if she were going to have his child.

Not since his beloved Lillian was alive could Gordon remember enjoying himself as much as he had over the past five months. The weather had remained beautiful, his great grandson would be born soon, and Addie had blossomed into a spectacular lady. Trust and friendship had come first. That, along with the circus, flowers, plays, riding lessons, excellent food, wine, clothiers, and all the pleasures that Paris had to offer, had combined to break down her starched exterior. Of course he liked to believe that it was his personal influence that had created the biggest transformation. After all, it was because of him that a smile now came readily to her marvelous full lips. Even though she appeared to be pregnant, men still seemed to be at her beck and call.

Gordon knew that in all truthfulness, Addie had done more for him than he for her. She made him feel alive again, and he loved seeing things through her eyes.

He released a grunt and shifted his position on the bench. He may have been feeling young and alive, but for the past couple of days he'd felt old and tired. Something he wasn't accustomed to. Even Addie's soft laughter had failed to perk him up, but he'd managed to hide his discomfort. Knowing that it could be nothing more than a temporary chill, he hadn't said anything about it to his wife.

He watched Addie turn and walk toward him. It was a graceful, self-assured stroll. Her apricot-colored gown and large matching hat complemented her finely arched brows and flawless skin. It seemed almost sinful that a woman could be so absolutely perfect in body and face. Her lips were tilted in that half-cocked smile he'd come to know. It usually meant that she was contemplating some complexity.

"The birds are such lovely creatures, but quite messy," Addie proclaimed as she sat beside her husband. "I'm not sure I'd want them around all the time."

They sat for several minutes in comfortable silence, both lost in their own thoughts.

"Gordon, I'd hoped to spare you this, but we have a problem that I can no longer handle by myself."

Gordon raised his thick gray brows and stared at his wife. "Problem? Impossible. I've taken care of everything. There couldn't possibly be a problem."

Adelaide brushed an insect from her skirt. "It's Penelope. She has started sneaking out of the villa at night."

"What?" Gordon roared.

"Her maid, Eleonore, told me. We owe her a great deal. She has been an unending source of information. She saw Penelope leave, and came directly to me. I waited up until Penelope returned at daybreak. I confronted her and she swore it would never happen again. But it has happened at least two more times that I know of.''

Gordon frowned. ''You should have told me sooner, my dear. I'll look into the matter. If she persists in taking off at night, I'll hire a guard.'' He took her hand in his. ''Now don't look so concerned. It's all going to turn out just as I've planned.''

Addie wanted to tell her husband how haughty and spiteful Penelope had been as of late, but Gordon's complexion had seemed pale the past few days. If he was coming down with a cold, she didn't want him also worrying over something that would probably pass. She had heard from maids that a pregnant woman was often difficult to get along with.

When they had first arrived in France, Addie had made a determined effort to get to know the lovely brunette and develop a friendship. But Penelope wanted nothing to do with her. Nor did the spiteful woman associate with the servants. Other than whispering with her personal maid, Eleonore, Penelope chose to be by herself. She had made it quite clear that she was interested only in the financial side of her bargain.

Nearly two weeks later, Addie's amber eyes flashed with anger as she confronted the attractive brunette in her bedroom. ''You can't walk out! Gordon has taken good care of you. He's made sure you wanted for nothing. You owe him Will's child!''

''Ha! Will's child!'' Penelope sneered. She raised the skirt of her gown, then slowly, deliberately, pulled a small pillow from beneath and let it fall to the floor. ''You put on airs of being such a lady, Addie, but there isn't any difference between us. Neither one is pregnant and we're both out to get what money we can from that old fool.'' She kicked the pillow away.

''It's been a lie all along!'' Adelaide couldn't believe how gullible she and Gordon had been. ''There is no baby!''

"Don't look shocked for my benefit, dearie. I know exactly why you married Stockman. Well, I wanted money, too! If Stockman was stupid enough to buy my story, I'd have been crazy not to take advantage of it. And look where it's gotten me. I'm well fed, I have clothes, and thanks to the old man's generosity, I have accumulated a considerable amount of money. But the charade could only continue for so long. I'm tired of the whole affair. Now that I'm in a country where no one knows me, I can start life over again. I've even found a man who wants to marry me."

"You can't do this!" Eleonore yelled as she hurried forward from where she had been making the bed. "We made a bargain!"

As Penelope headed for the doorway, Adelaide reached out and grabbed the woman's arm. "You hussy! I'll not let you leave without facing Gordon," she hissed.

Penelope delivered a hard slap to Adelaide's cheek. The two women struggled, then seemingly out of nowhere, Penelope had a knife in her hand. Adelaide grabbed Penelope's wrist and yanked downward just as Eleonore came up behind and tripped over the pillow. Adelaide was shoved forward, Penelope's wrist still firmly gripped in her hand. As if in slow motion, Adelaide saw the blade headed for Penelope's stomach. Adelaide tried to pull backward, but it was too late. Penelope's face turned white, and her eyes bulged as she looked down at the knife embedded in her flesh. Her scream ricocheted around the room as she collapsed to the floor.

Adelaide backed away in horror. Penelope had gripped the knife and was pulling it out. She let it fall to the floor. "I curse you for doing this to me," she rasped before closing her eyes. Eleonore dropped to her knees beside her, crying and trying to stop the bleeding.

Adelaide was about to lend her assistance when she heard a deep male groan. She jerked around and saw Gordon leaning against the doorframe, his face as ashen as Penel-

ope's. Adelaide rushed forward, but she couldn't reach
Gordon before he slid and sprawled out on the floor. "So
it was a lie all along," he whispered. "She never carried my
great-grandson."

"Gordon!" His eyes rolled back into this head. Addie
tried shaking him, but she received no response. "Gordon! What's wrong? What's...?" Gordon wasn't listening. "Eleonore!" she screamed. "Run for the doctor!"
Addie dropped to the floor and rested Gordon's head in her
lap. "It's going to be all right," she soothed as she brushed
back the strands of gray hair from his forehead. Tears
rolled down her cheeks. He was so still. "Gordon! Do you
hear me? You have to be all right!"

By the time the doctor arrived, Gordon Bently Stockman and Penelope were dead. The doctor said he'd died
from a heart attack. Adelaide's grief was all-consuming, yet
at the same time she hated Gordon for dying. He had given
her a brief glimpse of happiness, then in less than one short
hour, he'd taken it all away. There wasn't even a child for
her to raise.

No charges were pressed against Adelaide after Eleonore's testimony that none of this had been the mistress's
fault.

Penelope was buried in a small cemetery and Addie sent
a message informing Will and Guy of their grandfather's
death. By the time she'd made arrangements to accompany her dead husband back to San Francisco, she was
drowning in self-pity and misgivings. She grieved deeply for
the man she'd truly come to love and blamed herself for his
demise. She should never have started the argument with
Penelope. And she had taken care of Gordon all these
years, then, when he needed her the most, she'd been too
busy savoring her own pleasures to pay attention to his
needs. She had known he was acting strangely and she
should have done something about it.

What was so sad was that all of Gordon's elaborate plans had been for nothing. Will had been right all along about Penelope, but once again she had allowed herself to believe he was guilty. The same as when she'd been convinced he was the father of Beth's child.

On the voyage home, Adelaide spent many evenings standing by the ship's rail, mentally trying to rebuild her life and recuperate from her loss. She stared across the vast ocean, watched the sunsets and contemplated her future.

She told herself she should have remained a house-keeper instead of reaching for the stars. But all she had to do was think about what she would have missed, and she had no regrets. Her short time with Gordon had been glorious, and she'd never forget the memories. It was because of Gordon that she contemplated marrying again.

But Adelaide also had to look realistically at what was facing her in San Francisco. Financially, she was comfortable, what with the account Gordon had opened for her in Paris. Though she would never be as wealthy as he had planned, she would never have to work again.

Two days before the ship was due to arrive in San Francisco, Adelaide stood at the ship's rail, paying little attention to the occasional sprays of salt water that dampened her face. The full moon reminded her of a beacon, guiding the ship home. She had procrastinated enough. Decisions had to be made. The more she had thought about what had happened during the past year, the more convinced she was that explaining the tale to Guy and Will wouldn't be easy. There were too many complications. Will would be more apt to be understanding, while Guy would undoubtedly make unwarranted accusations. This was just one of several problems that Gordon was supposed to have handled and had now fallen into her lap.

Thinking about her questionable welcome home brought forth other problems to contemplate. Eleonore could verify the accident, but what about her marriage to Gordon? She had no proof that everything had been Gordon's idea. In fact, she had no marriage certificate. She had made a thorough search of the villa but had come up empty-handed. She didn't even know how to contact the captain who had performed the wedding.

Adelaide raised her hand to brush back the strands of damp hair clinging to her face, and noticed her diamond-and-emerald bracelet sparkling in the moonlight. And what about her money, the gifts, clothes, and certainly the jewels Gordon had given her? They could easily be misconstrued as presents for reasons other than a husband trying to please his wife.

Adelaide suddenly knew what she had to do. It was so simple. No explaining would be necessary if she didn't say anything about marrying Gordon. Why stir dead coals? Gordon once said he'd change his will after their return. That meant the cousins were going to receive their inheritance after all. All she had to do was say she no longer wanted to work for them, and leave. They would never know what had happened in France.

Sadness once again lay heavy on Adelaide's shoulders. It wasn't going to be easy to turn her back on the only home she'd ever known. And what about Guy and Will? Like Gordon, they had been the only family she'd ever known, and it was unlikely that she would see them again.

Realizing it was getting too chilly to remain on the deck, Adelaide left the rail and headed for her stateroom. Strange how everything had worked out, she thought. Even after all the planning and sacrifices, she wouldn't be the rightful mistress of the manor, after all.

Adelaide forced a smile. It was time to start thinking about the good things in life. Gordon had told her that she should try at least once to experience everything life had to offer. He'd also said, "Feeling guilty about things that can't be prevented only serves to make one stagnant."

When Adelaide entered her stateroom, she had no idea she was entering a new year—1866 was gone forever.

Chapter Eight

Guy glared down at Adelaide. "You don't really expect us to accept that story, do you?"

Adelaide sat board straight, twisting her handkerchief in her lap. "Of course I do. It's the truth!" she answered. The parlor she'd once felt comfortable in now seemed dark and foreboding.

"I realize Grandfather wasn't a young man, but he was in the best of health," Guy reminded Adelaide as he moved away from her chair. "Yet you say that, for no apparent reason, he suddenly dropped dead?"

"Was he with another woman when it happened?" Will questioned from the divan. "I assure you that such a delicate situation would come as no shock."

That was a possibility Adelaide hadn't considered. She was worn-out from the long voyage, and the cousins weren't going to leave her alone until she supplied them with some answers. "Well—" she lowered her head "—it is rather difficult to talk about."

Will jumped to his feet. "I knew it! Some woman gave the old man more than he could handle."

Guy thought about how he had anxiously awaited his grandfather's return from France. He had wanted to see the look of pride in the old gentleman's face when he learned his grandson had made a killing in the stock market. And with that, and most of his inheritance, he'd turned around and purchased a shipping line that was already showing a profit. But because of Adelaide, Gordon Stockman could not be proud of the way his grandson had started making his own fortune.

"If you will excuse me, I'd like to go to my room and collect my things. I shan't be working here anymore."

Guy turned and studied the housekeeper for a brief moment. "May I ask why?"

Addie smiled weakly. "I think it would be better for everyone concerned. I would appreciate a letter of recommendation. After all, I was a faithful servant to Gor...Mr. Stockman."

"Where will you stay?" Guy inquired. "Won't you need a little time to make arrangements? Certainly there would be no harm in remaining here—at least until Grandfather's funeral, or until you find other employment. You'll have the house to yourself, and, of course, the servants."

"I need your assurance that I will be left alone." Addie didn't want to stay, but she couldn't think of an acceptable excuse for leaving.

"You will not be bothered by either of us. Try to remember we are in mourning."

"Very well, I'll stay until I can make other arrangements."

"You'll also need to be here for the reading of the will the day after the funeral," Guy informed her. "I've already made arrangements for the funeral. Actually, it's a good thing you were with our grandfather. There is no telling how long it would have taken for one of us to get him back home. Now he can rest in peace. You've been a faithful servant to our family. I'll see that you are properly rewarded for your efforts."

Adelaide's ire was immediate. After having been treated as part of this family by Gordon, she deeply resented Guy's tone, as well as the implication that he was better than she.

Guy's gaze followed Adelaide as she left the room. Upon receiving the note of her arrival from Europe, he'd hurried straight to the big house. Will had arrived a few minutes later. From the moment Guy had set eyes on the house-keeper, he'd wondered what had happened to the black uniform she used to wear. And though she was quite fetch-ing in a black silk traveling suit, where had she come by the money to procure such obviously expensive clothing? Even her boots were of the finest leather. Her pulled-back hair and snooty attitude had certainly remained the same, yet there was a different air about her. Something about all this wasn't right.

"You're not really going to let her go, are you?" Will asked in a disgruntled manner.

"Not if I can help it. She's the only one who knows how to keep the household running smoothly. But we are obli-gated to abide by her wishes."

"Well, at least one good thing has come from all this," Will said. "We'll finally come into the old man's money."

"Try to have enough respect not to sound so light-hearted, Cousin."

"Now don't go blowing steam, Guy. What would you have me do? Fall to my knees in sorrow?"

"No, I don't think that's necessary."

"Exactly my point." Will rose from the worn chair. "Everyone knows that Grandfather and I weren't exactly close."

Guy chose to drop the subject. Besides, his thoughts were still on Addie. The more he considered it the more he was convinced that she was hiding something. "I guess we'd better finalize the funeral arrangements."

As soon as Adelaide was closeted from the others, she sank onto the side of the narrow bed and looked around the small bedroom. Not until she'd become the housekeeper had she been bequeathed a room of her own. She had thought this room was truly a gift from heaven. For once in her life, she could do anything she wanted. She didn't have to listen to others snoring, and she didn't have to share a chest of drawers.

But that was before she'd gone to Europe. Now the room seemed dark and barren. It reminded her more of a tomb. Drab and colorless. She released a heavy sigh. Gordon may have meant well, but he had ruined her. She had experienced the life of the rich, and it was going to be difficult to find enjoyment from small pleasures again. Perhaps not for people who had been rich all their lives, but for her, wealth just made her want more.

She couldn't remember a day that she hadn't worked—until she'd left with Gordon. But Gordon had also kept her busy. She would be living in a fool's world if she thought she could now just sit back and do nothing. She didn't want to return to being a housekeeper, but she needed something to occupy her time. It was definitely something she was going to have to think about.

She thought of her comfortable suite where Eleonore awaited her return. Maybe she had been overly extravagant when she'd procured rooms at the Cosmopolitan Hotel, but she couldn't bear to part with all the clothes—especially the Charles Worth gowns—jewelry and other fine things she'd accumulated. After all, she had to have some place to deposit them, at least until she could find a small house to buy. The rooms in the less ostentatious hotels had been too small to accommodate her needs. And unless she admitted to her marriage, she couldn't possibly store them here. She didn't want to incur the cousins' wrath.

After Eleonore had stood by her side, Adelaide had hired the petite redhead as her personal maid. There was only a couple of years' difference in their ages, and they suited each other just fine.

Though loath to do so, Adelaide stood and went to the armoire. Gordon had once said he never again wanted to see her clothed in one of the black uniforms. "I'm sorry, Gordon," she whispered, "but I have no choice." She opened the doors and pulled out one of the three gowns hanging inside.

"Addie, you're too hard on yourself."

Adelaide spun around, her gaze scanning the small room. She would have sworn she had heard Gordon's voice, but that was impossible. The room was empty. Now she'd started to hear things, or perhaps she'd become addled. Still unsettled, she returned to the bed and placed the black gown on top of the bedspread.

Before unbuttoning her gown, Adelaide again glanced around the room. She quickly discovered that removing her fine clothes without help was quite an undertaking.

Adelaide stood in the back with the other servants, only hearing bits and pieces of the words being spoken over Gordon's coffin. The entire town of San Francisco seemed to have arrived at the Lone Mountain Cemetery.

With so many standing in front, Addie couldn't see Gordon being lowered into his grave. Unchecked tears ran down her cheeks, and it was all she could do to keep from shoving everyone aside and declaring she should be the one standing in front. But she had chosen her fate and she had to abide by it.

Adelaide knew the service was over when the people began moving away. As the mourners climbed into their fancy carriages and left the cemetery, Addie waited quietly beneath an old oak tree. Finally she moved forward until she stood at the side of the grave. She leaned over, dropping a single red rose on the coffin's lid, smiled.

"After you passed away, I didn't know whether to hate or love you, Gordon Stockman. But I've come to realize you'll always retain a special place in my heart. I'll never forget you, or the things you taught me."

"Don't let the boys have my money!"

* * *

Upon catching sight of Adelaide moving to the grave, Guy Stockman lowered the foot he'd already placed on the carriage step. Curious, he stood and watched. He tried telling himself that Adelaide had been in his grandfather's employment for many years, and that her grief was only natural. But there was still that elusive something that made him believe it was deeper than that. Had they been lovers?

When Adelaide suddenly stood, her face was pale, as if she'd been frightened by something. Guy was completely taken aback. What was the matter with her? If he didn't know better, he'd think she'd seen a ghost. Almost at a run, she hurried off toward the cemetery entrance.

"Noble, follow Miss Thompkins, but remain far enough back that she doesn't notice us," Guy instructed his coachman.

"Yes, sir."

Guy climbed inside the carriage. The transportation that had been provided for the servants had already departed, and it was a very long walk back to the house. So at some point, the housekeeper was going to have to hire transportation. And just where was she going to do that? He considered giving her a ride, but a sixth sense told him to wait.

Five minutes later, Guy watched Adelaide enter a buggy that had obviously been waiting for her. It was soon moving down Geary Street.

"Do you still want me to follow?" Noble asked.

Guy thought for a minute. "Yes. Continue on."

Guy's curiosity was piqued even more when Addie's buggy reached Taylor Street and continued straight ahead instead of turning toward Nob Hill. When it did come to a halt, it was in front of the Cosmopolitan Hotel. Possibly she was meeting someone to interview for a housekeeper's position. But why did the doorman appear to recognize her? After telling Noble to wait around the corner, Guy hurried forward.

As Guy entered the ornate lobby, he glanced about to see which direction Addie had taken. She was already ascending the wide staircase.

Deciding he wasn't going to gather any more information regarding Addie's behavior, Guy headed back toward the door. He had only gone a few steps when he came to an abrupt halt. He glanced over his shoulder at the registration desk. Addie hadn't had time to make inquiries, so she had to have known exactly where she was going. Was it employment she was looking for or something else? The frigid woman certainly wouldn't be on her way to meet a gentleman.

Guy paused only a moment before going to the long counter with a backdrop of an uncountable number of small box openings for keys.

"May I be of assistance, sir?"

Guy smiled at the pale-faced clerk. "I have been out of town, and I wanted to see if my sister had checked in yet. She would be coming from Europe," he added as an afterthought. "Blond, and very pretty. Her name is—"

The clerk smiled knowingly. "No one but Miss Thompkins and her entourage could fit that description."

Guy lifted a black brow. "Entourage?"

The clerk raised his nose in a most snobbish manner, and Guy was tempted to flatten it for him.

"Perhaps that isn't the best choice of words, but had you seen the number of men carrying her twenty-some pieces of luggage, plus a maid—"

"What room is she in?" It was all Guy could do to keep his tone of voice civil.

As soon as Guy had the room number, he headed for the stairs. He took them two at a time. There was only one way Adelaide could afford all this. It had to have come from his grandfather. He and Will had been the fools. They'd actually believed she was a virgin! The Jezebel had to be damn good at her trade to get Gordon Stockman to keep such fancy quarters.

By the time Guy reached the right room, he was furious at how the wench had tricked them all. Rather than knocking, he turned the door handle. The door was locked. Without a second thought, he raised his foot and kicked. When the door flew open, a dog as big as a calf began barking and charging toward him. Some woman he'd never set eyes on started screaming. Adelaide Thompkins stared at him in wide-eyed shock, while holding some piece of clothing in front of her partially clad body.

"I want an expla—" Guy couldn't hear his own voice over all the noise. He tried to ward off the dog with his arm, but the confounded beast grabbed his sleeve and pulled backward, successfully ripping the fine material. He saw Adelaide march into another room and bang the door behind her. The other woman had snatched up a vase and was now swinging it at him. He had never realized a woman so small could make so much noise! The barking dog charged again. He grabbed Guy's pant leg and began demonstrating the game of tug-of-war.

After several hard tugs while dodging the vase, Guy finally got free and rushed for the door. The moment he made it into the hall, he slammed the door shut behind him. Even after reaching the stairs, he could still hear the skinny dog barking, and the woman carrying on.

When Guy stomped out of the hotel, he was in a fit of anger the likes of which he hadn't known in years. He climbed into his carriage and ordered Noble to take him to his cousin's residence.

Addie sat in the middle of the big bed, listening to the noise in the other room finally come to a halt. A few minutes later, the door opened and Eleonore quietly entered the bedroom, her head down, and looking as guilty as a stagecoach robber.

The Russian wolfhound came in behind Eleonore and jumped up on the spread. Addie had to pull the uniform out from under him when he plopped down, taking up the largest portion of the bed. Obviously proud of what he'd done, he eagerly wagged his tail, placed his head on her lap and rolled his eyes up at her, waiting for a pet. She couldn't help smiling at his antics. After all, he had been trying to protect her.

"The hotel clerk just left," Eleonore said. "I told him about the intruder. He's sending someone to repair the door."

"When did you say the dog's owner would return?" Addie asked.

"It should be anytime now. Had I known you would return today, I wouldn't have agreed to watch him."

Suddenly seeing the ridiculousness of what had happened, Adelaide broke out laughing. She would have sworn she heard Gordon laughing with her.

"What's so funny?"

Still in a fit of humor, Addie finally managed to say, "I knew the man. Next time you might try not to scream until—" Remembering the startled look on Guy's face, Addie broke out laughing again. Eleonore left the room.

It didn't take long for Addie to sober up when she considered the consequences of Guy's discovery. There was no doubt that a confrontation with the cousins would be forthcoming. They were going to demand an accounting for her sudden show of wealth. How was she going to explain? She couldn't even say the funeral had proven to be trying and that her grief was still raw, or explain that hearing what sounded like Gordon's voice had been the catalyst for a stressful situation. The cousins would have her committed to a crazy house.

Addie slid off the bed. She'd returned to the hotel so she could have Eleonore massage her tight neck and shoulders, and hopefully take a short nap on a comfortable bed. She looked at the lapel watch still pinned to the front of her uniform. There was no use avoiding the inevitable. The cat was out of the bag. She could no longer hide what Gordon had given her.

Addie considered putting her clothes back on, then going to Guy's residence and getting the confrontation over with. On the other hand, why rush matters? Everyone would be at the house tomorrow for the reading of her husband's will. In the meantime she could get a good night's sleep and arrive at the house looking completely rested.

Addie tossed the uniform onto a brocade armchair. Tomorrow she'd wear a black gown of her own and never again allow Guy or Will to look down on her! Gordon had told her to always hold her head high. She had nothing to be ashamed of.

It was two o'clock the following afternoon when Addie had her driver stop the buggy in front of the big mansion. The two carriages parked in front belonged to William and Guymour Stockman. The lawyer hadn't yet arrived.

With as much dignity as she could muster, Addie left the confines of her conveyance and walked majestically to the front door. It was a walk she'd had many years to perfect. Rather than go straight in, she rang the bell, then waited for the butler to answer.

"Good morning, Miss Thompkins," Roger said respectfully. "I hardly recognized you. I believe Mr. Guymour and Mr. William are awaiting your arrival."

"Oh, I'm sure they are." She gave him a friendly wink. "Hopefully Mr. Stockman left you something special in the testament, Roger."

Roger smiled and nodded. "And the same to you, miss."

Addie returned the smile. She and Roger had always gotten along well. She followed him to the parlor.

Addie found Will and Guy at the far end of the large room, talking quietly. She thought it interesting that it was still early afternoon, yet each held a drink of spirits. The looks they gave her were not friendly, but she hadn't expected them to be. Neither man moved toward her.

"We were just wondering if you would have the nerve to show your face today," Will commented dryly. "I must say, I hadn't expected such a transformation."

"Thank you for the compliment." Addie gracefully glided to one of the deep chairs and sat. She was thinking about the hour Eleonore had spent working on her hair, making sure the coiffure was soft and appealing. It took another hour to get dressed, apply perfume to just the right areas and lightly brush rouge across the tops of her high cheekbones and touch it to her lips. Addie knew she was stunning, and she was enjoying the look of appreciation that continued to spread across Will's face as his eyes scanned her from head to toe. Guy's expression remained set in stone.

"Let's don't bother beating around the bush." Guy's words were clipped. "I want to know how you can afford quarters in the Cosmopolitan Hotel. The apartment was registered in your name. And while you're at it, you might explain who that other woman was in your rooms. And don't bother trying to deny it. I have already obtained confirmation to what I've said from the hotel clerk!"

"It is none of your business."

"The hell it isn't!" Guy roared. "You've worked for this household and been taken care of since you were a child. Then all of a sudden, Grandfather travels to Europe, taking you with him. He comes back dead and you're mysteriously a woman of wealth. What do you expect us to think? How do we even know that the doctor's claim that Grandfather died of a heart attack is correct? You owe us an explanation, Miss Thompkins, and I want it now!"

Though Addie kept reminding herself that there was nothing they could do to her, Guy's hard, accusing voice was indeed unsettling. She took two deep breaths and looked Guy straight in the eye. "Mr. Stockman gave me the money. He said I was like a daughter to him, and he wanted me to enjoy myself while in France."

Guy slowly moved toward her. "And apparently that is exactly what you did, since you needed twenty-some trunks to carry your belongings."

"Twenty?" William blurted out in shock. "You didn't tell me that." He finished off his drink. "No wonder you wouldn't let us into your bed, sweet Addie. You weren't about to jeopardize your position with Grandfather. Apparently you were playing mistress of the house in every sense of the word."

At hearing the demeaning accusation, Addie's temper snapped. "How dare you accuse me of such! You of all people know I'm not promiscuous. I didn't tell either of you anything before because I knew you wouldn't believe what I said. And you haven't. But I never thought you would stoop so low as to accuse me of being your grandfather's mistress!"

"Acting innocent won't gain you a thing. Why don't you just come out and admit you fornicated?" Will asked.

Addie jumped to her feet. "I'm guilty of nothing, and I'll not listen to another word!" She turned to leave, but Guy had moved to the doorway, blocking her exit. "Get out of my way," she warned.

"Gladly. Just tell us one thing. How much of Grandfather's money did you take after his death?"

"What money I have was given to me."

"You mean you whored for it," William accused. "Well, enjoy what you have, because you're not getting another cent. If you've been left one penny of the estate, you're going to sign it back over to us."

"And if I don't?"

"I'll personally take you to court, and everything you've done will be exposed to the public," William said, seemingly offhandedly. "You can't win."

"Again you refuse to listen. You already have me accused and hung."

"Oh, I'm listening," Guy stated impatiently, "but so far you've offered no plausible explanation. I find it hard to believe that Grandfather would dress a beautiful woman in expensive gowns, then only think of her as a daughter.''

Addie gave him a cold smile. ''You're of the same mind as William. Maybe Gordon was right about the two of you.''

''Gordon?''

''He insisted I call him that.''

''Oh, really,'' Guy said sarcastically. ''And what else did you call him—or do to him? Did you kill him? And just what did you mean about my grandfather being right about the two of us?''

Don't let them get the better of you, Addie. Addie tried to ignore the words that Gordon seemed to be whispering in her ear. ''Now you are accusing me of murder? How could I kill a man I thought so highly of?''

Will and Guy moved forward at the same time.

''Of all the—''

Hearing someone clear his throat, they all turned in unison. The family lawyer stood in the doorway. He was a tall, slender man of about fifty-five, with gray streaks in his hair, which added to a most dignified appearance. His features were sharp and his expression one of withheld anger.

Aggravated at allowing his temper to get away with him, Guy ran his fingers through his hair. ''We've been waiting for you,'' he stated.

''Are you all right?'' Jason Harper asked Adelaide kindly.

His thoughtfulness helped bolster Addie's determination not to let the cousins ride over her. ''Yes, I'm fine. Thank you for asking.''

Will and Guy looked at the attorney, then Addie, then back to the attorney. Each wondered why the gentleman would show concern for the housekeeper.

''Guymour, please have the servants come in,'' Jason said quietly. ''I'll read that part of the will first.''

''We'll finish this conversation later,'' Guy said to Addie before leaving the room.

* * *

When all were gathered in the parlor, the attorney stood and proceeded to read what each servant was to receive in appreciation of their long and faithful service.

Standing off to the side of the room, Guy watched the servants file out as soon as their portion of the will had been read. His grandfather had been quite generous, and they all sported faint smiles of contentment. Especially the older ones, who now had enough money to retire.

Though still determined to find out what Adelaide had been up to, Guy found it strange that after so many years of faithful service, she wasn't even mentioned in the will. It suddenly occurred to Guy that he hadn't seen Hubert. During all that had happened, Guy had completely forgotten about the manservant. Why wasn't he mentioned in the will, either, and where the hell was he?

"I suggest you leave now," Will said unkindly to Addie. "There is no need for you to hear the rest. And don't expect that letter of recommendation you asked for."

Addie flinched. She had worked in this house and known this family for seventeen years. Now she was being carelessly dismissed, treated as if she were nothing more than a cur. And it damned well hurt. She turned to leave.

"No, please stay." Mr. Harper spoke up. "There is more." He glanced at each of the three remaining people, then cleared his throat to get their attention. "As for my two grandsons," he continued reading, "William and Guymour Stockman, they are to each receive the total sum of two thousand dollars and nothing more."

"But that can't be!" Will charged toward the attorney. "You have to have read it wrong!"

"Please allow me to continue. 'They throw away their money as if it were of no consequence, then expect me to replenish their pockets. The time has come for them to learn to stand alone. Therefore, I leave the rest of my estate in its entirety to my beloved wife, Adelaide Louise Thompkins Stockman.'"

Will's face twisted with anger. "Wife?" He looked accusingly at Addie, then back at the attorney. "That's impossible! Can't you see what she's done? She seduced the old man and got him to take her to France so she could get his money. I doubt that it was difficult to find someone to forge a marriage certificate. Grandfather would never be stupid enough to marry her! It's all a lie! You can't let her get away with this!"

"You are quite wrong," the lawyer said firmly. "Gordon personally informed me of his plans before leaving for Europe. At the same time, he revised his will. Affidavits were sent to me all along, including the marriage certificate. All proof that the wedding had indeed taken place." He looked toward Adelaide, who was clutching the back of a chair so hard her knuckles were white.

"As of now, Mrs. Stockman, the house and everything else belongs to you." Jason Harper looked at Will with disgust. "And, Mrs. Stockman, should you choose to evict these two... *gentlemen,* you would be perfectly in your right."

Addie wasn't sure she could even speak. She'd had no idea that Gordon... she'd assumed... "Mr. Harper, I'm not the one—"

"Mrs. Stockman, your late husband said that in case of his demise, I am to remind you that this was his wish." Mr. Harper walked over to Addie's side. "Before making any rash decisions, why don't you take a month or two to think about this? I would be pleased to remain your attorney, and if any questions arise—or should you need advice—just send a servant to fetch me."

"She has no right to inherit one single damn thing! I'm his blood kin! The..." Will restrained himself from saying the accusation that had been on the tip of his tongue. Addie had everything now and he could scarcely afford to alienate her any more than he already had. He'd have to find a way to get back into her good graces. In the meantime, surely Guy could find some evidence that could nullify everything.

Jason patted Addie's shoulder. "Do you need me to stay?"

Addie glanced at Guy, who so far had remained silent. The angry look on his face would be enough to make even the best of men squirm. "No, I'll be fine. Thank you, Mr. Harper. You'll hear from me in a couple of weeks."

The lawyer nodded. "Gordon thought very highly of you."

As soon as the attorney had left, Will hurried forward. "Addie, surely you're not going to take what is rightfully mine?"

Addie continued to stare at him. How could she have ever desired him or fantasized about what it would be like to be married to him?

"Until this is all settled properly, you do plan to continue giving me the allowance Grandfather provided, don't you?"

"What do you mean by 'settled properly'?" For the first time, she was beginning to see why Gordon was concerned about leaving his money to his grandsons. "No. I will not provide an allowance."

"But you can't do that! I have creditors to pay!"

"I will see that all your bills prior to today are taken care of. But from here on, you'll have to handle those matters on your own. I suggest you start by finding work."

"Work? How do you expect me to do that? I have no experience."

"You're a lawyer. If you haven't any experience in the field of law, I guess you'll have to start from the bottom and learn. However, if you can't find work elsewhere, you might consider working for me."

"You don't plan to relinquish our inheritance, do you?" Guy asked from across the room.

Addie looked him straight in the eye. "I considered it, but now I don't think so. My husband wanted me to have everything, and I'm going to stand by his wishes."

"His wishes hell!" Will crossed over to the crystal whiskey decanter near Addie and poured himself another drink. "You can't convince me that my grandfather had any intention of keeping the family money from us. How many years have you been working on him to give you everything?"

Even Addie was shocked at herself when she moved forward and slapped the glass from Will's hand, sending whiskey in every direction.

"You should have listened to the attorney," Addie said between clenched teeth. "That whiskey is now mine and if you want a drink, ask for it. And when you're in *my* house, you will keep a civil tongue. Only because you are Gordon's grandsons am I going to give you the courtesy of explaining what happened. I don't care whether you believe me or not. The wedding—everything—was Gordon's idea. He wanted a great-grandchild who would appreciate the value of money and carry on the Stockman name. I simply agreed to raise the child as my own. I had nothing more to do with it."

"Ha!" Guy exclaimed. "Had nothing to do with it? That's quite impossible."

Addie gave him a chilling look. "I did agree to raise the child—"

"How magnanimous of you," Guy said in disgust.

Addie's smile dripped with loathing. "Gordon couldn't tolerate the thought of leaving his fortune to the two of you, then have it squandered away. He wanted everything to go to me and the baby. Sadly to say, as it turned out, there was no pregnancy."

"Why, you slut!" Will accused.

"How dare you continue to call me such a thing!" Furious and hurt, Addie was having difficulty thinking. "It's plain to see why my husband felt the need to leave his grandsons practically nothing. You make me sick. You aren't even concerned about the loss of a wonderful man. Nothing matters but your blasted money!''

"You of all people can hardly cast stones," Guy said in a low, deadly tone of voice. "You just said you told him you were pregnant with his child so he would marry you. Now you conveniently state that it was a mistake."

Addie gasped. "I said no such thing! You're deliberately twisting my words. Whether you believe it or not, I was very fond of Gordon, and never once did I consider doing anything without his knowledge or consent. The twenty-*four* trunks you mentioned are full of gifts from him. Now, be so kind as to leave my house."

Will slammed his glass down on the harp table and hurried out of the room. Guy took his time.

Before he made it to the doorway, he gave Addie a hard look.

Addie raised her chin in defiance. "You've been awfully quiet for a man who usually likes to talk people into doing what he wants. Have you no comments?"

"None whatsoever. You'll be hearing from us."

Once she was alone, Addie allowed her tears to flow. She had always thought of the Stockman family as her family, even if she was only the housekeeper. She had loved Guy and Will for nearly her entire life. Though it was not her place to verbalize her concerns, she had shared Gordon's anxieties, hurts and tragedies and all else that went along with being a concerned grandparent. For nearly four years she had constantly worried that Guy would be killed in the war, and she had been sad when Will's wife died in a fire. The family had been her life.

Adelaide sent a servant with instructions for Eleonore to move to the house. Guy and Will would continue to think of her as less than nothing only if she permitted it. That wasn't going to happen. The gentlemen were going to find out they were no longer dealing with Addie the housekeeper, but with Mrs. Gordon Bently Stockman. An ex-

tremely wealthy widow who was soon going to be in the
social whirl of San Francisco.

But first she would have to restore the mansion to its
former glory. It had been dormant too long. She almost
wished she had told Will and Guy that shipments of
household items were due to arrive from Europe. It would
have put them in an even bigger tizzy.

How quickly things change, Adelaide thought. The boys
had declared war when they made their wager then followed that with false accusations. Now it was her turn to
retaliate.

That night, two people stood in an alley in the Barbary
Coast district, talking in whispers.

"Everything has changed."

"We're not going to kill her after all?"

"Oh, we'll kill her, but not right away. The old man left
her all the money. I want that money, *then* Mrs. Adelaide
Stockman can be taken care of. She owes me, and I want to
see her pay."

"How are you going to do that?"

"I have a plan. Though I'd as soon get right to it, it's
going to take money and time to set it up."

"But—"

"I'll be getting in touch with you."

Money was exchanged, then the two left the alley in different directions.

Chapter Nine

Nearly two months later, Will sat in Guy's house, waving his hands in frustration. "Who would have believed this could happen? Perhaps we should consult another lawyer."

"We've always managed to handle our problems. This is no different."

"We're discussing law now."

"You were the best legal mind in school," Guy reminded him.

"Books. All books. I have no experience."

"You know what is and what isn't acceptable evidence. She admitted she tricked Grandfather into marriage by claiming to be pregnant. Do we have a case?"

"No. Seduction alone is not a crime, and she could turn right around and change her story. We have no proof of anything. As it stands, the will is incontestable. However, if we can prove there was no wedding—or that Grandfather was coerced into marrying her—or that illegal procedure was used to procure the inheritance, we may have a justifiable case. Now, how we're supposed to do that is another matter. Do you know that we are quite the fashionable joke? Everyone is talking about 'Gordon's Folly'! My blood bloody well boils when I think of her giving pleasure to Grandfather all these years, while we treated her as some innocent waif!"

"I don't think she did that. She's more cunning than that. From what we know of Addie, I doubt that she allowed him to bed her until the wedding ring was on her finger. She probably waved her virginity in front of him like some banner, daring him to grab hold." Guy waved a piece of paper.

Will paused and stared at his cousin. Though Guy appeared to be unaffected by all this, his eyes had turned black, denoting his anger. "What is that?"

"It's from Hubert. Grandfather's manservant. I received the missive this morning. It seems Grandfather left Hubert in England to visit relatives, with the understanding that he would be picked back up when the old man returned home. I have sent money for Hubert's passage back. I'm curious as to why Addie apparently didn't want him around. I'd also like to know if he can shed light on what actually took place between the *dear* housekeeper and our grandfather. One way or another, I'm going to prove she seduced him. I don't give a damn about the jokesters. The woman is going to pay for what she's pulled. When we retrieve what is rightfully ours, I'm going to personally make sure everyone within a hundred miles knows of her trickery. She won't be taking another poor fool's fortune."

"Thank the Lord." Will's hands were a bit steadier now that he knew Guy was handling the problem. Once the Black Raven made his mind up to do something, he was undaunted by anything. A faint grin passed across Will's lips. He hadn't called Guy by that name since they were boys.

"Have you stopped to think what would happen if some rogue caught Addie's fancy and she up and married the bloke? He'd become wealthy with *our* money!"

"Not if I have my way."

Will smoothed his mustache with his finger. "Do you think she'll change her mind about giving us our allowance?"

"No. She's going to hang on to every penny."

Will paused in the middle of the room. "What am I going to do for money?"

"Take her up on her offer of employment." Guy stood, then went to the window and looked out. "At least we'd be able to keep an eye on her."

"Or woo her."

Guy slowly turned around. "What do you mean by that?"

"It's very simple, Cousin. If we can't get our money back by proving she used underhanded methods to procure the Stockman wealth, then there's always marriage. She may even confess to her treacherous ways before the wedding."

"I wish you luck."

"I still have a five-thousand-wager to collect. Come, come, Guy. Not even for a moment do I believe your show of disinterest. The woman has a body that's begging for a man. Now that she's no longer a virgin—and presuming Grandfather did right by her in bed—the coupling will be all the more pleasurable."

"You think so? Then you weren't watching her during the reading of the will. Her expression never changed. There wasn't even a twitch of her eyebrow. I'll agree that she has a most desirable body, plus the face of an angel. But she's feelingless. She's colder than a frozen pond."

Will grinned. "I don't agree. She had to have given Grandfather one hell of a romp for him to leave her everything."

"Some women are awfully good at pretending. I'm sure she's one of them. I would even venture to say the Iron Maiden doesn't care much for men. But it makes no difference. Pursue your romantic interest if it pleases you. Personally, I'm going for the jugular vein."

A week later, the butler knocked then stepped into the study. He took a deep breath, enjoying the combined smells of beeswax, leather and lingering odor of fine tobacco. "Mr. William Stockman is here to see you, madam."

Addie was immediately infused with adrenaline. It had seemed like a lifetime of waiting for the cousins to come begging. She walked behind the imposing desk, sat on the marquetry chair, then withdrew a stack of bills from the desk drawer. They had amounted to a tidy sum. "Thank you, Roger. You can send Mr. Stockman in now."

When Roger opened the door to leave, Adelaide caught a whiff of fresh paint. With each passing day, the house was feeling more like hers instead of Gordon and Lillian's. The old carpet and furniture had already been replaced in several of the rooms. At this very moment the laborers were redoing Gordon's bedroom. When it was completed, she'd move in. The large suite would make her feel important, and at this point in time, she could use a little self-assurance.

Adelaide glanced around the office. This room would stay the same. How many times had she seen Gordon sitting in this very spot, going over bills and household allotments with her? Or what about the hours when he just wanted to talk or get her opinion on a business matter? He had always said she was good at reading people's characters, and she had an excellent head for business.

William quietly stepped into the room.

"I wouldn't have thought you capable of rising so early in the morning," Addie said sarcastically.

Will smiled. "You might be surprised at what I'm capable of doing if I set my mind to it. May I be seated?"

"But of course."

Will made himself comfortable. "You look quite at home behind that desk."

Addie shoved the stack of bills toward him. "I'm now devoid of any obligations. The accountant has paid all your bills."

"Thank you. I glanced in the parlor and was surprised at how comfortable the room looks now. You must be very fond of Queen Anne furniture." Actually, the sight had caused him to clench his teeth. Though tastefully furnished and much brighter, it was his money she had spent to make the changes. He also resented having to act like a guest in a house that he'd practically been raised in.

"I plan to eventually refurbish the entire house." Even after the way Will had treated her, Addie couldn't deny that the man was extremely handsome. His eyes still twinkled with the old charm, but she knew how deceiving that look could be.

"It's been quite a while since we've seen each other." Will crossed his legs. "The last time was at the reading of the will."

"How could I forget? You said such nice things to me."

"I was understandably upset at the time. My inheritance had just been given away."

"Why are you here?"

"I'd hoped you had reconsidered giving me an allotment?"

Addie shook her head. "No."

"I see."

"So, you've already gone through the money your grandfather left you," she accused.

"You underestimate me." Will looked around the study. "When do you plan to redo this room?"

"*If* I do anything, it will be very little. This study reminds me of Gordon."

"Enough chitchat. You have left me with no option but to accept your offer of a position. There is little doubt in my mind that my income will be minimal, but I can use my small inheritance to help subsidize that. At least until I receive a wage that will be in accordance with my ability and knowledge."

For a brief moment, Addie stared blankly at him. "What ability and knowledge?"

"I am a lawyer and quite good at numbers and business matters."

Addie smirked. "You've given no indication of either. I must admit I didn't expect you to take me up on my proposition, however, I will honor my offer." Addie stood. "But there are stipulations. If you report late to work or leave early, your pay will be reduced accordingly. If this occurs often, or you prove to be inept—and most importantly—should you try to commandeer money from the company, you will be immediately fired."

A hurt look spread across Will's face. "You think I would steal?"

"Yes, and you would justify it by saying that you were only taking what was rightfully yours. Do we have an understanding?"

"Most certainly, though I can't believe you would think me capable of so base a crime."

"Also, you will no longer try to get me into your bed. This is a business venture, nothing more."

Will nodded.

"Good. There are some things we can learn together."

Addie didn't see Will's grin.

"As I said, I didn't expect you to accept my terms, nevertheless, I did discuss it with Jason Harper. He has agreed to let you work under him so you can gain experience as a lawyer. He won't always be able to handle Stockman enterprises, and it would be nice to know a capable attorney could take his place on down the road. Also, you and I will work directly with the accountants. They will be here a week from Monday. I know of most of the companies Gordon owned, but I want to learn more of the details." Addie stood and walked around the desk. "Have you been with Guy since I last saw him?"

"Quite a few times. That was over two months ago." Will bowed his head. "Addie, I sincerely want to apologize for the things I said back then. I had no right to make such uncalled-for accusations. But surely you must realize how distraught I was."

"I understand completely. And how is Guy managing to pay his bills?"

"I have no idea, but he doesn't appear to be in need. A while back he was even discussing investing in stocks."

"Oh." Addie was quite disappointed at not being able to control him, as well. "And what has he said about me?"

Will's mouth spread into a broad smile. "Something about grabbing you by the jugular vein."

"The nerve of the man!" Addie snatched up her gloves. She'd known all along that it was Guy who would give her the most trouble. "Come along. We might as well go to Jason's office downtown and get you started. Oh, and while I'm thinking about it, from now on you are to call me Mrs. Stockman. It's time you accepted my position as your employer. Or should I say grandmother? If you say the name often enough, you might learn to get used to it."

As they left the room, Addie was feeling quite pleased with herself. The satisfaction would have been twofold if she could get both cousins under her thumb. She wanted to see them crawl and squirm like they'd made her do before she married Gordon. One way or another, they were going to pay for that wager they'd made to bed her, plus all the unkind accusations that they'd so carelessly thrown about. Guy couldn't possibly have as much money as Will seemed to think. He'd eventually come around. She could wait.

"I didn't see a wedding!" Hubert said, slurring his words.

Guy glanced at Will then back at Hubert. The manservant was seated on the divan with his legs stretched out and his bulbous nose even redder after enjoying his forth brandy.

"Addie's attorney has affidavits stating the wedding took place." Guy spoke curtly.

"Like I said, I didn't see it. Maybe she forged the documents. I wouldn't put it past her."

Guy couldn't decide whether the man was telling the truth or not. "Why do you say that?"

"She had her eye on Mr. Stockman for years."

Even though he was to the point of wringing the woman's neck, Guy somehow found that hard to believe.

"I guess she was around sixteen when she told me she intended to be his mistress and that I'd best not get in her way. I can't tell you how many times I caught her stealing things from the house. I tried telling Mr. Stockman, but he was so taken with the slut, he wouldn't believe me. He had to have told her about it. She warned me that if I tried that again, she'd make sure that I would have to go out of San Francisco to find employment."

Guy noticed that Hubert had become unusually coarse in his drunken state. "Would you swear to that?" he asked.

"I certainly would. I've had more than one grudge with that woman. I'll be happy to see her pay for what she's done." Hubert lifted his glass toward Will, who still held the decanter.

Will automatically walked over and refilled the glass. "What else did she do to you?"

"Mr. Stockman told me many a time that because I had been a loyal servant for so many years, he was going to leave his house to me. From what you've said, she apparently had that changed, also."

Will and Guy looked at each other in disbelief.

"The house to you?" William snapped.

"That doesn't seem very likely," Guy said, joining in.

"It's the truth," Hubert insisted.

Will placed the decanter back on the sideboard. "Did you ever see our grandfather and Adelaide copulating?"

"I caught them once in his bed. She jumped up and left immediately. I got hell for that, I can tell you." He took several sips of his drink. "They spent an awful lot of time together in that office of his."

"And what about the ship?" Guy asked.

"They had adjoining rooms, but I didn't see anything except a lot of kissing and feeling. Mr. Stockman told me not to show my face unless I was sent for." Hubert pursed his lips. "Addie's maid spoke some foreign language, so I never got any information out of her. She—"

To Will and Guy's surprise, the bald manservant closed his eyes and slowly fell to the side, spilling his drink on the divan. By the time Guy reached him and had removed the glass from his had, Hubert was out cold.

"He certainly can't hold his liquor worth a damn," Will said with disgust.

"Go tell Noble to bring my carriage to the front."

As Will left to get the coachman, Guy picked Hubert up and slung the drunk man over his shoulder. "For someone who had supposedly been destitute in England, you sure are fat." He headed for the front door.

The following morning, Guy took Hubert to an attorney named Hempt, and had sworn affidavits drawn up. Satisfied, Guy returned the manservant to the same hotel Hubert had spent the night in. He was given a purse of money and told to stay out of sight until he and William could come up with some further information.

Slowly but surely, Guy was starting to pull a rope around Adelaide's lovely neck.

The coach moved down the brick street toward the wharf area at a rather brisk pace. Adelaide had given her driver explicit instructions to avoid the Barbary Coast. The district was a cauldron of bordellos, bars, gambling houses, dance halls and general depravity.

Adelaide glanced at Eleonore, who sat across from her. Now that the men had gotten their eight-hour workdays, would servants start demanding the same privileges?

When they arrived at their destination, Addie and Eleonore left the conveyance and walked out on the wharf, looking at the various fish stands. As she moved about, Addie was quite careful not to snag the hem of her new candy-striped skirt on the grainy wood beneath her feet.

After purchasing some rock cod, Addie and Eleonore went in search of crab. Unfortunately, they had arrived too late. The better selections had been picked over by servants who had already left.

The few ladies of wealth who still lingered turned their back to Adelaide as she passed by. This was something she had become accustomed to. Society was not going to take her graciously into their fold. It was a beautiful day and Addie had felt the need to take her nose out of Gordon's ledgers and enjoy the fresh air. She inhaled the smell of the briny water, and enjoyed the San Francisco Bay breeze caressing her cheeks. She'd be damned if she would allow a group of society biddies to spoil her outing.

Unnoticed by Addie, Eleonore, who walked beside her mistress, flirted outrageously with the seamen. More than one sailor had offered to carry her basket. Each time, they received a scathing look from Adelaide and a sweet "no thank you" from Eleonore.

"Why do those men keep pestering you?"

Eleonore's green eyes were the picture of innocence. "Why…why, I have no idea." She came to an abrupt halt. "Isn't that the man who barged into your hotel room?"

Addie looked in the direction Eleonore was pointing. Ahead, stood Guy talking to a seaman.

"Oh," Eleonore purred. "If I hadn't been so frightened when he entered, I would have welcomed him much differently."

"You and every other woman in San Francisco." But Addie couldn't stop staring, either. It wasn't just because his thick black hair was blowing appealingly in the breeze, or that his handsome looks took her breath away. Nor did it have to do with him looking exceptionally tall and broad shouldered. She was feeling a momentary bout of guilt at the way he was dressed. She had never seen him in anything other than the finest clothes and hats. Yet there he was, wearing a worn pair of those pants Mr. Levi Strauss made for miners, soiled boots of indeterminable age, and a green-and-blue-striped shirt with the sleeves rolled up.

"Perhaps you'll introduce me so I can apologize for my conduct."

"An apology is hardly appropriate, Eleonore, since *he* broke into *our* room." So this was how Guy was making his living, Adelaide thought. Her mouth curved into a hint of a smile. Apparently his dabbling in the stock exchange had been a disaster. Was he a stevedore, or was he working on a fishing boat? Suddenly she saw no humor in Guy's situation. Seeing him like this was starting to make her feel guilty about taking the Stockman fortune.

Adelaide squared her shoulders and raised her chin. Why was she acting this way? Soon Guy would be coming to her for money, and she would have him exactly where she wanted him. He had been raised a gentleman and would soon tire of manual labor. Before much longer, he'd learn to treat her with respect. "Come, Eleonore. We'll not find any crab to my liking today. It's been picked over."

Addie had waited too long. Guy had already caught sight of her. Their eyes locked in an ungiving battle of nerves. "Don't move," she whispered to Eleonore.

"But you said there was no reason to stay."

"I've changed my mind." Addie wasn't about to give Guy the satisfaction of thinking his presence had caused her to leave. She turned to the vendor on her right. "Can you tell me if there are other boats coming in with crab?" She kept her head turned, pretending not to notice the handsome rogue headed in her direction.

The dirty woman gave Addie a toothless grin. "It ain't likely, ma'am. But if'n you come back in the mornin', I'll save you some of my best."

"Fine. That will be fine." Addie could see from the corner of her eye that Guy was almost upon them. "I'll..." She pulled some money from her reticule. "Here." She didn't bother to count the change she handed over. "I'll have my—"

"Have her give you more than that, Sally," Guy inter-rupted. He raised a booted foot and rested it on one of the wooden crates that acted as a low table. "Mrs. Stockman is a wealthy woman, but unreliable. She may not return, and you'll be left with spoiled crab."

How dare the man say such things! But rather than ar-gue, Addie handed over more money to the vendor. When she looked up, she caught Guy's eyes brazenly roving over Eleonore's body like gravy covering a biscuit. She knew that look well. On more than one occasion he'd used it on her. At the time, she'd thought he considered her someone special. Now she knew that look applied to any female.

"You're a very fetching little thing when you're not screaming."

Eleonore gave Guy a coquettish smile.

"Leave my maid alone!" Addie grabbed Eleonore's arm and shoved the petite woman behind her.

Guy raised a dark eyebrow. "Don't be jealous, Addie. You had your chance."

Addie stood straight as a post. "Jealous? You misjudge me." She felt the need to say something scathing. "I sim-ply do not want her around someone who won't even be able to scrub off the smell of fish."

"Oh? Do I smell of fish?"

"Well . . . no. But working down here, you soon will. Besides, that's not the point."

"Pray tell, what is the point?"

Addie hated being caught making a stupid statement, especially to Guy. She turned to Sally, the vendor. "I'll be here in the morning."

"You know, Mrs. Stockman," Guy said, "I never real-ized what a snob you are." He lowered his foot. "And a thief to boot."

"A thief?" Addie's amber eyes flashed at the false ac-cusation. "Why would I steal from this woman?"

"Why not? You had no problem stealing from me and my cousin."

Addie delivered a hard slap to Guy's cheek.

Guy's cold, dangerous smile didn't reach his eyes. "Don't ever do that unless you're willing to accept the consequences," he threatened.

Addie grabbed Eleonore's arm and hurried back the way they'd come. Though still angry, Addie was shocked at her display of temper. She had actually slapped a man! It was a wonder she hadn't been killed!

"Have a pleasant day, *Mrs. Stockman,*" she heard Guy call. Addie stopped and turned. She'd be damned if she'd let him have the last word. She smiled sweetly. "And the same to you, Mr. Stockman."

"Guy, darling!"

A lovely redhead hurried past Addie. She had on a flowing yellow creation and didn't seem to be the least bit concerned about the hem getting snagged on the wharf planks. When she reached Guy, she rose up on tiptoes and kissed his cheek, right where Addie had delivered the slap.

"Constance, this isn't a proper place for a lady of your breeding to come alone." Guy looked at Addie, his smile broadening.

Addie curled her lip. They looked ridiculous together. The woman couldn't have been more than five foot one or two, and against Guy's tall frame she looked like a misplaced lemon.

"I am, after all, a widow, darling." Constance held up her basket. "I brought lunch for the two of us."

"I can't wait to feast my eyes on it," Guy replied with a sudden sparkle in his eye. "The lunch, that is."

The redhead giggled.

Addie found their behavior disgusting. Refusing to watch a minute longer, she hurried on her way. "He doesn't have to go about flaunting his women friends."

"I thought it was the other way around," Eleonore commented.

"I didn't ask for your opinion!"

Not wanting to undergo another confrontation with Guy, the following morning Addie sent Eleonore to fetch the crab. Then, for the next two hours, she waited impatiently in the kitchen for the maid's return.

"What took you so long?" Addie demanded when Eleonore finally drifted in through the back door.

"Some of the servants from other homes stopped to talk to me."

"And did they ask the same questions that the others have?"

"Yes." Eleonore handed the cook the basket of crabs.

Addie knew how the servants exchanged gossip when they visited one another. "Della," she called to the cook.

The heavy woman turned and looked at her mistress.

"Have the servants from the other homes been asking questions about me?"

Della nodded. "But I never tell them a thing unless it's something good."

"Thank you, Della. Did you happen to see Mr. Stockman on the wharf?" she asked Eleonore.

"No."

"Are you sure?"

"I looked everywhere. I would have recognized that one."

Addie left the kitchen. Now Guy was deliberately avoiding her. Of course she had deliberately avoided him, but that was different. Her eyes suddenly became bright. Perhaps he was embarrassed about his line of work. She shook her head. No, Guymour Stockman would never hang his head, no matter what his occupation. He just wanted nothing to do with her.

Addie entered the conservatory and yanked on her work gloves. She already knew the questions the servants were asking about her. What was it like having to work for Mrs. Stockman, and how many men does she entertain? The information wasn't nearly as important to the servants as it was to the women they worked for. Of course, under their breaths the biddies were probably saying, "What can you expect from a servant? She undoubtedly took poor Mr. Stockman under the covers and tricked him into leaving her all his money."

Adelaide reached for the trowel just as the floor began to shake. Her heart pounding, she grabbed hold of a large post to stabilize herself. Several of her plants fell to the floor, dirt flew in every direction and windows rattled in their casements. Though she knew only seconds had passed, it seemed to take forever for the tremor to end.

Still quivering, Addie carefully released her grip on the post. Her only complaint about living in San Francisco was the tremors. She would never become accustomed to them. She walked to the old wooden chair and plopped down.

"Things aren't as bad as you make them out to be, Addie."

Addie was getting used to hearing Gordon's little messages. She didn't know if they were real or just in her mind, but she was past the point of caring. "Did you cause the earthquake, Gordon? Because if you did, you can stop. And how can you say things aren't bad? I'm spurned by everyone, plus today I'm another year older! This is all your fault!" Adelaide glanced around the humid room, daring Gordon to appear. "And to top everything off, if anyone heard me talking to myself like this, I would be put in a crazy house. At least your grandsons would be happy!"

An idea seemed to come to her out of nowhere. It might not be cricket, as Will would say, but she no longer cared. She'd had her fill of being rejected and talked about. All along, she had suspected that many of the upper class were afraid of her. After all, she knew which women had had affairs with Gordon, and the husbands certainly didn't want their wives to find out the many times they'd tried to bed her.

There was little doubt that the Stockman cousins were busily informing their aristocrat friends that she was not the type they cared to mingle with. Will was sure to have also added his personal insight to those who would listen. Well, none of them were going to be allowed to ignore her anymore.

The days passed quickly for Addie. Every other morning was spent with Will and the accountants, discovering the extent of her wealth and what it was composed of. At the beginning, the three crotchety old men showed their disapproval with comments and supposed slips of the tongue. Not only had she come seemingly out of nowhere, she'd dared to enter a man's domain. More than once she'd had to snap at them for constantly addressing Will and ignoring her. It didn't take long for the gentlemen to change their ways, especially when they came to realize that Adelaide—and only Adelaide—made the decisions.

Chapter Ten

Jason Harper stepped into the large parlor, amazed at the drastic change. With light streaming through the windows, and colorful furnishings, the once-dreary room seemed to have come alive.

"How nice of you to arrive so soon."

The attorney turned and discovered Adelaide sitting near the fireplace. He couldn't help staring. Adelaide Stockman had shed her cocoon and had emerged as a butterfly. Her silken blond hair was looped so it hung smoothly to her shoulders, then the ends had been rolled into a soft knot at the top of her head, reminding him of a halo. The high-necked forest green gown acted as a picture frame for an amazingly beautiful face. Apparently Mrs. Stockman considered her short mourning period over. The diamond pendent at her throat and small, matching earrings gave only a tasteful hint of wealth. Even her long, full skirt had been perfectly arranged at the base of her chair. Everything was perfect, and he knew immediately that the woman wanted something of him. Nevertheless, knowing didn't keep him from enjoying the view.

Jason made a slight bow. "Good afternoon, Mrs. Stockman."

"Good afternoon, Mr. Harper. Do be seated. Didn't you call Mr. Stockman 'Gordon'?" Addie asked as soon as the attorney was settled.

"Yes, I did."

She gave him a winning smile and enjoyed seeing how his face lit up with interest. He was every bit as attractive as she had remembered. "Then I see no reason why you shouldn't call me 'Adelaide,' or 'Addie.' And henceforth, I shall call you 'Jason.'"

"Very well."

"May I have the maid bring you something to drink?"

"I think not. Your message said you had an urgent matter to discuss."

Addie anointed him with another smile. "Well, not exactly urgent, but it did get you here, didn't it?"

"That it did." Jason rested his back against the tufted divan, still trying to adjust to what he was seeing—and hearing. He had spent many hours in this house with his close friend Gordon, either playing chess or attending a lavish soiree. Never had he thought of Addie as being anything more than a housekeeper who moved silently about. Yet here was the very same woman, using female wiles with the ability of someone who had been doing it for years.

"It *has* been a while since we last talked. Tell me, how is William doing? Has he been prompt over the past several months? Does he attend to his work? When I asked you to hire him, I truly didn't mean for him to be a hindrance."

"It is I who should be thanking you."

"Oh? Why?"

"He is very prompt, and I have never met anyone with such an aptitude for law. He has the ability to become one of the best legal minds this country has ever known."

Addie blinked. "We are talking about William Stockman, aren't we?"

"Indeed, we are. I've even considered offering him a partnership. I would hate to lose him."

Addie had noticed a change in William, but she'd credited it to his no longer trying to coax her into his bed. But Will wasn't the reason she had sent for Jason. "If I remember correctly, aren't you single?"

Jason cleared his throat. "Yes. I hope you're not think-ing about—"

Addie's laughter burst forth. "No, I'm not looking to marry again." She dabbed the corners of her eyes with the delicate linen handkerchief she'd been holding. "You have no need to worry." *At least not now,* she thought. "What I want from you is far more dangerous. I want you to ac-company me to the next big social event."

"To the Mastersons' formal dinner?" he asked, seem-ingly unabashed by the question. He hadn't missed the twinkle in those beautiful eyes.

"Yes." Adelaide was quite pleased with the information he'd just supplied. "You have received an invitation, haven't you?"

He nodded.

"I believe it's time I made my debut into San Francisco society. Don't you?"

Jason was chuckling as he left the Stockman mansion. Gordon had told him that Adelaide could be quite beguil-ing, and that she was as sharp as a tack. Traits seldom found in women, especially beautiful ones. But Gordon had never mentioned the strong dash of determination that went along with her other attributes. The lady knew how to go about getting what she wanted. Jason thought about the men he had admired who had such qualities, including Gordon Stockman. Now he had a woman to add to his list.

Jason climbed into his waiting coach. Before going to Europe, he and Gordon had had a violent argument about the Stockman fortune being left to a housekeeper. It was beginning to appear that his old friend may have been wiser than he'd given Gordon credit for.

"This arrived only minutes ago," Roger said as Ade-laide entered the house. He handed her a white envelope.

Adelaide had gone for a walk to clear her head and had been looking forward to a short nap upon her return. It had been another hectic day of going through old logs that gave particulars on some of the companies Gordon had bought years ago. "Thank you, Roger."

After allowing the butler to remove the wool cape from her shoulders, Addie broke the seal on the letter and read. It was the date and time when Jason Harper would pick her up for the dinner. Suddenly Addie didn't feel the least bit tired. In one week, she would present herself to San Francisco's society.

Addie removed her bonnet of lilac silk and handed it to a waiting maid. Her meeting with Jason a week ago had turned out to be far different than she had anticipated. She had thought pressure would be needed to get the attorney to escort her to a social function. Why he had been so willing remained a mystery, but she certainly wasn't going to stir the water by asking.

She dearly hoped that Guy Stockman would also attend the dinner. She could already taste the satisfaction of putting him in his place. She intended to inform him that if he said one more degrading thing about her, everyone on Nob Hill would know he had been diminished to a dock laborer.

She tapped the envelope in the palm of her hand. With the passing of time, she had come to realize that it wasn't only the boys she wanted to get even with. There were also the snobbish women who had turned their backs on her, as well as the husbands who had left bruises on her fanny. She moved forward. Yes, yes. The dinner should be interesting.

While in France, Gordon had paid the great couturiers to instruct Addie in fashion and explain how differently styled clothes gave varying impressions. Therefore, the pink silk taffeta gown had been carefully selected.

When her toilette was finished, Addie stepped in front of the mirror to see the overall effect. The off-the-shoulder, tight-fitting bodice and skirt were adorned with tiny diamonds that had been sewn into designs of flowers. Diamond earrings graced her ears. A pink-feathered fan and matching long-sleeved gloves completed her costume. The pink ribbons, worked around a coiffure of many curls, were the only added features. Nothing about her appearance could possibly cause unfavorable gossip.

Addie glanced at Eleonore. "Everything is perfect."

"You have never looked lovelier, madam," Eleonore said proudly.

Addie squeezed the maid's hand fondly, then left the room. Jason was already waiting.

The look on the attorney's face when Addie descended the stairs to the entry removed any remaining doubts she may have harbored regarding her attire for the evening.

"My dear, you are absolutely ravishing." Jason took the ermine cloak she handed him and placed it around her shoulders. "Perhaps we should reconsider my eligibility as a husband." He led her to the front door, where Roger handed him his top hat.

"Permit me to return the compliment, Jason," Addie said as they stepped outside. "You cut a most dashing figure in your evening clothes." The gentleman grinned and she realized a consideration of marriage wasn't the least bit unheard-of. Being married to so distinguished a man would absolutely be to her advantage.

Jason helped her inside his carriage.

"Did you inform Mrs. Masterson as to my attendance?"

"No, she didn't ask. It was very kind of them to rearrange the seating when I said I would be bringing a companion."

"Are you trying to make me feel guilty?" Addie asked capriciously.

"Not at all. I was merely making conversation."

"Will you be embarrassed at having me on your arm?"

"Flattered would be more accurate. I haven't had anything this exciting happen in years. Believe me, I'm quite looking forward to the evening."

Addie suddenly had a different impression of her lawyer. She hadn't realized the man had such a delightfully dry wit. Now she could understand why he and Gordon had been such fast friends, even though Jason had to be twenty years Gordon's junior.

It gave Adelaide a considerable sense of satisfaction when she discovered the Masterson house was nothing compared to the Stockman house. Nor was the interior as elegant as her newly decorated home. After the couple were ushered into the salon, Kenneth and Jewel Masterson graciously welcomed them. Adelaide didn't miss the momentary shock that touched Jewel's face when it occurred to her who Jason's dinner partner was. But the plump woman was the immediate recipient of Adelaide's respect. Even after she recognized Addie's name, Jewel's gracious attitude never altered.

However, the other female guests were of an entirely different frame of mind. Addie was engulfed in pure delight when she watched jealousy leap into each woman's eyes as introductions were made. Three of them Addie recognized as ladies who had spent more than one night in Gordon's company. She also watched the men fidget. She didn't even try to remember the number of times each had asked her to be his mistress.

In all, Adelaide couldn't have asked for a better introduction into society. Word would quickly spread about her attendance. She had met the upper crust on their own doorstep. With the knowledge she possessed, they would be fools to turn their backs on her again.

"Mrs. Stockman—"

Addie turned to her hostess. "Please, call me Adelaide."

Jewel smiled. "I would like to introduce our daughter, Mary Masterson Clark."

"I have so wanted to meet you," Mary said excitedly.

Adelaide was surprised by Mary's attitude of acceptance. In the carriage Jason said she would like Mary. He'd been right. Addie took an immediate liking to the lovely woman. Maybe it was her straightforwardness, or the inquisitive green eyes and the open smile she gave Addie. "How very nice of you, but why would you want to meet me?"

Mary lowered her voice so as not to be overheard. "Because I've been told so much about you. You are even more beautiful than I thought you would be."

"I'm sorry I'm late, Jewel...Kenneth. I hope I didn't delay your dinner?"

Blindfolded, Adelaide would have recognized that deep voice.

"Not at all," Kenneth replied.

"Guymour," Mary called, a definite twinkle in her eye. "Come and meet Mr. Harper's dinner partner."

As he moved into Addie's view, she relished his startled look. His gaze immediately shifted to the lawyer. Addie knew exactly what he was thinking.

"Be careful, Jason," Guy said with a cocked grin. "She devours older men."

Jason met him eye to eye. "I hope you're right."

Adelaide smothered her laughter at Jason's rebuttal.

"Shame on you, Guymour," Mary chastised sweetly. "Have you misplaced your manners?"

"Dinner is served," a butler announced.

Addie took Jason's offered elbow and allowed him to escort her into the large dining room.

The first course of the meal was eaten in relative silence. Adelaide knew it was because of her presence, and she made no effort to alleviate the tension. Instead, she encouraged it. On two separate occasions, she deliberately winked at one of two stately gentlemen who had overstepped their bounds more than once. Then there were the women she gave knowing smiles to while asking to be passed a saltcellar, or some other insignificant item.

"Tell me, Jason," Kenneth Masterson said, "do you think the legal system is going to do anything about what happened over on Townsend Street and later at the rope works of Tubbs & Co.?"

"I have no idea, but I contend that mob shouldn't have been allowed to drive the Chinese laborers from their work and shanties. Nor should their provisions have been destroyed. I'm also against the anticoolie clubs that are being organized."

"I think they should all be shipped back to their country," Freda Powazik firmly stated.

"You don't know what you're talking about," her husband rebuffed.

Everyone started speaking at the same time.

Addie looked across the table at Guy, who had hardly taken his cold eyes off her since the meal began. She smiled and innocently blinked her lashes. "Have you seen Constance lately?"

Guy frowned. "Constance?" It took a moment for him to realize Constance was the redhead Addie had seen at the wharf.

"There are so many women in your life that you've probably forgotten about the one I'm referring to."

The table had become hushed again and everyone was staring at Guy.

"Surely not Constance Brackman, Guymour?" Lorna Walker uttered in shock. "She just remarried!"

"What color is her hair?" Addie inquired sweetly.

"She's a redhead."

Addie appeared to be thinking about it, then looked toward Guy. His jaw muscles were taut and she knew he was furious. "No, the woman I saw him with had brown hair," she lied. "I probably shouldn't have even brought it up. We all know how my grandson skits from one woman to another." She made it sound like a secret that everyone was privy to. She looked at her hostess. "Do you have a French chef?"

"Yes, I do," Jewel said proudly.

"I just knew it. I haven't had such wonderful crepes since leaving Paris."

A few minutes later, Addie complimented another woman on her gown, and even went so far as to ask the name of her dressmaker. Soon everyone had relaxed and a variety of conversations were going on at the same time. Adelaide smiled inwardly. She had controlled everything. Well, nearly everything. Those cold eyes from across the table were still on her. Maybe now Mr. Guymour Stock-man would know just how unforgiving a woman could be. And she had only started.

Adelaide heard a gentleman at the end of the table say something, but it was the words, "calls himself the Black Raven," that turned her attention to the conversation. That was what William used to call Guy when they were young. The black represented Guy's hair, and the raven was be-cause Will swore Guy was always swooping down on him like the angry bird.

"How long has this been going on?" Guy suddenly asked.

"I have no idea," Kenneth replied. "Two of my friends have already been robbed. I find it unforgivable that gen-tlemen's carriages are being robbed at night and in all parts of town!"

"How frightening." Freda Powazik placed her hand over her heart, as if she were about to swoon.

Guy set his fork on his plate. "Is there a description of the gentleman?"

Addie knew Guy had to be the bandit! How else would he have enough money to survive all this time? Certainly not on a fisherman's wages. Now she really had something to hold over his head.

"I'm told he uses a disguise. Black clothes and gloves, and a black hood, making it nearly impossible to see him in the dark. He seemingly appears from nowhere, and after the gentleman stops his coach, he robs his victim and disappears into the night."

That sounds like something Guy would do, Addie thought. She was feeling quite smug with her newfound information.

It wasn't until after the meal, when everyone had left the table, that Guy took hold of Addie's arm and pulled her away from the others.

"Turn loose of me," Addie demanded in a hushed voice.

"You didn't even have the courtesy to wear black tonight? My grandfather is barely in his grave."

"I—"

"What are you doing here?"

Addie would have sworn she heard him snarl. "I suggest you stay away from any social functions if you don't care to be in the same company. From tonight on, I *will* be part of society whether you like it or not."

"Are you now determined to also marry Jason and take his money? Then what? Will he be found mysteriously dead?"

"You listen to me, Guy Stockman. If you plant so much as a hint of such a thing—or spread any more degrading gossip about me—I *will* reciprocate!" Though his grip tightened, she refused to say how much it hurt her arm. He suddenly released her, but she didn't like the grin on his face.

"My dear Adelaide, I'm not the least concerned about what you say or to whom you say it. But be careful. You're getting in way over your head." He walked away.

During the ride back home, the excitement of the evening returned. Addie could hardly sit still. She felt like a cat licking its whiskers as it watched a mouse struggling in a trap. Tomorrow she'd send Guy a message to come to the house. She wanted to prove to him that from now on, she would be controlling the strings.

It took a few minutes for Addie to realize that Jason was especially quiet. "You're displeased with me, aren't you?"

"Does it matter?"

"Yes, for some reason it does."

"It's not displeasure I feel, it's concern."

"Why would you say that? Tonight everything went exactly as I had planned."

"I can understand your need to get back at certain people for the way they've treated you, but be careful, Addie. Sometimes we're not as clever as we think."

"What do you mean?"

"I'm simply saying that when we seek revenge, we become the same as those we retaliate against. You're much too young and beautiful to get caught up in such a waspish affair."

"You don't think I have a right to be angry and pay them back for their injustice?"

"I didn't say that. However, it is a proven fact that kindness makes a person feel far more guilty than threats."

"If you think that way, why did you agree to escort me tonight? Surely you knew what I was up to."

"The one thing I love the most in this world—besides my sisters, nieces and nephews—is women. There is nothing about them I don't find fascinating. I'm especially fascinated by their quick tongues and manipulative abilities, and I must say you gave a wonderful performance when you asked me to take you to the dinner. I would not have missed your exhibition at the Masterson home for anything."

"Then why—"

"It was simply a word to the wise. Nothing more. I do believe you need a man in your life, Adelaide."

"Only a man would make that comment."

"Possibly."

"You forget, I loved Gordon."

Jason laughed and patted her hand resting on the seat. "My dear, you haven't the least idea what love is."

Addie couldn't help laughing at the ridiculousness of the conversation. "You know nothing about me."

"I know everything about you. Including your arrangement with Gordon."

Addie was grateful for the darkness inside the coach. She didn't want Jason to see her blush. "Are you suggesting yourself as an answer to my so-called problems?"

"Let's just say that should you need a confidant or someone to escort you about town and to various affairs, I would be more than happy to oblige."

Addie grinned, quite enjoying the gentle bantering. "And by all means, should you hear of anything you think would be of interest to me, please don't hesitate to mention it."

Guy leaped out of his carriage and pounded on the door. When there was no immediate response, he pounded again. As soon as the butler appeared, Guy shoved him aside and entered. "Where is my cousin?"

"Sir, Mr. William is unavailable." Seeing Guy headed for the stairs, the butler hurried forward. "Sir, you can't go up there. Mr. William is indisposed!" There was nothing that irritated Morris more than to be ignored, but he knew that any more effort to dissuade Mr. Guymour would be futile.

Upstairs, Guy barged into Will's room without so much as a knock. The two naked people on the bed jerked around to see who had interrupted their pleasure.

"Ah, Susan. You do get around." Guy hooked his cane beneath Will's trousers, then flipped the pants onto the bed.

"What the hell are you doing here?" Will demanded.

"Get dressed, Cousin, we have things to discuss."

"You can plainly see I'm busy."

"You can resume after we've had our talk. I'll be waiting in your study." Guy tipped his hat and smiled at the voluptuous woman on the bed. "Susan," he acknowledged before retreating from the room.

"Damn the man," Will growled. He grabbed his trousers and climbed off the bed. "Don't worry, precious," he assured the woman, "I shan't be long." Without even bothering to don a shirt, he hurried after Guy.

Will stormed into his study.

"Close the doors behind you," Guy ordered. "We don't want to be overheard."

Guy finally had Will's attention. He closed the door.

"You've procured new evidence against Addie?" Will asked anxiously.

"No. I'm here for an entirely different reason. What the hell are you doing going about robbing carriages?"

"What?" Will started to laugh. "You mean you interrupted me for that? If I were going to rob something it would probably be a bank. It would be far less vigorous than what you're accusing me of."

"You know nothing about the Black Raven?"

"Of course I do. I used to call you that."

"A man using that name has been robbing coaches all over town. Don't you find that to be a bit too coincidental?"

They each slumped down into a chair.

"It seems to me that of the two of us, you would be the one more apt to do such a thing." Will looked keenly at his cousin. "No," he finally said, "if it were you, you wouldn't have charged over here accusing me."

"Only three of us knew the nickname. You, Addie and I. If I didn't know the lady, I'd give serious thought to her being the scoundrel. But I can't come up with any reason for her to do so. As the matriarch of our family, she wouldn't be about to do such a thing."

"Matriarch?"

"I'm convinced that is the way she presently sees herself."

William smoothed back his tousled hair. "Are you sure the name was the Black Raven?"

"I'm sure."

"Then it must be coincidental."

"As much as I would like to believe she was the culprit, I'm sure you're right."

They remained silent, trying to come up with a solution.

"Have you been able to go through all the records regarding Grandfather's will and the marriage?" Guy asked.

"Like I told you, Jason keeps them in his personal files." Will grinned. "However, while you were milling at the Mastersons' dinner party tonight, I was able to sneak into his office and read them. As much as I regret having to say this, Addie's case is airtight. Grandfather even provided a list of names, as well as the addresses, of those who attended the wedding party. There is no question as to the marriage. I also found out that Hubert witnessed the wedding. I went to confront him with his lie, but he's no longer at the hotel. We have his affidavit, but I think he was lying through his teeth."

"Why do you say that?"

"He lied about the wedding, and he said he wanted to get even with Addie keeping him out of the will. I suspect he contacted you so he could have a means of getting back to America." Will reached for the decanter sitting on the table beside his chair, then filled two small glasses with whiskey. He handed one to Guy.

"We've apparently come to a crossroad with no idea as to which direction to go."

"I've been working closely with Addie for nearly three months, and I've seen no indication of a seductive nature. She may have been telling the truth about it being Grandfather's idea all along."

Guy's eyes narrowed. "Do I detect feelings of forgiveness on your part, as well as hers? Is it possible that you may even believe Addie no longer holds our accusations against us?"

"I'm quite sure of it. We've misjudged her, Cousin. I have accepted my plight, but that doesn't mean I'm not going to do something about it. I intend to make Addie my wife."

"Have you already won our wager?"

"Not yet."

"Is she aware of your intentions?"

"Of course not. Right now I'm concentrating on gaining her trust. When that happens, love should follow. She's an idealist and it's not likely she'd marry without love."

"She already has."

"That's exactly why I don't believe she'll do it again."

Guy handed Will his glass and waited until it was refilled and returned. "Don't count on it. I believe you already have competition. Jason accompanied Addie to the dinner party tonight."

The light tap on the door startled both of them. When Susan entered, she was completely clothed. Both men had forgotten all about her.

"It's getting late, William," she said angrily, "and I must leave. I need to get home before Adam returns from his trip."

Will jumped to his bare feet. "I'm sorry, dearest, but we had important business to discuss that couldn't be avoided. Say you'll forgive me, and that we can get together soon."

Seeing the woebegone look on Will's handsome face, she smiled. "Do you mean it?"

"With all my heart." Will raised her hand and kissed her knuckles. "I shall count the minutes until you will once again be in my arms. Now hurry, I wouldn't want you to get into trouble and not be able to return."

Susan threw her arms around Will's neck, kissed him passionately, then rushed off.

Will quickly returned to his chair, his paramour already forgotten. "Why would Addie do that?"

"Do what?"

"You know damn well what I'm talking about."

"She seems to prefer older men." Guy downed his liquor and stood.

Will suddenly wondered if Guy was starting to have feelings for Addie. He sounded a lot more bitter and angry than vindictive.

"Neither the answer to the Black Raven nor the situation with Adelaide is going to be solved tonight. A word to the wise, Cousin. Watch out for Addie. She was out to draw blood tonight. Believe me, she hasn't forgotten a thing."

"Perhaps that applies to you, but not me."

"Don't say I didn't warn you."

"And Guy," Will said as the tall man was about to depart, "the wager still stands."

Guy slowly turned. His grin was one of pure pleasure. "Good. I think you both need to be taught a lesson, and I'm just the man to do it." He placed his glass on the table and left.

As he stepped out into the night air, Guy took a deep breath and paused a moment. He wanted Addie in his bed, but it had nothing to do with the wager. She'd created a fire in him with her constant challenging, and each time she confronted him she was only stoking the flame. He and Addie had an appointment. Maybe not tomorrow or the next day, but eventually. The waiting only made the victory all the more pleasurable.

"Why did you send for me?" The hooded figure made a point of remaining in the shadows of the dimly lit room, and away from the window.

"You hadn't gotten in touch with me and I thought something might have gone wrong or you'd changed your mind about killing the woman."

"Nothing has gone wrong, and you should know I will never change my mind about Adelaide Stockman's death. I told you it would take time for me to accumulate enough money. Well, it doesn't matter now. You'll be pleased to know I now have the finances necessary for my plan. At last we can make our move.''

''I'm having second thoughts about all this.''

''How can you have second thoughts? It's something that has to be done. Once we put my plan into action, you'll feel differently. The idleness hasn't been easy on either of us. The first thing tomorrow, I want you to...''

Chapter Eleven

Adelaide stood holding the calling card Eleonore had just handed her. It seemed as if every eligible gentleman in San Francisco had discovered her doorstep. Not that she was complaining. On the contrary. She was delighted. Even William had fallen into place. His manners were impeccable and he treated her with the utmost respect. Since she had refused his proposal of marriage and scoffed at his declaration of love, he'd never brought either subject up again. She'd finally gotten even with him for all the nasty accusations he'd made.

Everything had turned out even better than she'd anticipated. At last she was being given the respect she deserved from those who had hurt her. All but one. Guymour.

"Will there be anything else, madam?"

Adelaide looked in the mirror to check her appearance. "Mr. Guymour still hasn't responded to my messages?"

"No, ma'am."

"Give my regrets to the gentleman downstairs. Tell him I can't be disturbed and to call another day. As soon as..." Adelaide glanced at the name on the card, blinked, then read it again. "Prince Rupert Stalinsky? A prince is downstairs?"

"No, it is his representative. He said Prince Stalinsky will be arriving in San Francisco soon and would like to call on you?"

"A real prince?"

"That is what his gentleman said."

"What does he rule?"

"What do you mean?"

Addie chewed on a thumbnail. "There are so many questions to ask. How does he know about me? What country is he from? How do I know he's real? Am I expected to bow or what? What if he's only after my money?"

Eleonore giggled. "You'll have to ask the gentleman downstairs those questions."

"I'm sorry, Eleonore, but I've never known anyone of nobility." Addie thought a minute. "You said the gentleman is waiting for an answer?"

Eleonore nodded.

"Tell him I am too busy. Perhaps another time." Addie was convinced Eleonore's wide eyes had doubled in size.

"But you can't do that. He represents his majesty!"

"He has no authority in America. Besides, his highness could be eighty and wrinkled, with a barrel for a stomach."

"Why do you not trust men?"

"Because I know what they can be like. Now hurry back down with the message. If the prince is interested, he'll think of some way for us to meet properly. Oh, and as soon as the man has left, see that my carriage is brought around to the front. I have business to take care of this morning."

When Adelaide stepped into her brougham, she was still feeling smug about a prince wanting to call on her. Assuming he was real royalty. Wouldn't it be a feather in her cap if she arrived on his arm at some soiree and he hadn't yet been introduced to the local society? She'd ask her new friend, Mary Masterson Clark, about the mysterious man when the pleasant widow arrived for tea that afternoon.

Addie stared out the small window as the conveyance turned onto Sacramento Street. The steady rhythm of the horses' hooves reminded her of a clock. And a clock reminded her it was long past time to put Guy in his place, something she should have already taken care of. She was through putting up with his lack of respect. How dare he belittle her by refusing to call! It would soon be two years since she'd married Gordon, and still Guy refused to accept her position in the family. Well, she was about to stop that! She reached up to be sure her new straw hat with a bluebird was still sitting at just the right angle on her head.

When the carriage came to a halt, Adelaide didn't bother waiting for the footman to open the door. She bounced out of the conveyance, ready to give Guy her planned ultimatum. To her dismay, she found herself facing a grand house. It wasn't nearly as large as hers, but far too large for a bachelor who was supposed to be without funds!

"Vincent, are you sure this is the right address?" she called to her coachman.

"Yes, ma'am."

Addie pinched her cheeks for color, raised her skirts a smidgen, then proceeded forward. If Guy wouldn't come to her, she would go to him! She was startled when the front door swung open before she'd had an opportunity to knock.

"May I be of service?" the portly butler asked.

"I wish to see Mr. Stockman immediately."

"I'm sorry, madam, but Mr. Stockman is indisposed. If you will come back—"

"I'll see him right now!" Adelaide shoved the rail-thin man aside.

"I—"

"Where is his room?" Addie demanded. "Up the stairs?" She was already headed in that direction.

"Yes . . . but—"

"Never mind. I'll handle this myself."

By the time Addie reached the second floor, she had worked herself into a tizzy. From the way the butler had acted, she could only assume Guy was entertaining some woman. Well, that wasn't going to last long. How dare he do such a thing while deliberately avoiding her efforts to contact him? It had been over a month since she'd seen him at the Masterson house, and he hadn't been to any of the other social functions she'd attended.

Addie banged open one... two... three... doors before locating the right room. She barged in, ready to take on anyone.

A soiled shirt lay on the mussed-up spread, but the room appeared to be empty. The butler had said he was up here, and she'd already made enough noise to awake the dead. Was he hiding?

"Where are you, Guy Stockman?" she called. "I warn you, if you don't show your face you are going to be in serious trouble!"

"*Grandmother!* How nice of you to come calling."

Adelaide swung around just in time to see Guy rise from his bath. She should have had the sense to wait downstairs. Realizing she had made a horrible mistake, Addie was hard put not to panic. She quickly shifted her gaze, but not before she'd seen the water running off Guy's glistening muscled body and back into the metal tub.

It was essential that she get out of here now! Addie turned, but in her haste to get away, she failed to see the chaise longue beside her. The instant her knees struck the side, they buckled. Quite ungracefully, she toppled onto the heavy piece of furniture.

"My, my. Haven't you become the capricious one?" Without bothering to dry off, Guy reached for his trousers and pulled them on. He was delighted with the spectacle Addie was unintentionally providing. An ear-to-ear grin spread across his face as Adelaide wrestled frantically with the skirts she'd become tangled in. Unbeknownst to the lady, her effort was drawing her closer to the edge of the chaise, until she finally plummeted off the side. A gust of air was expelled when she hit the floor.

Guy laughed uproariously. Everything about *dear Adelaide* was in disarray. A thick strand of golden hair had already escaped its pins and hung quite delightfully down the side of her face. He was fascinated at how her hat tenaciously clung to the side of her head, the bird looking as if it had been shot.

When Addie worked her way to a sitting position, her crinoline cage lifted straight up in front causing her skirts to slide back toward her waist. That she refused to look at him made the situation all the more amusing. She undoubtedly thought he was still naked. "Your pantalets are most becoming," he commented wickedly. What a joy it was to see Addie's face turn scarlet.

"A gentleman wouldn't mention such things!" She was having no success at trying to cover herself, or stand.

"And a lady would never barge into a gentleman's room. But since you did, and because you're so cognizant of proper etiquette, I can only assume you've decided to take advantage of my offer to end the wager. I must admit though, I hadn't expected you to be quite so eager. And such a clever woman at that. Tell me, how did you guess I would insist we lie naked in the daylight?"

"Shut up!"

"Shall I help you to your feet?"

"Stay away! I can do it myself."

"But you don't seem to be having any success, Grandmother. Won't you at least permit me to be of assistance?" Guy couldn't remember when he'd had such an enjoyable morning.

"What you can do is—"

"Uh-uh. Be careful you don't say something indelicate."

"I was going to insist you put on some clothes!"

"I have."

"Oh."

She finally managed to raise the flexible crinoline and was about to roll onto her knees when she was lifted up by two large hands encircling her waist. With Guy behind her, at least she didn't have to keep avoiding looking at him. Then he molded his body against her back. She didn't dare move.

"Mmm. You smell good," Guy whispered. He leaned down and nibbled at an inviting earlobe. "What is it you wanted to talk to me about?"

How was she expected to think when his hands had slid up to just below her breasts and he was planting soft, delicious kisses at the curve of her neck? They seemed to be dissolving into one as the moisture left on his body soaked into her suit.

"The wager is still on, my lovely. Why don't we end it here and now?"

Addie stopped breathing. His hands were cupping her breasts, making the light material of her town suit seem nonexistent. A need was building within her that was nearly as terrifying as Guy's touch. He was igniting strange feelings that she couldn't deal with. "How dare you treat me like this. Turn me loose immediately." She had meant it to sound like a command, but it came out as a murmur.

"No one need know what goes on between us. Let me undress you. Let me make you come alive."

He brushed his thumbs across the tempting buds of her breasts. He could feel their firmness and hear her shallow breathing. He turned her around so she was facing him. Her amber eyes had turned to large orbs of fear and wonder. "I want you more than I've ever wanted any woman," he said softly before claiming her ripe lips. He felt her lean into him. At last she was surrendering.

Guy was certain of his success when she kissed him back. Tentatively at first, then her hungry need started taking over as her confidence grew. Carefully he edged her toward the bed. Then, to his dismay, Addie laughed. Not a nervous laugh, but a full laugh drenched with humor. He stepped back and looked down at her.

"What a delightful experience." Addie reached up and pulled the pin from her hat. It wasn't easy keeping her hands from shaking. "I have often wondered how a man of your notoriety seduced women." She waved a hand in front of her face as if to cool off. "You are indeed very good at it." She was careful not to let her gaze drift downward. The top half of his body was devastating enough.

Guy chuckled, quite enjoying the hunt. "But not good enough to draw you to my bed?"

"Precisely. I hope you are now convinced of that. The reason for my being here has nothing to do with... promiscuity. I came to give you a warning. Never again ignore my request. When I want your presence at the house, you will come immediately. Also, you are never again to say one uncomplimentary thing about me."

Guy stared at her in disbelief. "You're threatening me?" he stated in awe.

"I most certainly am. And last, but certainly not least, you are never to touch me again!" Addie put her hat back on as best she could. She ignored the bird that fell to the floor.

"Or what?"

"Or I'll ruin you in this town!"

Guy's smile disappeared. "Now the real Adelaide has stepped forward."

"I don't forget an injustice. You and Will were the ones who started all this, now it's my turn. I'm certain a good many people would like to know who the Black Raven is. Is robbing people of their money all you do now, or are you still working as a fisherman? I wonder how your so-called friends would feel if they discovered that you steal from them? Assuming you wouldn't have already been caught for your crimes..." She watched his brown eyes turn black with anger. "But that isn't all I'll do if you don't heed my warning. I will also discourage anyone from hiring you. You will become financially destitute. Have I made your position clear?"

"Well, I'll be."

"What is that supposed to mean?"

"You really do consider yourself the matriarch of the family! I didn't think it possible, but you've become an even bigger snob than you were before marrying Grandfather."

Addie lifted her skirts slightly to be sure they hung correctly, then allowed them fall back down. "There is nothing wrong with wanting to be someone."

"Sudden wealth has a strange effect on some people."

"Perhaps, but do not forget that money allows me to do what I please. Do we have an understanding?"

"Oh, indeed we do."

"Good." Addie started to leave the room.

"Just one other thing," Guy called.

Addie stopped with her back turned to him.

"What if William is the Black Raven?"

"Impossible!"

"Why?"

"I keep him too busy." Addie marched out, her head reeling. Upon reaching the stairs, she was sure her legs would give out from under her. She had just given her greatest performance. She held tightly to the banister and started downward. She'd been within an eyelash of succumbing to Guy's masculinity. Pulling herself back to reality had taken a monumental effort. She had wanted to feel his hands on her . . . she had wanted his kisses . . . she had wanted him to make love to her . . . and she had even wanted to hear his words of desire.

How totally naive she had been. At one time, she'd honestly thought she could go through with his offer to end the bet and feel nothing. She knew now that she'd only been fooling herself. There was no longer any doubt that once she succumbed to Guy, she'd never be able to walk away. He was too experienced and she was still naive in many ways.

It occurred to Addie that there was another reason for not coupling, and perhaps the most important one. It would prove her marriage hadn't been consummated. Why, by all that's holy, hadn't she thought about that before? Gordon had made sure that no one would suspect they hadn't had a marital relationship. Could Guy use the information to overturn Gordon's will?

As she left the house and walked out into the bright sunlight, Addie's mouth suddenly teetered on a smile. Why was she having such devastating thoughts? It was a beautiful day, and now that she thought about it, everything had turned out even better than she had anticipated. Falling, then wallowing on the floor had been embarrassing, but she had persevered. And, though she was certainly no authority, she was almost certain Guy had been aroused when he'd romanced her. For once, someone had turned their back on him. And more importantly, she had been the one to do it.

Her lips blossomed into a full smile. She had been the victor! How did Guy and Will feel now that the table was turned? What if she placed a wager on them? An interesting thought.

Standing in front of the window, Guy slowly shook his head as he watched Addie step into her carriage. To say he was perplexed would be putting it mildly. Addie had not only rebuked him, she'd proceeded to lay down rules she apparently expected him to follow! It seemed to him that her offensive air of superiority had increased since she'd elevated herself in society, making her fall all the more comical.

Hearing a light tap, he glanced at the butler who had entered the bedroom.

"Sir, I apologize for the lady's intrusion, but she wouldn't listen to me."

"It's all right, Henry. Short of tackling her, I doubt that you could have prevented it from happening."

Henry made a short bow, then disappeared.

Guy looked back out the window. Only minutes ago he'd thought everything was going just the way he wanted. Addie had acted pliable and had even started returning his advances. Had she reacted favorably to his kisses and touch, or was it all an act? Dammit, she *had* wanted him! Yet again she'd slipped from his hands.

Guy thought about William's plans to marry the elusive woman. It would certainly be a way of getting their money back. Unfortunately, it would never happen. Why should she marry William when everything was going just the way she wanted it? She'd keep William well tucked under her thumb. First she had put Grandfather under her spell, then Jason Harper, and now William. She was like the spider who wrapped a web around her prey then let it sit until she was ready to devour it. It made the game all the more enticing.

Guy turned and peered at the servants who had entered his room to empty his tub. What was he going to do with Adelaide? The lady certainly had a propensity for avoiding a man's bed. He still found it hard to believe that she'd actually tried to blackmail him! It was apparent the spider hadn't heard anything about his growing wealth.

With Will resigned to Addie's innocence, Guy knew he could no longer count on his cousin's help. He sighed. So now he was the only one left to make sure the spider didn't get away with her kill. Would she also try to end his life if he didn't fall into line? Was that why his grandfather now lay in a casket? One way or another, the lady was going to pay for her crimes.

Guy left the window as his manservant started laying out his clothes.

"The correspondence that arrived while I was gone, is it in my study?"

"Yes, sir."

"After I go through it, I'll be away all day."

"Will you be back in time for supper, sir?"

"No. I have too much business to attend to." He unbuttoned his worn trousers and let them fall to the floor. "Did my cousin come by while I was away on business?"

"Yes, sir. Quite a few times."

"What did you say to him?"

"Only that you were entertaining a lady friend out of town."

Guy chuckled. "That was one excuse William would believe."

During the time it took him to dress, Guy had concluded that there was only one way to handle Adelaide Thompkins Stockman. He was going to have to woo her, and he was going to have to do it properly. Though she'd managed to avoid him so far, he was still convinced she was susceptible to his charm. He just had to take his time and get her past her reservations. He'd had his fill of losing their ongoing battle. He released a chuckle. As strange as it seemed, his admiration for the woman continued to grow. Few people were capable of outwitting him. But eventually the tide had to turn in the other direction, and Jason would be saved from an untimely death. There was no doubt in Guy's mind that Adelaide had selected the distinguished gentleman for her next husband. Guy didn't want her to grace any man's bed but his.

Determined to relax and enjoy her afternoon with Mary, Addie had managed to shove aside the embarrassing confrontation she'd had earlier with Guy. Never having had a close friend, Addie always relished Mary's visits. To further her resolve, she'd chosen to wear a flowing white gown with ells of silk. She had also selected the garden as the ideal place to serve tea because of its peacefulness. Most of the flowers were still in bloom, and the sweet fragrances permeated the air.

When Mary arrived, Addie thought her friend looked particularly lovely. Soft curls bounced about her cheeks when she walked, and she had a fashionable straw hat perched on the back of her head. The white dress with blue vertical stripes made her rather thick waist look considerably smaller.

"Adelaide," Mary said when they had finished exchanging gossip, "I want you to volunteer your time at the hospital. Now, you need not flinch. If not once a week, then once every other week. They can use all the help they can get."

"I don't think—"

"Then let me put it differently. You would be an inspiration to other ladies of wealth who sit for hours doing nothing but needlework. If not an inspiration, they certainly would do it just so you wouldn't outshine them."

Adelaide grinned. "You do have a way about you for getting what you want. Very well, once every two weeks."

Mary grinned.

Adelaide sipped her tea. "Mary, have you heard of a Prince Rupert Stalinsky?"

"Yes. Just last night at supper, Father said he'd heard a prince had arrived in the city." Mary smiled. "Of course Father eagerly raised his brows and asked if I plan on remarrying anytime soon. He and Mother would do anything to add real royalty to the family. Or has he already been added to your list of admirers?"

Addie couldn't resist a bit of bragging. "His envoy arrived at my house, requesting I meet with him."

"Oh, how exciting!"

"Would you like to wed again?"

Mary set her cup and saucer down on the small round table. "I suppose so, if the right man came along. But for now, I'm quite content to spend my time with my two children."

"I had assumed that you and Guymour were..."

Mary laughed. "I'm fond of him, but he's more like a brother to me."

For some reason, Addie was quite pleased to hear there were no attachments. At least the lovely brunette wouldn't be involved in her vendetta against Guy.

"Guymour, William and I have known each other since we were children." Mary grinned. "Besides, Guymour is more than I could handle. You are quite welcome to him."

"I don't want him."

"I had an entirely different impression."

Addie refilled Mary's cup. "How could you think such a thing? We do nothing but yowl at each other like a pair to tomcats."

"That's what made me suspicious."

"What a strange thing to say. We hate each other."

"*Hate* is an awfully strong word."

Addie picked up the silver platter and held it toward Mary, waiting for her to select another delectable delight. "Guy is determined to prove I gained the family fortune by unorthodox means."

Mary nodded. "I must admit I've heard the stories. I was quite eager to meet such a notoriously wicked woman." She giggled before taking a bite of the sweet cake she'd selected.

"Some would be even more convinced of my wicked ways if they'd seen what happened this morning."

Mary was all attentive. "Do tell me about your latest escapade."

"I would hardly call it an escapade. I went to Guy's home—"

"You what? Surely you didn't go alone?"

"Of course I did. He's my—"

"How deliciously daring. Especially with it being Guymour. Does he know yet that you're still a virgin?"

"No."

Mary leaned forward. "Why haven't you told him? Surely then he'd realize that all his suspicions are unfounded."

"I doubt it. He thinks that besides coaxing Gordon out of his money, I had something to do with his death."

"Hmm." Mary waved a fly away. "I'm sorry I interrupted. How wicked of you to go to his house alone. What happened?"

Addie cleared her throat. She couldn't tell about how she'd fallen over the lounge, or Guy's kisses. "I saw nothing wrong with what I did, Mary. You're making more of this than necessary. Though we may not act like it, we are family. When Gordon passed away, he not only gave me his money, he left me with a big responsibility. I feel that since he isn't here, it has become my duty to watch after William and Guymour, and to try and make responsible citizens out of them. I have William working now, and he's become an entirely different man. As for Guymour..." She had been about to mention the robberies. "I'll soon have him right where I want him. It won't be much longer before he comes to me for money."

"I don't understand what you're talking about." Mary wiped her hands on her linen napkin. "Why would Guymour come to you for money?"

Addie could see the confusion in Mary's eyes. "I'm saying that I intend to put an end to William and Guymour's spending and carousing. They need to start taking responsibility for their own lives."

"But..." Mary dabbed her mouth. "Surely you know that with the help of Guymour, William has made several real estate investments that have already brought him profit."

"But that's impossible. Guymour doesn't have anything to give William. Are you sure that isn't a lie Guy told?"

"I know it's true. Father helped select the property, and Guymour lent the money."

Addie was furious. Guy was stealing then giving his take to William to invest! "It would be interesting to see what happened if Guymour's means of income ceased."

"Well, we both know that isn't likely to happen. Father so admires Guymour for what he's managed to do on his own. Father says in the very near future, Guymour will be one of the wealthiest men in San Francisco."

Addie was shocked. "You know how Guy procures his money, yet Kenneth admires him?"

Mary thought for a minute. "Addie, why do I get the distinct feeling that we're talking about two different things?"

"Perhaps you're right." Addie nervously shifted her cup around on the saucer. She didn't dare say anything about the Black Raven until she was sure that was what Mary had referred to. "I know he and William received an allowance when Gordon was alive, but that has long since ceased. So if Guymour is supposed to become so wealthy, where is he getting the financial backing he would need?"

"I'm sure he didn't need any backing. After all, he had his inheritance."

"Gordon only left him two thousand dollars."

"Not that inheritance. I'm speaking of the one his parents left him. They were wealthy in their own right, and with Guymour's keen business sense, he knew how to invest it."

Addie mopped her forehead.

"Addie, are you feeling all right? Your face is so flushed."

Addie was mortified. "It must be the unseasonable August heat. And what about William's inheritance?"

"It's my understanding that he spent his inheritance on pleasure. But you'll have to admit, that certainly doesn't detract from his charm."

"And..." Addie was having difficulty speaking. Her embarrassment that morning had been bad enough, and now she'd discovered that her accusations of Guy being the Black Raven—plus threatening to turn his friends against him—amounted to nothing! "How much money do you think Guy has?"

"I have no idea, but with those shipping companies he bought, the bank in Sacramento and the railroad investments Father said he has, I wouldn't be out of place saying he is exceedingly well-to-do. And, of course, I doubt that I even know half of what his income is derived from. Addie... are you sure you're all right? Now your face is almost white."

Out of the corner of her eye, Addie saw a man walking toward them. When she turned to look, the tree shadowed him. It looked like Guy! This was more than she could take in one day. She'd die of humiliation... she needed time to prepare herself....

Mary wasn't fast enough to catch Adelaide as she slid off the chair in a faint.

Adelaide heard the whispering before her eyes fluttered open. She was lying on her bed and a damp cloth had been placed across her forehead. She raised up on her elbows and looked around the room. "How long have I been here?" she called to Eleonore, who appeared to be tidying up on the other side of the room.

The smiling maid hurried over with a glass of water. "Mr. William carried you up here only minutes ago. Do you feel all right?"

"Mr. William? It wasn't Guymour?"

"I haven't seen Mr. Guymour today."

Adelaide sat up, swung her legs over the side of the bed, and took the glass. She suddenly remembered what Mary had told her, and groaned. "And to think Guy just let me ramble, knowing all the time there was nothing I could do to him!" She scooted off the bed. "Where are the others?"

"They left after deciding you'd be fine."

"They couldn't even wait until I came to?" Addie handed her the damp cloth. Maybe it was a good thing they'd left. She could think of nothing she wanted more than for the day to end, though it was doubtful she could make herself look any bigger a fool than she already had.

"Mr. William thought you'd just had too much sun. Mrs. Clark told me privately that women's tight corsets were the reason they swooned so often. Isn't that the most ridiculous thing you have ever heard?"

Adelaide was too busy thinking about how Guy must have laughed to the point of tears after she'd departed this morning. That he had allowed her to make threats, without saying a word, was unforgivable. Damn the man!

"Did you say something, madam?" Eleonore asked.

Addie wondered if she'd spoken aloud. "Did Mr. William say why he was here?"

"No, ma'am. Are you sure you're all right?"

"No, I'm not all right. If I were smart, I'd leap off a cliff into the ocean and drown."

"All women faint. It is nothing to be embarrassed about."

"That's what you think!" Addie walked out of the bedroom.

Chapter Twelve

"Not again!" Susan protested.

William looked up. Seeing his cousin standing in the doorway of his bedroom somehow seemed fatalistic. Will climbed out of bed, knowing Guy wasn't going to leave until he joined his cousin in the study.

"When did you return?" William asked. "That woman must have really been a lioness to detain you so long."

"I've been out of town on business."

"This is the second time in a row!" Susan seethed. "I warn you, William, if you leave this time I won't be back!"

Will looked down at the lovely woman partially covered with a sheet. "I can assure you, my dear, this is harder on me than it is on you."

"Very well!" Susan jumped off the bed and reached for her dress.

"Now, darling," Will said as he pulled on his own clothes, "you told me Adam isn't due home for three days. Why don't you climb back in bed and get a little rest? You know I plan to keep you up all night."

"Well . . . if you're sure you won't be long . . ."

Will pulled her into his arms and kissed her passionately. "I'll be back as soon as I can."

Susan pouted prettily. "Very well, I'll wait. But not long!" She returned to the bed, paying no heed to the full view she'd given both men.

Guy walked over and took hold of William's arm. "Come along before you change your mind."

"Whatever you have to say, make it quick. I intend to have my pleasure tonight."

"My house has been robbed by the Black Raven."

"Were you home?"

"No."

"How do you know it was him?"

"He had the nerve to give his name to my butler. I haven't assessed the loss yet, but Henry said it wasn't much."

"Is that all you wanted to tell me?" William headed back toward the bedroom door.

"I'm not finished. I found a lace handkerchief on the floor with the initials A.S. embroidered in the corner."

William took another step before it suddenly occurred to him what Guy was alluding to. "It can't be Adelaide!"

"The initials fit. I find it difficult to believe a man would carry so delicate an item simply for the pleasure of it."

"Couldn't Henry tell if it was a man or a woman's voice?"

"Apparently he was too worried about his own life to pay attention."

"There could be other reasons for Addie's initials to be on the handkerchief. Perhaps she gave it to the gentleman. No one knows who he is. He could even be one of our friends or associates." His brows furrowed. "Or your thief deliberately left a false clue."

"Well, well. A war or a woman. Two sure ways to cause trouble among relatives. Adelaide has you just where she wants you."

"You have no right to say that."

"The hell I don't! When you tell her about this, which I'm sure you will, you might also mention that I've hired a very capable man to get to the bottom of all this. You're a fool, Will. Women always were your weakness."

"You're a fine one to talk! You knew damn well we'd get into a fight when you told me those lies about Olivia. Because of a woman, you ran back to America to fight in a damn war! At least you had the decency to tell mutual friends you were leaving because it was your patriotic duty."

"They weren't lies."

"She told me how much you loved her and of your bitterness upon finding out she'd chosen me to marry. I believed her."

Guy shoved his top hat back and stared at his cousin. "I've wondered how long it would take for you to bring up my relationship with Olivia. I left so you'd have to get out of your own mess, and I didn't want to stay and watch how the marriage turned out. It had nothing to do with love or loss. I told you then that I refused to marry her and she went straight to you vowing it was you she loved. You wanted to believe Olivia, and she knew how to use that to her advantage. Just like Adelaide."

"Is there a point to all this? Olivia is dead."

"But Adelaide isn't." Guy rested his hands on the ivory lion adorning the top of his cane. "I'm sure you know now that I was right about Olivia. It's not likely, but maybe she even admitted her lies. I never loved her and she knew it. Now you're allowing Adelaide to do the same thing. As Olivia did, Adelaide has you convinced she's innocent of any wrongdoing. She's manipulating you."

"Are you finished? If so, I'll rejoin Susan."

"Is that all you have to say? You're just going to stand back and let Adelaide get away with everything?"

"Because of all the things I said in England, I'm trying damn hard to not plant a fist in your face. Just because Adelaide is a female has nothing to do with how I feel. Off and on, she and I have talked. Bit by bit, I'm finding out what actually happened with her and Grandfather. It's quite an interesting story. And if you would stop and think about it, the Stockman men have always been prone to doing unorthodox things. Where do you think our fathers' wildness came from? Our grandfather's loin. So for him to up and ask Addie to marry him makes perfect sense to me."

William repeated everything Addie had told him. "So you see, it was that bitch Penelope and her story about being pregnant that started everything."

"And you believed that?"

"Yes, but that doesn't mean I'm willing to let Addie keep what's mine."

"She won't marry you, Will."

William cocked an eyebrow. "I'll try my way to get back my inheritance, you try yours. In the meantime, I'm learning about law, as well as my future estate. Something that I've discovered is quite to my liking."

"Your future estate, hell!" Guy still didn't believe Adelaide was innocent, but apparently she had managed to get Will interested in law. Something no one else had done. He could already see a big change in his cousin. Will was willing to stand on his own two feet now.

Guy shook his head. He shouldn't have come here tonight. "Go back to Susan, Will. I'll see myself out."

As Addie bid each guest good-night, she was pleased at how successful her dinner party had been. Not a single person had sent regrets. It still amused her to see how the wealthy families of San Francisco had suddenly taken her to their breasts. Or so they claimed. She had thought about inviting Guymour, but she still wasn't ready to face him.

Jason was the last to leave. He leaned over and kissed Addie's cheek. "A most enjoyable evening, my dear."

"Thank you. I thought it went very well."

The butler handed Jason his top hat and helped him with his cape.

"You should start seeing other men, Addie."

"Why would I want to do that when I have you?" she teased.

"I want to ask you something."

"You sound serious."

"I'm sure you're aware that I'm very fond of you."

"Yes, but you don't love me."

"True." He adjusted his cape on his shoulders, then pulled his cane from the hall tree well. The butler had apparently forgotten it.

"If you are concerned that I might misinterpret your willingness to escort me to social functions, you can ease your mind."

"You've come to know me well."

"I will admit that at one time I did consider you for a second husband, until I discovered you're in love with Ursela Warren."

Jason became very still. "I must be more careful. How did you find out?"

"The look in both your eyes when you think no one is watching. She adores you. It is because of the two of you that I've come to believe there really is such a thing as true love." In her mind's eye, Addie pictured Ursela's husband. His stiff, ungiving manner was all the more evident next to her sweet tenderness.

Again the silence.

"I don't suppose you'd tell me about it?" Addie asked.

"No. And you?"

"What about me?"

"Are you going to tell me about your prince?"

"I've never met him."

They strolled across the wide entry floor toward the front door.

"A month or so ago, a man claiming to be representing his highness began talking to Gordon's old friends. He asked about your character, your relationship with William and Guymour, and your financial status."

"How strange. I don't know whether I should feel complimented or angered."

"With all the trouble the man seems to be going to, I'd say you'll be finding out soon. Don't let the fact that he is a prince sweep you off your feet."

"Don't worry. I have no intention of letting that happen."

"Good girl."

Addie closed the door behind Jason, then leaned against it. Was Jason right? Would his highness be contacting her soon? She hadn't said anything, but her curiosity was driving her insane.

"Miss Addie. Wake up!" Eleonore called excitedly.

Addie opened one eye and looked at the maid. She was bent over so low that they were practically nose to nose. "Why are you waking me so early?"

"It's nearly noon. Besides, that same gentleman is back that came before. He is waiting in the entry. He said his highness, the prince, wanted to know if he could call at three this afternoon."

Adelaide opened the other eye and sat up, almost knocking heads with Eleonore. "Yes!" Just last night she had wondered when the prince would present himself. She hadn't expected it to be this soon. "But when you repeat that, don't sound so excited. Now hurry. Go! Wait! After you deliver the message, run to the kitchen and have water heated for my bath." She threw the cover off. "At last I'm going to meet the mysterious prince!"

At five minutes to three, Adelaide sat in the parlor, watching the clock hands move. It had taken nearly the entire three hours she'd been given to go through her clothes—at least five times before finally choosing a dress—eat the breakfast Eleonore had forced down her, then attend to her toilette. The last minutes of waiting were the worst. Would the prince be fat and short, or tall and handsome?

The knock on the door made her jump. She reached up to check her curls in the back, pinched her cheeks, then glanced down to be certain her skirt was still properly draped. Because she hadn't the vaguest idea as to the proper etiquette for greeting royalty, she had already chosen to do nothing. After all, this was America, and he was seeking her out, not the other way around.

When the gentleman stepped into the parlor, there was no question in Addie's mind that he was a true prince. His regal bearing demanded attention. He was wonderfully handsome with dark auburn hair, strong features and long, purposeful strides. He wasn't as tall as Guy or William, but that didn't detract from her attraction.

"Permit me to introduce myself. I am Prince Rupert Stalinsky II. At last we meet."

How could she not be impressed when he stopped in front of her, clicked his heels, made an impressive bow and handed her a magnificent bouquet of red roses?

"How beautiful!" Addie accepted the gift. She'd been given flowers by other suitors, but they had only been posies. "Won't you be seated . . . what am I supposed to call you? Your royal highness?"

"We are in America. I would like my new friends to call me by my Christian name. Rupert. It seems as if I have waited a lifetime for this day."

Everything about him was perfect, including his dashing black and red uniform. Even his teeth were straight and his black boots polished to perfection. She hadn't expected him to be dressed in so dashing a manner, but it was probably a symbol of his country. "Please be seated. You sound as if you've seen me before."

"Indeed, I have." He took the chair next to hers. "On quite a few occasions."

"Now I am curious."

"The first time was in Paris. I was captivated with your beauty even then. I happened to pass by in my coach and saw you feeding pigeons. I stopped and watched for some time, though you were obviously in a family way. It took but a few inquiries to find out who you were and, alas, that you were married."

Adelaide smiled nervously. Though immensely flattered, she needed to get his mind off the part about being pregnant. "Where are you from?"

"Dubaine. It is a very small country. When I first saw you, I was in Paris attending to some political matters. You were a charming distraction."

The maid entered, carrying the tea service.

"I hope you don't mind, Prince Rupert, but I took the liberty of serving."

"I am honored."

Doesn't he know how to smile? Adelaide wondered. For a man who appeared to be only in his early thirties, he certainly had a serious nature. Perhaps that would change once they became better acquainted. She perused the plate of delectable tidbits the maid had placed on the table in front of her. The cook had quite outdone herself, Addie thought. She handed the bouquet of roses to the maid, Gwen. "See that they are put in a vase and placed in the entrance."

"Yes, ma'am."

Gwen left as quietly as she had arrived, and Addie proceeded to pour for the prince and herself.

"Excellent," Rupert commented after tasting the hot brew.

Was he referring to the tea? His gaze hadn't left Addie since Gwen had entered the room.

"Tell me. Did you have a boy or a girl?"

"I beg your pardon?"

"The child you were carrying. Was it a boy or a girl?"

"Oh. Ah . . . neither. The child died at birth. I have no children."

"My apologies for having brought up so delicate a subject. You must have been devastated."

"Yes . . . yes, I was." She cleared her throat. "I hope you're enjoying your visit to America."

"Indeed, I am. I attended Oxford, but this country is very different from England."

Addie had wondered about his British accent and perfect diction. She looked down at the tempting goodies on the plate. She knew it wasn't good for her waistline, but she could no longer resist one of Della's sweet tarts.

"I came to America to see you."

The sweet tart didn't reach Addie's mouth. "But that's impossible. We've never met before." She placed the tart back on the plate just in time to keep the strawberry filling from dripping onto her dress. "How did you know where to find me?"

"I have loved you from that first day when you were with the pigeons, and I made a point of finding out everything I could about you."

Addie gulped.

"I was insanely jealous of your husband, and even considered killing him. Instead, I wisely left Paris."

"Kill Gordon?"

"Try to understand. I had never felt this way before. In my country, the men are very passionate about their women. But you are not from my country and I knew that if I did such a thing you would never forgive me. I left France for the same reason I came to San Francisco. You."

Addie was nonplussed.

"While in Paris the first part of this year, I inquired about you and was told your husband had died. I sent my representative ahead to see if it was true and to discover where you were living." He raised his cup and drank the now-tepid tea. "I have told you all this because in my country, it is customary for a man to declare himself to a woman. Do not worry, I lived in England long enough to know your customs. I cannot carry you off on my horse, and women are allowed to make their own decisions as to the men they want to be with."

Adelaide's fingers toyed with the diamond cross hanging from a chain around her neck. Carry her off on his horse? How exciting!

"I discussed this in great detail with my advisers and they felt I should also inform you that I have had extensive instructions in the art of pleasure, and considerable experience. I will give you nights of indescribable passion."

Adelaide choked on her drink. Somehow she managed to set her cup down while grabbing for the napkin resting on her lap. After a short coughing spell that brought tears to her eyes, she regained control of herself.

"Are you all right?" Rupert asked, his handsome face mirroring his concern.

"Yes, I'm fine." Addie dabbed the corner of her eyes. Prince Stalinsky could not be referred to as shy. Only one other man had spoken so openly to her.

"Are there any questions you care to ask?"

Addie cleared her throat. "Just one. What is the purpose of all this?"

"I thought you knew. Marriage. I have every intention of convincing you to become Princess of Dubaine."

One of the few things Eleonore had known about royalty was to never do anything until they did it first. Adelaide slowly rose to her feet, almost expecting someone to yell at her. "I . . . I am very honored, but marriage is out of the question."

Addie watched him stand. She was prepared to scream if necessary. However, the thought of screaming quickly vanished when Rupert's shoulders seemed to relax and he bestowed upon her a devastatingly warm smile.

"What I had to say wasn't easy for me, either. In my position I am not accustomed to explaining myself. But with that out of the way, surely we can now take the time to at least become friends."

Adelaide was having a difficult time adjusting to the sudden transition. Now Rupert was exuding total charm.

"I would be most honored if you would accompany me to the theater tomorrow night. I assure you, you will be quite safe."

"Prince Stalinsky, at present I have no intention of committing myself to anyone."

"Yet my representative tells me you go out with only one gentleman. Your attorney, Jason Harper."

Addie was furious. "How dare you spy on me?"

"You have such beautiful amber eyes when you're angry. I simply wanted to know who my competition was."

"I have no idea what women are like in your country, but I choose whom I care to go out with and I have different gentlemen coming to call."

"I am aware of that. I also admire your independence."

"And I refuse to have any gentleman tell me whom I should, or should not, be with. I hate displays of jealousy."

"I assure you, I will not disappoint you."

What a sweet plum it would be to have a prince escort me about San Francisco, Addie thought. Everyone would be absolutely pea green with envy. Still, she hesitated. She was thinking about the impassioned thoughts that had tempted him to kill Gordon. He raised an eyebrow, waiting for an answer. She couldn't help but smile. No doubt about it. He was a charmer. "Very well, I'll go to the theater with you. However, I shall bring a friend."

"Male or female?"

Addie laughed. "I haven't decided."

Rupert again clicked his heels and bowed. "Until tomorrow."

For the following two weeks, Addie saw Rupert at least once a day. He went shopping with her, they played cards, attended dinners and talked about everything. Though his kisses weren't as devastating as Guy's had been, Rupert was showing her an enchanted world. She delighted in hearing words of love and being treated as his princess. And how could she not enjoy being the envy of every woman they met? None of whom could boast of having a prince on their arm.

However, when she received an invitation to the Brookmore ball, she was relieved when Rupert couldn't escort her. She had become too fond of him. Deep in her heart, she knew it wasn't love. She wasn't looking forward to telling him that marriage was out of the question.

Once again it was Jason to whom she turned. Dear Jason wanted nothing from her.

Chapter Thirteen

Adelaide continued fanning herself, even though the night air was considerably cooler than that inside the Brook-more house. It was delightful to be whirled around the ballroom floor by one handsome bachelor after another, but fresh air had become a necessity. She knew she should have told Jason she was going for a stroll in the garden, but having to smile so much had become tiresome and she'd felt the need for a few minutes alone.

"You are indeed a most beautiful woman."

Addie's fanning slowed as she scanned the shadows. "Do I know you?"

She should have recognized that deep, husky voice. She hadn't known Guymour was at the ball, and even if she had she wouldn't have expected the excitement that trailed up her spine when he stepped out of the shadows. "Had I known you would be here I would have reconsidered my invitation," she stated defensively. This was their first meeting since their confrontation at his house. She should never have threatened him. This was the man who one time said he believed in an eye for an eye. "How long have you been standing there watching me?"

"From the moment you stepped outside. Even if I hadn't seen you, I would have recognized your intoxicating perfume."

"Oh."

"Actually, I thought this an excellent opportunity for me to apologize." *Especially after hearing all the gossip about you and that prince! Damn if I'm going to allow another man to get in my way or lay claim to the Stockman fortune!*

"You apologize? For what?" Her fanning became more brisk. The evening seemed to have heated up considerably.

"For everything. I have failed to give you the respect you deserve. Stockman men have always treated their women with the highest esteem and expect everyone else to do the same."

Taken aback by his gentle words, Addie didn't pull away when he circled her arm in his and continued to stroll down the path. She wasn't about to mention their last meeting.

"I have given this a lot of thought, and I've come to realize my bad attitude started when I returned from the war. It was your unapproachable demeanor and cutting remarks that eventually set my nerves on edge and drove home the need to retaliate."

Adelaide was about to defend her actions, but he continued on.

"When Will suggested the wager, I thought it a perfect way to take you down a peg or two. I finally did some logical thinking and realized that it was probably my scar that repulsed—"

"Oh, no," Addie quickly assured him. "It had nothing to do with that. The day that you walked into the house, I thought you were extremely handsome."

Guymour smiled inwardly. The wooing might not be as difficult as he'd anticipated. Maybe it was a good thing that her prince's attention had spurred him into action. "You're too kind. What I'm trying to say—and doing a poor job of it—is that we started off on the wrong foot, and if possible, I'd like us to begin again."

"I'd like that very much," Adelaide said sincerely. She blessed Mary for telling her of Guy's wealth. Otherwise, Addie would have been certain he had said this because of her threats. He had apologized, and after all, wasn't being treated with respect what this had all been about? It was much better than the constant bickering.

"Even though I still have a bitter taste in my mouth at the family estate being left to you, I've come to accept that it was all Grandfather's doing, not yours. I should never have accused you of unfair—"

"Why have you changed your mind?"

"If we're to be friends, I guess I have to admit that William went through Jason's files on Grandfather. They corroborated everything you'd said."

Addie's soft laughter drifted through the air. "Wouldn't Jason have a tizzy if he knew?"

"Harper is an intelligent man, and I'm sure he's already figured it out. Who knows, he may have even planned it. Tell me, Addie, did Grandfather ever teach you to ride a horse?"

"Yes. In fact, I'm quite good at it. Gordon and I used to ride every morning in France."

"He always enjoyed a morning ride. Perhaps I can persuade you to ride in the park with me Sunday."

Addie's senses were suddenly alerted. She was positive Guy was up to something. Had all this been an act? "I'd be delighted, but I haven't a steed or a saddle."

"I'll furnish everything. Shall we make it about ten?"

"Ten would be fine. Guy, about the things I said last—"

"Remember? We're starting over. That day never happened." He couldn't choke back a laugh when he remembered the sight of her falling off the chaise.

"Is something funny?"

"I guess I was just feeling good now that we've made peace with each other. Though you may find it hard to believe, I've felt guilty about trying to force you into my bed. I'm really not the type of man who would think about doing or saying such things. I was just angry."

Addie struck the toe of her slipper on something hard, causing a groan of pain. She looked down but it was too dark to see anything. She hadn't realized they had moved well into the shadows and the house was a considerable distance away.

"Are you all right?" Guy asked.

"I . . . I stubbed my toe." She stepped back down on her foot. "Yes, it seems to be fine." She wasn't thinking about her toe, she was thinking about Guy's nearness, and the simple apology that had so quickly nullified all the pent-up bitterness she'd clung to tenaciously. She had to know if he was sincere or not, because right now she was feeling both suspicious and yet very vulnerable. She was about to move away when he suddenly scooped her up in his arms.

"I hadn't realized we had drifted so far. I'll carry you back. You don't want to do more damage to your foot."

When Guy didn't move, Addie felt spellbound. Having his strong arms about her, smelling the faint, pleasing odor of his after-shave lotion, and especially his nearness sent her mind reeling. She knew her thoughts were dangerous, but she'd never had a man carry her before, at least not while she was conscious.

Guy stared down at the beautiful face captured in the moonlight. He could clearly see the look of desire as her arm came up and circled his neck. Her lips slowly parted, and he leaned down, unable to resist the full, ripe mouth that was waiting to be kissed. He was astonished at how the simple movement sent fire surging through his body. Her breasts were pressed against his chest, and she was returning his kisses—seducing him—driving his desire to the point of no return.

His lips moved to her inviting neck, and she leaned her head back onto his arm, giving him complete access to do what he pleased. Her nipples were barely contained by the low-cut neckline of her dress, and were just waiting to be claimed. But not tonight. It was the wrong time and place, and he had to remember that with Adelaide, he must take it slow in order to assure an eventual victory. He drew his head back and started walking to the house. Besides, he wanted her completely. He wanted to take his time and take them both beyond the point of thinking. But if he didn't get away from her soon, the lovemaking would be short and not so sweet.

"Do you know what you're doing to me?" Guy asked, his voice husky with desire. "Again I must ask you to forgive my blatant ways." He chuckled. "And, even as tempted as I am, it wouldn't be ethical for a gentleman to take advantage of a lady. I want our new friendship to start off right."

"Thank you for your consideration." Addie wanted to scream. The man was aggravatingly unpredictable. She wanted his kisses. Couldn't he tell? As they neared the lit area of the lawn, he lowered her to her feet and stepped away. It wasn't fair! She suddenly wondered if her earlier suspicion had been right. She had heard of women teasing men, so why couldn't a man tease a woman to get what he wanted?

"I thought I saw your driver atop a new coupé."

"You did." *Didn't he feel anything when they kissed? How could he discuss her coach?* "Isn't it beautiful? I haven't seen another like it. I insisted Jason and I use it tonight."

Guy was more inclined to believe she just wanted to show it off. "I was thinking about your safety."

"Safety?"

"What with the charities you have funded, as well as donating time at the hospital, you have become quite well-known. Is your coachman armed?"

"Well...no. I hadn't thought about it being necessary."

"My coachman is. One can't be too careful. The Black Raven has yet to be caught. May I suggest you take my drag home? I'll see that yours is returned early tomorrow."

Addie thought of the diamonds and emeralds she was wearing. "Perhaps you're right. Thank you. I accept your thoughtful offer."

Guy smiled broadly. "I'm already looking forward to our outing Sunday. I'll be there promptly at ten."

Addie rubbed her bare arms as she watched Guy disappear into the house. With him no longer keeping her warm, the night seemed uncomfortably chilly. She was still in a quandary as to why he had released her. It didn't at all fit the pattern of the man she thought she'd come to know.

As Addie headed back toward the house, she considered her ride with Guy. Actually, she was suddenly looking forward to Sunday. Not just because of the ride, but also because she was now curious as to what Guy would come up with next. She quite liked having two strong, passionate men vying for her attention! What more could a lady ask for?

It hadn't been too long ago that Adelaide had known exactly the type of man she would pick to marry. Quiet and responsible. How much she had changed in so short a time. She wondered if Gordon knew what he had started. And why didn't he speak to her anymore? Apparently she had been right. It had all been her imagination.

She'd covered only half the distance to the house when Jason appeared in the open doorway that led to the ballroom. Standing tall and looking very distinguished, he waited for her to join him.

"So there you are. I thought I had searched everywhere. I didn't think about the garden." Jason took her hand and escorted her inside.

"I became overly heated and decided to take a stroll."

"Did you lose your fan?"

"Oh! I guess I did. It was so lovely out I hadn't paid attention."

"I'll go find it for you."

"No, no. That won't be necessary. I'll send a servant over tomorrow to retrieve it." She hadn't even realized it was missing. "Jason, would you be terribly upset if I went home?"

"Is anything the matter?"

"I have a headache. Probably due to becoming overheated." She surreptitiously glanced around the large room. There were too many people for her to locate Guy. However, during her quick perusal, she had deliberately smiled at Mr. Fancher because he still couldn't get up the nerve to speak to her. She'd long since lost count of how many times the pudgy man had tried to bed her when she was a lowly housekeeper.

"I'm ready to leave, also. I'm getting too old to keep up with the social pace you've set over the last few months."

"Nonsense." Surprisingly, Addie was also tiring of the constant parties. Only a short time ago she had commented to Eleonore how much she was enjoying all her male suitors.

"I'll tell Minnie and Coleman we're leaving, then I'll meet you at the front door."

Addie nodded. "I saw Guymour awhile ago, and he mentioned the danger of being robbed and offered his drag for our use. I hope you don't mind, but I accepted."

"Probably a wise move."

By the time the coachman had Addie headed home, she was already having difficulty smothering yawns. They had left early, but even so, it was after two in the morning. Adelaide thought about Guy's kiss. If she closed her eyes, she was sure she could still feel his lips on hers. Why didn't other men's kisses make her feel light-headed and weak in the knees? He still had an effect on her even when she was positive he was up to something.

Adelaide suddenly remembered something. "Jason, you said Gordon had told you of our arrangement. What did you mean by that?"

"I was aware the marriage was to be platonic."

"I have another question. Since the marriage wasn't consummated, can that information be used to contest the will?"

Jason chuckled. "No, my dear. You have no reason to worry about Guymour, William or anyone else taking your money from you." He took Addie's hand in his. "While we're asking questions, I have one for you. How serious is your relationship with the prince?" He'd always liked the way Addie's eyes would light up when she smiled.

"As a husband, he would be an excellent feather in my cap. Every biddy in town would be pea green with jealousy."

"I take that to mean you're not in love with him."

Addie sobered. "I don't know. I've never been in love." Her smile returned. "Perhaps you would be more interested to know that Guymour asked me to go riding with him Sunday."

"That is indeed more interesting. Apparently he's changed his attitude toward you."

"Just because he asked me to a Sunday outing? No, he wants something."

"You're too suspicious, Addie."

"Whoa there!" the driver suddenly yelled.

Something hit the side of their vehicle, then Adelaide was unmercifully tossed from side to side in the conveyance. The pain! Was that her screaming? The pain! She was so cold. Everything went black.

Guymour hurried into the house, brushed by the butler, then took the stairs two at a time. When he'd arrived home, a sobbing servant from the manor had been waiting to tell him Miss Adelaide had been in a horrible accident.

Adelaide's bedroom door was closed, but that didn't keep Guy from barging in.

"What do you think you are doing, young man?" questioned a short, bald man. He remained by the side of the bed, blocking Guy's view of Adelaide. "Leave this room immediately!"

"I have a right to be here. I'm family!"

"I don't give a damn who you are. If you want this woman to live, you'll get out of here and let me do my work."

Guy was tempted to ignore the doctor but thought better of it.

Knowing he couldn't be of any help, Guymour left the house. He wanted information, and a servant had told him his footman, Stanley, was out back in the carriage house.

Guy found the young man sitting on a bale of hay, bent over, one boot lying to the side. His ankle was badly swollen, but other than that, he appeared none the worse for his experience.

"What the hell happened," Guy demanded. "I haven't been permitted to see Adelaide. Is it true? Are my driver and Jason Harper dead?"

"Yes, sir, that's the truth of it."

"Good God." Guy rubbed his temple.

"It weren't Noble's fault, it was the driver of that delivery wagon that done it. I swear, Mr. Stockman, it seemed to come out of nowhere, hit your coach hard in the side, then disappeared into the night."

"Was there a company name on the side?"

"I only got a glimpse of it just in time to yell a warning to Noble and jump clear."

Guy reached out and patted Stanley's shoulder. There were pauses when the young man spoke, and his voice kept cracking. The retelling wasn't coming easily. "I'm sorry, Stanley, but I need to know whatever you can remember."

"I understand, Mr. Stockman." Stanley wiped his mouth with the back of his hand. "It's just that everything happened so quickly. The drag rode on two wheels for some distance, and I could hear Mrs. Stockman screaming. Then it tilted over, rolled and hit a tree. Everything seemed to stand still, yet I could hear wood splintering and the horses galloping away."

Stanley had buried his face in his hands, and Guy had to strain to hear what was being said.

"Then I came to my senses and ran to see if I could be of any help. The first thing I could make out was that older man's head. It was a bloody mess. The rest of his body was under the coach. His eyes was open, but he was dead. Next I found Mrs. Stockman. She'd been thrown some distance. There was lots of blood and her body was twisted, but she was breathing. I was afraid to move her. Then I found Noble. I ran as fast as I could to get help, Mr. Stockman."

"I'm sure you did, Stanley, and you shall be justly compensated for what you've done. I know it wasn't easy for you to relive the accident."

"Funny, I don't so much remember the runnin' as I remember the sweat drippin' into my eyes. Is Mrs. Stockman goin' to be all right?"

"I don't know. I haven't talked to the doctor yet. He's still attending her. I have a feeling it's going to be a while before I'm allowed to see her."

"You'll let me know?"

Guy nodded.

"Noble was a good man, sir. I'm gonna miss him."

Guy knew it would be quite some time before Stanley had another decent night's sleep. Seeing death for the first time wasn't easy. He wished he could get his hands on the man who had caused the accident. He'd personally see that the bastard was hung. The coward hadn't even stopped to see if he could help.

"I been sittin' here thinking, Mr. Stockman. Something wasn't right. How did that coupé pull loose from the horses? They should have gone down, too. Something wasn't attached properly."

Guy nodded. "Look into it after you feel better."

* * *

William and Guymour were playing baseball on the lawn, then Gordon joined them. Laughing, the threesome looked up to where Addie stood by the window, and waved. Why were the boys so much younger than she? It didn't matter. What was more important, Gordon was alive! But just as her excitement soared, the three faded from view. "Gordon," Adelaide called, "come back! I won't let you die. I'll take care of you!"

Standing in the doorway, Guymour watched the doctor hold Adelaide down on the bed when she again tried to rise up. Even unconscious, she appeared to be trying to say something.

Guy clenched his teeth to control the overpowering emotion he was feeling. Addie had been cleaned and nightclothes had been put on, but it didn't help. The swelling, cuts and bruises on her face made her unrecognizable. The doctor had informed him that besides her many lacerations, she had a broken leg and arm. He was able to re-set the arm, but the leg had been broken in several places, and he wasn't sure if he had managed to align the bone properly. It was possible Adelaide could be crippled for the rest of her life. But for the present, it was the deep wound on the back of her head that concerned him the most. She still wasn't out of danger.

Guy turned away and went back downstairs. He was angry and hurt. His longtime driver, Noble, and Jason were dead, and there wasn't a damn thing he could do about it. Worse yet, he couldn't even do anything for Adelaide except get in the way. He'd never felt so helpless.

Earlier Eleonore had run into her mistress's room screaming, "No, no, no," then she had fainted. It had been up to him to carry her to the kitchen where she was quickly revived. Since then, it seemed Eleonore appeared every fifteen minutes or so, asking if Addie was going to live.

Guymour entered the study and turned up the lantern. After pouring a tall glass of whiskey, he took several long drinks before trying to relax in one of the deep leather chairs. He leaned his head back and closed his eyes.

"Mr. Stockman. Is there any news?"

Guy's eyes flew open. "Eleonore, when I know anything I'll make a point of telling you. Until then, I don't want to be disturbed."

"I'm sorry, sir, but I am so worried."

"We all are." Guy was sorry he'd snapped at the pretty redhead. She was only trying to be of help, and all this certainly wasn't her fault.

Hearing her departing footsteps, Guy stood and went to the window. The sky was starting to turn gray, and before long, the sun would rise. Where the hell was William? He'd sent a servant with a note hours ago. Will was probably sleeping peacefully in some woman's bed.

"Where is Guymour?"

Recognizing William's booming voice, Guy went to join him.

After being told what had happened, William hurried upstairs. It wasn't long before he came back down, his face ashen. "She was so beautiful," he whispered. He looked sharply at Guy. "If you say one word about her deserving this, we're going to get into another fight. Then we can go another four or more years without speaking."

Guy rubbed his aching temples. "I haven't changed my mind about how she procured the family fortune, but I wouldn't put this kind of curse on her. During the war, I saw similar wounds. The hardest part is yet to come."

"I love her, Guy."

Guy looked up at the ceiling and swallowed the snide remark that was on the tip of his tongue. "I see." He'd left England not only because of Olivia and his fight with Will, but also to force Will to get out of his own problems. He needed to back off again. "Let's get some breakfast."

They strolled toward the kitchen, neither in any hurry.

"You're not going to make any comment?" Will asked.

"Nope, I'd rather talk about the Black Raven. I believe I know who he is."

"Who?"

"Grandfather's manservant, Hubert."

"Hubert? Of course! I had forgotten all about him."

"We've been so wrapped up in other things that we totally missed the obvious."

"And he knew about your nickname. It would also explain Addie's handkerchief in your house. He'd said he wanted to get even with her."

"It will probably do little good, but I'll give the authorities his description."

When they entered the kitchen, the smell of yeast buns perked their appetites.

"You poor boys," Della soothed. "You must be starving yourselves. It wouldn't hurt either of you to put on some weight."

The cousins sat at the big table. Guy thought about the delicious meals they'd had here when they were young. He couldn't remember a time that Della hadn't been his grandfather's cook.

"I'll have breakfast ready in no time." Della took ham and eggs from the larder. "How's Mrs. Stockman doing?"

"Not well," Guy replied.

"Oh, that poor baby. I'm saying my prayers, and when I go to church I'm going to ask the Lord to look down kindly on her. They don't come any better than that lady."

"I'm sure she would appreciate it," William said.

Guy hadn't failed to notice that all the servants seemed very fond of their mistress. It was hard to believe that they hadn't felt her sharp tongue on more than one occasion. He turned to Will. "What about Jason and Noble?"

"When I arrived home and read your message, I went straight to the undertaker and made arrangements for the burials. Noble will be quietly buried this afternoon at three. I also started the arrangements for Jason's funeral. It will be a big affair. He was not only well-known but also well liked. He has no family, but he did leave a will. I'll read it when I get to the office to see if he left any special instructions.''

''So now you'll be handling the legal side of the Stockman fortune.''

''That will have to be Addie's decision, if she's ever well enough. Jason had said he would leave me his law practice. Did I tell you he made me a partner?''

''No.'' Guy thought about Will's declaration of love. ''Will, when Addie is on the road to recovery, I'm going back to England.''

''Why? Your home is in San Francisco now!''

''I shouldn't be gone over a year. I need to get together with my contacts and pick up more shipping contracts.''

''Does that mean you've given up on accusing Addie?''

''Here you are, boys,'' Della said as she placed a large plate of food in front of each man. ''I want you to eat every last bite. If you want more, you just let me know.''

As Della shuffled away, Will looked at his cousin. ''Well?''

''Do I have a choice? With this accident, she's beaten me, though I'm still not convinced she didn't trick Grandfather into marrying her.'' He cut a bite of the thick, savory ham. ''I talked to Grandfather's doctor, and he said Grandfather had had trouble with his heart before. I've chosen to give Adelaide the benefit of my doubts about how the grand gentleman died.'' He took several more bites of food.

Will buttered his bun and smothered it with strawberry jam. ''How can you be so apathetic?''

''Toward Addie?''

''Not only Addie, but Jason and Noble.''

''Do you have something on your mind, Will?''

''Adelaide doesn't need your attitude. She needs someone who cares and believes in her.''

''And that someone is you.''

"Yes. That someone is me."

"You're wrong, William. I'm not as devoid of feeling as you seem to think. I just don't let it show." Guy shoved his plate away and stood. "That was a wonderful breakfast, Della, but I can't eat another bite."

For Guy, the following days passed slowly. The funerals were held, and the bodies laid to rest. Jason's will was read, and to Guy and Will's shock, the bulk of the estate was left to them. There was a side note saying he wished Gordon had lived long enough to see what fine gentlemen his grandsons had turned out to be. And, as promised, Will also inherited the law firm along with the wealthy clientele.

For the first time in years, William could once again be called a wealthy man. He had seen what it was like to not have money, and he vowed to never let it happen again.

Guy and Will were allowed to visit Addie only once a day. The swelling of her face had gone down considerably, but the red welts, lacerations, black eye and bruises seemed even more apparent. But she was coherent now, and would live. Again she drew Guy's admiration with her lack of complaining, even though she had to be in pain, emotionally and physically. When Will had told her of Jason's death, she didn't cry, but Guy had seen the way her eyes grew dull from her deep sadness.

Guy and Will were furious when they found out that Addie had requested a mirror, and Eleonore had stupidly given it to her. Something about Adelaide seemed to die after seeing the results of the accident. Addie would survive, and Guy knew the time had come for him to leave for England. Will had declared his love for Adelaide, and this time Guy would make sure he didn't interfere. He had no place here. William could and would handle everything. Besides, if he didn't leave, he was going to pound down Addie's door and give her a sound lecture. He was too aware of what happened if an injured person stopped fighting. Yes, it was time to go.

* * *

"How could you have done such a stupid thing?" The question was asked with barely controlled anger. The dark figure moved off to the side. "I told you to get rid of Guymour Stockman and that lawyer, but I sure as hell didn't tell you to hurt Adelaide Stockman! Had she died we would have lost everything!"

"I'm sorry. I didn't know they were in the carriage. At least the lawyer is out of the way."

"Just pray to God that you haven't ruined everything."

Even after the doctor had told Addie that with a wheel-chair she could return to her normal activities, she was discontent. She couldn't stand the thought of never being able to walk again, and to prove she could, she tried on several different occasions to get to her feet, only to fall on her face and require someone to help her up.

The doctor had also said her scars would eventually fade, but all she could think about was the image she'd seen in the hand mirror. God was paying her back for becoming so vain and caring only about herself. Nevertheless, her vanity still hadn't died. She refused to receive visitors until she could see the final results of her injuries. She also needed time to recover from the loss of Jason.

For weeks after her accident, Eleonore pleaded for Prince Rupert to be allowed to see Addie. Eleonore told of his broken heart and how close he'd come at one time to killing himself over his loss. Addie had finally told the maid that she had enough problems of her own without having to hear Rupert's. And, if Eleonore said one more thing about the prince, she could find other employment.

As one day followed another, Adelaide could no longer deny how lonesome she'd become. She yearned for Jason's counsel and company. But like Gordon, Jason was gone forever. She didn't want to talk to Will because she had allowed herself to believe that this might never have happened had the cousins welcomed her into the family.

And the only reason Will could possibly want to marry her was so he could get back the family money. As for Guy, he had taken off to England. He hadn't even cared enough to stay with her. She was glad she hadn't gone with him on that Sunday ride.

It was with considerable trepidation that Adelaide finally listened to Eleonore, and allowed the prince to call. When she realized Rupert wasn't at all disgusted with her appearance, she began to enjoy his visits and thoughtfulness.

Chapter Fourteen

London—Six months later

Standing at the long, polished bar in the men's club, Guy Stockman quickly opened the letter he had been handed. Mary Clark would have no reason to contact him unless something was wrong at home. He proceeded to read the delicate handwriting.

> Dear Guymour,
> Though it is not my place to write, I chose to do so anyway. William assures me that Adelaide's health is fine, but I still worry. I have not been permitted to see her since the accident. This is not at all like the dear friend that I've come to know. William will do nothing to advance my cause for fear of upsetting Adelaide, whom he feels is too fragile to undergo any changes. Especially since the doctor told her she would never walk again.

Guy snorted. Fragile? That would never be a word he'd use to describe Adelaide—under any circumstances.

> I'm afraid William no longer has any influence on Adelaide. He is now only permitted to talk business and he says Adelaide constantly snaps at him. He ex-

cuses this by saying her bitterness stems from being crippled, and that in time she will change. She also informed him that she will not see any visitors because she refuses to let the San Francisco biddies gloat over her misfortune. The only two she does seem to listen to are that intolerable maid, Eleonore, and Prince Rupert. Eleonore is not only uninformative, she's extremely abrasive when I call. As for Prince Rupert, I never see him at any social functions. Just yesterday, Adelaide told William that the prince has asked for her hand in marriage. William is extremely worried that she will accept.

The muscles in Guy's jaw flexed.

Perhaps I am being unduly concerned, but I would feel so much better knowing you were here to handle matters and to make sure Adelaide isn't being taken advantage of. I have no idea how you could go about doing this, but you always were the one who seemed to know all the answers. I realize you have never been fond of Adelaide, but I truly believe you might hold the secret to restoring her back to her old self. She certainly won't listen to anyone else.

Guy dropped his cigar into the spittoon.

Unfortunately, I have more bad news. When I informed William that I was going to write you whether he liked it or not, he insisted I tell you the harness on your drag had been cut. Surely he must be wrong. That would mean the fatal crash wasn't an accident.

Guy's nerves were pulled as tight as a bowstring. Why would someone want to kill Jason and Adelaide? Or perhaps it had been a mistake. Perhaps he had been the intended victim.

Guymour, I'm sure your business in London is of paramount importance, but I plead with you to come home. We all need you.

Your loving friend,
Mary

Guy crushed the paper in his large fists. Why the hell hadn't someone contacted him sooner? Why would anyone want to kill him or the others? Will wouldn't have said anything about the leather being cut if it wasn't so. As for Adelaide, her days of self-pity were about to come to an end. He had backed off and given Will free rein to convince Adelaide to marry him. That obviously wasn't going to happen. Now it was his turn. He hoped Addie hadn't changed too much, and would still refrain from readily committing herself to any man. It had suddenly occurred to him that there was only one answer to all of this. Perhaps it had been staring him in the eye all along. He was the one who would marry Addie.

Guy glanced around the men's club, searching for a particular face. His gaze came to rest on a rail-thin gentleman with unruly red hair and thick spectacles. As usual the Swedish doctor was enjoying his afternoon beer. Guy moved forward.

The docks were alive with stevedores loading waiting ships when Guy arrived in San Francisco. At three in the morning, it was still dark, but to his relief he had no trouble procuring a public cab. After giving directions to William's place, Guy tried settling back in the seat. But he was pushed for time. He had a lot to do and not much time to do it. There was only a glimmer of hope that his cousin would be home. By the time the cab came to a halt, the milkman was making deliveries.

It took incessant pounding on the front door before William's butler showed himself, holding a lantern in the doorway, Guy could clearly see resentment on Ivan's sour face at having been disturbed so early. That immediately changed when he recognized the caller.

"Mr. Guymour! I didn't know you had returned from England."

"Neither does anyone else, and I want it to stay that way. Is my cousin in his room?"

"Yes, sir."

Guy hurried forward.

Just when he had his lank, curly-headed cousin sitting on the side of the bed, Ivan arrived with coffee.

"Damn, Guymour! It's good to see you. At least I know you're alive and well, but couldn't this have waited until a bit later?" Will took a grateful drink of the black coffee.

"No, I'm only going to be here a short time. What's this about tampered trappings of my coupé?"

Will nodded. "So Mary *did* write you. Your footman discovered it and informed me."

"Have you come to any conclusions as to what this is all about?"

"Only hypotheses. The big question is who was the accident meant for? It's possible the guilty party didn't know you'd lent your coupé."

"I thought about that."

"I admit that over the years you and I have acquired more than a few enemies, but what purpose would killing Addie solve?"

"What if it was Hubert trying to get at Adelaide?"

"Hubert was caught a week after you sailed for England."

"Perhaps he escaped."

"No. Some very irate citizens wearing masks hung him."

Guy rubbed the dark stubble on his chin. He hadn't shaved since yesterday morning. "You definitely think it wasn't an accident?"

"I checked myself. The leather had been partially cut in all the right places. It had only to take a jar of some kind to snap them all loose."

Guy pulled his watch from his vest pocket and checked the time.

"At least you can't blame Adelaide for this."

"I still think she used underhanded means to acquire our inheritance. I'll eventually find out the truth."

"I wouldn't advise you try to see Adelaide, Guy. She's...well, she's apt to have you dragged from her house. She refuses to even talk about you."

"I see. How healthy is she?"

"Fine, as far as I can tell. She lost quite a bit of weight from the accident, and strength from being confined to a wheelchair, but when she gets angry, she can certainly bellow out her words. I feel sorry for her."

"Feeling sorry for her isn't going to help." Guy pulled on his fine leather gloves. "Has she married the prince yet?"

"Not yet, but she's giving it serious consideration. I don't like it one damn bit. Sure as hell, he's going to get the family fortune, which I'm beginning to think he's been after all along. I don't know how to stop it, other than to put a bullet between his eyes, and believe me, I've thought about it. Perhaps between the two of us, we can come up with an answer to the problem."

"My ship is waiting to take me to the islands. Be careful, Cousin, and watch your backside. If someone is after me, they may also be after you."

"Why a business trip now? There are more important things to attend to."

"Business trip? Who said anything about a business trip?" Guy smiled wickedly. "I'm taking an old acquaintance on a voyage."

"If you're in danger, this is a hell of a time to be entertaining a woman! You were safe while in England."

Guy chortled. "How many times have I said that to
you?"

"We need to find out who's behind all this!"

"That's something you can be working on while I'm
gone. I made a promise quite some time ago, and I can no
longer put off keeping it. When I return, maybe one of us
will have figured out what this is all about."

Angry and bewildered at Guy's attitude, William could
only watch his cousin's smile broaden before he left. "Be
careful," Will called after him. It was Guy's smile that
worried Will the most. He knew it well, and it meant trouble.

Knowing cook's helper would already be up, Guy entered the large house by way of the back door. Without so
much as a hello to anyone, he marched straight through the
long room, across the entry, and up the wide stairs. Without a moment's pause he continued down the long hall.
When he came to the door he wanted, he shoved it open
and walked in.

"Who is there?" Adelaide asked angrily. "You know I
don't like being disturbed so early!"

Guymour continued on to the bed.

"It isn't even light out yet!"

Guy scooped Adelaide up in his arms, and marched back
out of the room. He couldn't believe how lightweight she
was.

"What do you think you're doing?" Adelaide demanded upon realizing who was committing so foul an act.
Furious, she tried to struggle, though she knew it was useless. Guy was too strong. "I demand you turn me loose! Do
you hear?" she yelled.

"Miss Addie!" Eleonore called.

"Get help!" Addie called back.

"Della! Ivy! Gwen!" Adelaide screamed as she was carried through the kitchen. "Get Roger! Get help! Dammit, don't just stand there with your..." It was too late. Guy had already marched outside. Again she screamed as he shoved her into a waiting carriage.

After several deep breaths, Addie asked in a somewhat more controlled voice, "Just where do you think you're taking me?"

"On a voyage, my dear. On a long voyage."

"I won't go. I'm not well. I have no clothes! Where is my wheelchair? And what about Eleonore? I can't possibly go anywhere without a maid!"

"I've had enough of hearing you give orders. So either keep quiet, in which case we will get along fine, or I'll clamp my hand over that mouth of yours. Something I've wanted to do for a long time." William had been right. Addie may have lost a great deal of strength, but not when it came to her mouth.

Adelaide sucked in her breath and her amber eyes grew large. She knew why Guy was doing this. "You're going to kill me!"

"Oh, no. But I assure you there will soon come a time that you would prefer I did. No, Mrs. Stockman, I have other plans for you. Your days of hiding and feeling sorry for yourself have come to an end. No more being mollycoddled. You are going to have more sun, fresh air, and ocean than you've ever known in your entire life."

"You can't do this to me! My face, my...don't you know it is impossible for me to walk. Please, Guy," she pleaded, "don't do this." His silence infuriated her. "Damn you, I have no clothes for a trip!"

"How do you know you can't walk? You've never really given it a try."

"That's a lie. I tried. The doctor said I will never walk again." Addie grabbed the door handle, ready to throw it open and fling herself onto the road. She wasn't fast enough. Guy's big hand was immediately on hers, forcing her to turn loose of the knob.

"I never knew you were such a coward, Addie," he snapped.

"So help me, I'll get even with you for this, Guymour Stockman."

"How familiar that threat sounds. Now there is the real Addie I'd come to know." He pulled a flask from his pocket and handed it to her. "Here, have a drink of wine to calm yourself."

Addie grabbed the sterling container, opened it and took a long drink.

William stared impatiently at the petite maid. It was hard to believe that he had yet another visitor so early in the morning. "If you would calm down, I might understand what you're trying to say!" He wanted to grab her by the shoulders and give her a good shaking. "Dammit, you keep saying Addie's name. Is something wrong with her?"

"Yes ... I mean, no ... I don't know." Eleonore continued to wring her hands. "Mr. Guymour took her!"

"He what?" William exploded. "You can't be serious."

"Gwen and Ivy both said he bounded into the house and disappeared. When he reappeared, he was carrying Miss Addie. She was yelling for someone's help, but those who saw it said they weren't about to try messing with Mr. Stockman. Then he left and I hurried over here. Oh, Mr. William, you're the only one who can go after her! She's too weak to be treated like that."

William remembered Guy's parting words. *It isn't exactly a business trip. I'm taking an old friend.* Now he knew who that old friend was.

"Why do you just stand there? You must do something before that terrible man harms her!"

"It's too late to do anything. I believe it is safe to assume that your mistress is already out to sea, and I have lost a fine stallion." William broke out laughing. Only his cousin would be bold enough to walk into a house and kidnap a woman.

"At sea?" Eleonore collapsed onto the nearest chair. "He has no mercy. He will kill her. What am I going to tell the prince? He is going to be heartbroken!"

Hearing her sniffle, William pulled a handkerchief from his sleeve and handed it to her. He shouldn't have laughed but he couldn't help himself. "If I know Guy, I'm afraid the prince is going to be in for a big disappointment. And you needn't worry about Addie. Though Guy might like to apply his hand to her backside, he would never do any harm to Addie." He took her by the hand and pulled her to her feet. "You need not worry, Adelaide will be watched after. Though I'm loath to admit it, this may very well be the best thing that could have happened to her."

Her thick eyelashes still wet with tears, Eleonore looked up at the handsome gentleman. "He will kill her," she repeated.

Their eyes locked and, for a brief moment, time seemed to stand still.

"Perhaps you can convince me she will be all right," Eleonore whispered. "We can console each other. You for losing your money and me for losing my mistress."

William's gaze traveled to her parted, cherry red lips. Inviting lips. She moved up against him, leaving no doubt as to what she meant by consoling. The redhead was beautiful and tempting, but for some reason that even he couldn't understand, Will wasn't interested. Besides, he loved Adelaide. At least he thought he did. He backed away from the temptation. "You'll feel much better when your mistress returns. I suggest you take advantage of this and go visit relatives or friends."

He pulled the tassel hanging down the wall. A minute later Ivan appeared. "The young lady is ready to leave." Will turned to Eleonore. "Mark my word, everything is going to be fine."

William left the room, already chastising himself for not taking advantage of promises offered. Yet, even though Eleonore was genuinely upset over her mistress's kidnapping, he didn't trust her. He shrugged his shoulders. He had no idea why he would feel like that.

Chapter Fifteen

It was a strange...heavy...flapping sound that brought Adelaide to her senses. As groggy as she felt, it seemed to take forever before she could manage to open her eyes. When she did, the blinding sunlight caused her to shut them again. It took several tries and a lot of eye fluttering before she was finally able to see clearly.

Her head pounding, Adelaide pulled herself into a sitting position. Where was she? She didn't recognize the bed she was on or the room that was even smaller than her quarters when she'd been a housekeeper. There was only the bed, a commode...those were trousers and a shirt draped over the back of the single chair! The bunk swayed. "No!" she yelled.

Collecting her strength, Adelaide hoisted herself onto her good knee and was able to peek out the porthole. For as far as the eye could see, there was nothing but ocean. Lord Almighty, she was on a sea vessel! Guy must have put something in that wine she'd drunk. She had heard of such things being done when men were needed for a ship's crew.

Adelaide glanced again at the clothes draped over the chair. Fear surged through her body like melted silver. Guy had sold her because of her ugliness and she was going to be sharing the bed with a sailor! This was how Guy intended to regain the Stockman fortune. No one would ever know what happened to her.

Frantic, Adelaide reached up and, with shaking fingers, unlatched the porthole. Commanding herself to be calm, she grasped the opening and tried pulling herself up. She fell back onto the bunk. Her panic grew. She had no way of knowing when the seaman would return. She had to get her body through the hole. Drowning was far better than being forced to share a stranger's bed. Her only regret was that she couldn't kill Guymour before taking her own life.

Somehow she had to stand on her good foot. It was the only way she could get her body through the hole. This time she clasped both hands on the opening and pulled with all her might. She was weak, and her efforts already had her perspiring. At last she had her leg under her, but she hadn't used it in so long it had little strength! She was about to release a cry of accomplishment when she felt her damp palms starting to slip and her leg gave out. She tried tightening her hold, but it was no use. Again she fell backward. She hit the bed hard, groaned, then lay still on her side, her chest heaving as she fought to catch her breath.

"Do you need help?"

Guy! Addie thought with relief. He hadn't deserted her after all! She had been so engrossed in what she was doing that she hadn't even heard him enter. Suddenly she remembered he had to have been the one to bring her on board. And who did the clothes on the chair belong to? She was about to turn and demand some answers when she thought about her face. Her pride smarting, she didn't want him to see the scars. She rolled further onto her side.

"You wouldn't make much of a meal for the sharks, but I'm sure they'd still be grateful." Guy watched her shudder, then curl up in a ball as best she could. "Well, my dear, let me see if I'm understanding this correctly. You refuse to talk to me, you don't want me to look at you, and you're ready to die. Am I right?"

No reply.

"I'm sorry to disappoint you, *your ladyship,* but that isn't the way it's going to be. The tables have turned. I am now giving the orders and you will follow them. Don't expect pity, because I don't know the meaning of the word. I have had enough of your reclusiveness, and more than enough of you wallowing in self-pity.''

"You know nothing! You've been in England."

Though her words were muffled, Guy had no trouble understanding bullheadedness. Especially hers. As he moved forward, Addie tried tucking herself into a tighter ball. If he hadn't been so angry, he would have thought her effort to avoid him amusing. He easily rolled her onto her back. She tried fighting, but her strength had already been depleted. Effortlessly he climbed on top of her and straddled her waist. Holding her arms over her head with one hand, he used the other hand to clamp his fingers around her jaw, making it impossible for her to turn away.

Furious, Addie opened her eyes and stared up at him.

"I'm looking at you. Now what? Are you Mors, the god of death? Or perhaps you're Medusa, and any minute I'm going to turn to stone?"

"If you're finished staring, then turn me loose." The look of horror she'd expected to see in Guy's eyes wasn't there.

"Oh, no. We're going to talk about this right now. Are those few scars what all this is about?" he raved. "Damn woman, if you hadn't become so vain, you'd know those scars are nothing. There isn't a thing wrong with you that weight wouldn't help." He climbed off her. "You look like a skeleton! I once told you a story about a bully. You should have taken heed. You're a lot of talk, Addie, but inside you're one of the biggest cowards I have ever met."

"What I do is none of your business. Why have you brought me here?"

"I've decided to take matters into my own hands. There will be no more hiding."

"Don't you understand? I'm not well!"

"Furthermore, you will eat everything you're served, or at least make a noticeable attempt. In other words, my dear, you are going to rejoin the living."

"I'll kill myself before I'll let you order me around."

Guy was amused. What would Adelaide have to say if she knew he had contemplated marrying her and putting a proper end to her floundering about?

Guy placed his hand on his narrow hips and looked down at the woman on the bunk. Her thick, blond hair had come loose from the pins and was lying in disarray on the pillow. But it was her gaunt face that continued to trigger his anger. "You truly amaze me. I find it hard to believe that someone so vain could allow herself to get into this condition. Perhaps your vanity will be appeased if you remember that none of the crew have ever set eyes on you before, and have no expectations. I left some clothes for you to wear."

"You mean ... surely you're not ... I'll not be seen dead in men's trappings!" Addie blurted out.

"The cabin boy wasn't pleased at having to share, so I suggest you guard them with your life. There is nothing to replace them with. Of course it's up to you as to what the crew will see when you go on deck. Your nightdress isn't made of the thickest material."

Addie crossed her arms over her breasts. "I'm not leaving this cabin!"

"Oh, yes, you are, because I'm going to carry you out no matter what you do or do not have on." Guy walked to the chair, picked up the clothes and returned. "Now get dressed. I'll assist you until you're capable of doing it yourself."

"Don't you dare touch me!"

Guy shrugged. "I'll wait outside no longer than ten minutes. If you're not ready, I'll come in and dress you myself."

"I need to bathe."

"There is water right there by your bed, soap and a cloth to clean yourself."

"But that's not adequate."

"There is another choice." He raised a dark eyebrow.

Addie was horrified. "Surely you wouldn't..."

"Throw you in the ocean? No. However, I wouldn't be averse to taking you on deck and having a barrel of salt water poured over you. I'm no different than the crew. Seeing that wet nightgown clinging—"

"I've heard enough!"

"Then perhaps you've come to realize that I have no intention of putting up with your refusals. Ten minutes. Don't try the porthole again. I have a man watching it." He left the room.

Adelaide released one long, ear-splitting scream. What made him think she'd kowtow to his demands? She thought about his threats. Didn't he realize she wasn't capable of doing anything? Oh, how she loathed him. What made him think he had the right to take over her life? If she had a gun she'd shoot him! A weapon. That's what she needed. She glanced around the room but couldn't see anything useful. Guy had left her with no choices. She'd have to do what he said, at least until she could find a way to escape. Perhaps she could get one of the crew to help. But that would never happen if she stayed in her cabin. She'd have to let him take her above.

Addie's hand touched the cabin boy's clothes. How long had it been since Guy left the room? She pulled her nightclothes over her head.

Putting on the shirt and pants proved to be more difficult than Adelaide had anticipated. Since her accident, Eleonore had always dressed her.

It seemed to have taken a lifetime before the task was finished. Her strength once again depleted, Addie fell back onto the bed. She felt indecent. Though the trousers were loose, they still left her legs outlined. And the shirt! She couldn't possibly allow anyone to see her like this. There were no undergarments! She was about to take the shirt off when Guy returned.

"I will not be seen looking like this!" Addie said determinedly.

"As I stated before, it's purely your decision. Make up your mind fast, because your throne is awaiting you and I have other things to do besides standing here arguing."

Addie sneered. "The men aren't going to see me, because I'm not going anywhere! And while I'm thinking about it, these are terrible accommodations. The steamship I—"

"To hell with your steamship!" Guy roared. "These *are* your accommodations! You might as well get used to them! You are on the *Francisca,* lady. My clipper ship. It wasn't built to accommodate rich and haughty passengers like yourself."

As Guy leaned forward to pick her up, Addie delivered a sock right to his chin. He was furious. Never had he put up with a woman who caused as much trouble as this one. And he couldn't even retaliate. His only consolation had to be watching her rub her sore knuckles. He swooped her up in his arms. Damn if he was going to let a slip of a woman get the better of him. What had ever happened to the unemotional housekeeper he used to know?

"I can't find enough words to express how much I hate you for doing this to me," Addie wailed as Guy carried her out of the room.

"You're certainly giving it a good try."

"You want to get even for something I was never guilty of. Then you'll return to San Francisco acting the hero and saying you did everything possible to restore me to my old self!"

"*Lady Adelaide,* I swear that tongue of yours would drive the hardiest male to his grave. If you were a man, I'd have you whipped into submission." One more step and they were on the deck. "However, knowing you would un-

doubtedly relish the suffering—as well as playing the mar-
tyr—I shall forgo the temptation!"

Adelaide wasn't paying any attention to what Guy was
saying. She was too enthralled with the panorama that
suddenly stretched out before her. Three giant masts
reached up to the sky, with huge sails billowing in the wind.
Now she knew where the flapping sounds had come from.
Men seem to be everywhere, busy at work.

When Guy placed her on a wooden chair that had been
anchored down, Addie knew this was what he'd sarcastically referred to as her "throne."

"Welcome aboard, Mrs. Stockman."

Addie shadowed her eyes from the bright sun with her
hand, and looked up. Too late she remembered her scarred
face. Let them look, she thought bitterly. Her excitement
quickly faded. "I want to go back to my cabin."

"Please excuse her ill manners, Captain," Guy said.

Again Addie looked up. "Captain? Didn't you say you
were in charge of this ship, Guymour?"

"I only own her. It takes many years at sea to become a
captain. Captain Green, permit me to introduce my grandmother, Mrs. Stockman."

Adelaide flinched. Nevertheless, that was followed with
her best smile. "How do you do, sir," she said sweetly. "I
don't mean to be a bother, but is there by chance a tub
aboard?"

"Tub?" The captain looked at her as if she had lost her
mind.

"A tub to bathe in, Harold," Guy stated with a laugh in
his voice. "She's not used to a lack of accommodations and
doesn't realize the scarcity of fresh water. But it isn't of
importance. She'll learn."

Adelaide wished Guy would disappear and die. As the
two men became lost in a conversation about some kind of
fish, Addie's gaze was locked on a man carrying a tray of
vittles, headed in her direction. She licked her lips, already

anticipating the taste of steaming hot coffee and food. She couldn't remember the last time she had been so hungry.

And so Adelaide's life aboard the *Francisca* began. Every morning, noon and late afternoon, Guy took her to her "throne," and each day she was permitted to remain a little longer in the sun.

All Adelaide's worries seemed to disappear. She didn't even miss Rupert. The weather was wonderful, and grew warmer the farther they traveled. She discovered she truly loved sailing, and often found herself wishing she'd been born a man. Her life would have definitely been spent at sea.

On their third day out, Addie watched a sailor approaching. Guy was nowhere in sight, so she could only pray the huge bear of a man would pass on by. As he neared her, he smiled, showing chipped teeth. His beard was shaggy and long, he wore an eye patch, and Adelaide refused to look at the tattoos adorning his body. The rank smell alone was enough to make her want to faint. When he stopped in front of her, and it was apparent she wasn't going to pass out, she considered screaming. She decided not to. It might make him angry.

"Me name's McCregan."

Addie didn't know if that was his first or last name, and she didn't care. She was too frightened to reply.

"I been worryin' 'bout ye stayin' in the sun so much, lass, so I brung ye a gift." The Scotsman brought his huge hands from behind his back, and proudly presented a gentleman's top hat. "It won't protect your face a lot, but it'll keep your head from gettin' burned. I always fancied I'd like one, but after I bought it, I discovered I had nowhere to wear it."

Addie was deeply touched. Other than Gordon, she could never remember a time that someone had been so unselfishly kind to her. "I wouldn't think of wearing it. I might ruin it."

"What's it for if not to wear?"

Adelaide was starting to relax, and McCregan was less intimidating. "Very well, I would be proud to accept your gift." She placed the gray hat on her head. It fell to her ears.

"I didn't think about ye bein' so small and all." Clearly perplexed, McCregan thought a moment. "I'll make it smaller."

"But you'll destroy it."

"To have someone as pretty as ye wear it would be worth it."

The following day, the big Scotsman returned and showed her his handiwork. He had cut away part of the hat, then he'd sewn it back up. Though Addie said nothing, it looked atrocious. But it fit, and she treated it as she would a precious jewel.

Most of the time Adelaide was outside, she wore her hat. At first the others laughed, but she ignored them. She wanted McCregan to be proud.

Instead of her face repulsing the crew, it turned out to be the other way around. Many were scarred worse than she. Apparently Guy had been right. With no one having seen her before the accident, there were no expectations. Once that realization was met and accepted, she even agreed to eat her meals with the captain, the first mate and Guy.

Addie's life melted into an enjoyable routine. She was even grateful Guymour had brought her along. She loved the sun, the sea and especially the occasional sprays of salt water. And she became fond of the crew. One by one, the sailors managed to sneak forth and make her acquaintance.

For the first time in over six months, Addie had real friends to talk to. She learned the difference between the stern and bow and the names of the various sails. The word *mizzenmast,* the sail closest to the stern, fascinated her the most, probably because she'd never heard it before. It was the discovery that the ship didn't have a full crew aboard that interested her the most.

According to the men, the ship was being loaded with cargo when orders came to set sail, and word was that Mr. Stockman hadn't yet given the captain a destination. Obviously this voyage hadn't been planned. So why had Guy done this, and just how long ago had he returned to San Francisco? Since her accident, she had set down rules that no one was to speak of Guymour.

The sailors seemed to derive pleasure from presenting Addie with an occasional gift. She received whittled miniatures of animals and a small carved boat. One man even made her a comb, and another gave her a crimson ribbon that he'd kept tucked away for years. Both items were badly needed to keep some kind of control over her hair. She especially delighted in devouring the delicious pastries the cook occasionally brought as a special treat.

The captain had a good collection of books, so when Addie wasn't talking to the men or staring out over the vast ocean, she read. However, when Guy was about, she only pretended to read. Though she and Guy seldom spoke, he'd never said she couldn't look. She'd become fond of watching him stroll along the deck while talking in low tones with Captain Green, or when he'd decide to work alongside a sailor.

Guymour was magnificent with his black hair blowing in the wind, his boots, tight pants that showed muscled thighs, and a white, billowy-sleeved shirt. He reminded her of pirates she'd read about. But she knew she was fantasizing again. A curse that she'd always had. It was knowing that he would never again look at her with desire that always brought her back to reality.

With the warm, lulling breeze, Addie also napped and did a lot of thinking. She now realized that during her self-imposed hermitage, she'd missed being out in the fresh air and visiting with people. She'd missed her talks with Mary, Will and especially Jason. Maybe Guy had been right about her wallowing in self-pity.

* * *

A week and a half from the day they had set sail, Guy stood next to the rail with a partially smoked cigar clenched between his white teeth. As he watched the natives transporting cargo to shore in their colorful outrigger canoes, he was contemplating the financial costs of this voyage. What with only half a crew, he'd doubled the sailors' wages. Captain Green had to be paid the percentage he'd lost for not having a full cargo in the ship's hold. Even the cabin boy had managed to fill his pockets. Guy had been forced to dicker with him for his clothes. The curly-haired gnat had definitely gotten the better end of the deal.

Hearing the natives laughing, Guy was reminded that the captain and crew had gone ashore that morning. Most were undoubtedly partaking in debauchery while the others were passed out drunk. As many times as Guy had visited these islands, he would never have believed the day would come when he'd remain aboard ship to watch over a spoiled woman.

He should have realized a long time ago that it was impossible to outguess Adelaide. This morning she had insisted he hold her up so she could see the natives and canoes. He had suspected it was a ruse, and that as soon as she spotted the islanders, she'd make an outburst of some kind to draw their attention. That would be followed with accusations of kidnapping. So he'd been ready to clamp a hand over her mouth at any time. But that hadn't happened. Apparently Addie had come to accept her fate.

He hadn't even been right about her getting seasick! She not only didn't get sick, she didn't even complain about the food! Who would have thought she'd turn out to be a born sailor? Adelaide Stockman was actually enjoying herself. But why not? Everything she needed was taken care of for her, including being carried to and from the deck and meals in the captain's quarters.

Guy leaned against the ship's railing, his dark brows drawing into an ominous frown. What bothered him the most was Addie's attitude toward the crew. Though she was hostile toward him, she certainly seemed to have no problem with the men. She had each and every one wrapped around her little finger. If she told them to mutiny, they probably would. They treated her as some queen who had graciously bestowed her presence on them. If she dropped a thing, one of the men would be right there to hand it back to her. Something he'd wanted her to have to do for herself.

It was a good thing this voyage was going to be short. More than once Guy had come close to beating the hell out of a sailor for the way he looked at Addie. Guy knew exactly what the man had been thinking.

He tossed the cigar stub over the side and waited until it hit the blue water below before shifting his position so he could look at the "queen." Adelaide was perched on her throne some twenty feet away, a pillow stuffed behind her back and her bare feet resting on a sort of footstool someone had made for her. She was sound asleep. As much rest as she was getting, he doubted she had slept since recovering from her accident. How she managed to keep that godawful hat on her head was a mystery, and why she persisted in wearing it was beyond his understanding. But he'd made a point of not mentioning it. He didn't want her to know he'd even noticed.

As his gaze trailed the length of her, he slowly shook his head. Adelaide looked as if she belonged in the cabin boy's clothes. Or maybe he'd just become used to seeing her in them. The clothes had caused more difficulty than he'd anticipated. Carrying a woman fully dressed was one thing, but carrying a woman with only one layer of clothing separating her from him was an entirely different matter. From that first morning when he'd stolen her from her bed, he'd known exactly how thin she was and now he was well aware of how she was filling out again. So far he'd managed to keep his growing desire under control, a feat that he was beginning to find increasingly difficult.

He turned back and continued to watch the men loading the ship with fresh water and supplies. When all this came to an end, it was inevitable that he and Addie would have their final confrontation. When had their battle begun? Months after he'd returned from the war? Who was to say? Perhaps as far back as when they were young. Though Addie had a good heart, there had always been an aloofness about her. Maybe it was because of all the trouble he and Will used to get her into.

It had been her attitude, the wager, her marrying his grandfather, the accident...that wasn't exactly right. What needed to be settled was just between the two of them. More than once he had decided to take on the untouchable duchess and her haughty ways. He'd invariably backed away, but not this time. His determination to teach Mrs. Stockman a lesson or two about life had only been lying dormant until the time was right. When he'd received Mary's letter and had made the decision to take matters into his own hands, he'd set the wheels in motion. The Addie that left San Francisco wasn't going to be the same one who returned.

Guy took another look at Adelaide before going to the galley for a cup of coffee. All in all, he had little to complain about. His plan had worked smoothly. After leaving William's place, he'd gone straight to his grandfather's home. The opiate he'd purchased in England had already been poured into the flask of wine. With everything in readiness, there was just the matter of collecting Adelaide. The two gowns he'd purchased were his only miscalculation. But he hadn't realized just how much weight Addie had lost. The gowns were far too big. But in the end, even that had served his purpose. Now that she was close to regaining her normal weight, he could use the clothing as a bribe.

The hood for her dark cape was pulled over Eleonore's head as she continued east toward the Barbary Coast.

When she arrived at the run-down Seaman's Hotel, she went up the back stairs to the second floor. When she reached the right door, she knocked four times. A moment later the door swung open. She could smell the whiskey on the auburn-haired man's breath when he bid her enter. He was well on his way to being drunk, his clothes were sweaty and he was badly in need of a shave.

"I told you to leave this alone!" Eleonore grabbed the whiskey, went to the window and poured it out.

Rupert sneered. "What difference does it make? You said the charade was over. What a shame to go from a prince to this in so short a time." He flopped down onto the sagging bed.

Eleonore glanced at the black and red uniform carelessly tossed in the corner. It made her all the more furious to know that the hard-earned money she'd spent to make him look like a prince had been for nothing. "I have accommodations at that boardinghouse you told me about. I said we were husband and wife."

"I'm going east, Eleonore."

"You can't! We haven't finished what we set out to do."

"*You* set out to do!" he stormed at her. "I did everything you told me. I played the part of the prince, and I was close to winning Adelaide's hand in marriage. It appeared we were finally going to get the money."

"You make it sound so perfect." Eleonore tossed her hood back and glared at her brother. "You didn't do a damn thing right. You thought that because you're a man you could handle things your way. Instead of putting a bullet in the lawyer's head, you had to kill him in a carriage accident. Your scheme was so good you almost killed Adelaide! Where would that have left us? But you didn't stop there. Oh, no. Again you had to do it your way. I tried to get you to run off with Adelaide, just like Guymour Stockman did. You wanted to wait. You said she had fallen in love with you and it was only a matter of time before she agreed to the wedding."

Rupert rubbed his chin in frustration. "I had heard the Stockman cousins can be most formidable. I had no intention of being hanged."

Eleonore dusted the seat of the wooden chair with her hand, then sat. "Are you saying you wouldn't have killed her as we had planned once we had the money? Have you forgotten so soon about what happened to our sister? Maybe I should have let you go ahead and kill her to get even for Penelope's death before Addie inherited all that money. We would have been done with it. It is our vendetta, Rupert! An eye for an eye!"

"I haven't forgotten. You're the one who only sees what she wants to see. I told you from the beginning that this wouldn't work. You have too much hate and it will be our destruction."

"Hate?" she yelled at him. "She was our sister!"

"Half sister, and she only thought of herself. Think of how much she must have enjoyed having you to play her maid and wait on her. When you returned, you said Penelope had even planned to leave without giving you half of the money she'd made from the old man. I already have my fare to New York, Eleonore."

"We can steal things from the mansion, sell the bitch's jewelry... Rupert, there is still a lot of money to be had."

"No, I'm leaving tomorrow. I want to start a new life. Come with me, Eleonore."

Her eyes flashing with anger, Eleonore stood and glowered at her brother. "I don't need you. I can take care of everything myself. Go. I don't want to ever set eyes on you again." She yanked her hood up and rushed out of the room.

Chapter Sixteen

Guy hadn't thought about it being earlier than usual until he barged into Addie's cabin and caught her in the process of dressing. Her britches lay beside her.

"Get out of here," Addie demanded.

She managed to pull the blanket over her, but not before Guy had a good glimpse of her damaged leg. It was considerably thinner than her right one, but it wasn't deformed, as she had claimed.

"If you must stand there, at least turn around." Since he showed no inclination to do so, Addie quickly finished buttoning her shirt.

Guy wasn't listening. He was too busy taking his first real assessment of his prisoner. With all the arguing they did, he hadn't noticed how the right food, open air and a hard hand had accomplished everything he had counted on, and more. Her once pale skin now had a golden hue to it and the color had returned to her cheeks. The ocean air had also served to increase her appetite. The frail woman he'd brought aboard was gone. It hadn't taken as much effort to accomplish the transformation as he'd anticipated, but he knew the real battle was yet to begin.

"Did you lose all gentlemanly manners when you came aboard this ship?" Addie became very still when Guy walked up to her.

"We're going to start something new today," Guy finally said.

Addie looked at him suspiciously. "What?"

"Your health has returned, and now it is time we get to the real reason for your being here."

Addie scooted back onto the bunk. "What are you talking about?"

"Your leg, my dear."

"You leave my leg alone! I've done everything asked of me, Guy. Don't do this."

"I believe you can walk."

"I *know* I can't." She pounded her fist on the bed. "Don't you think I would if I could?" She fought back a threatening explosion of tears. "Do you think I like being a cripple? I don't understand. Do you hate me so much that you feel the need to punish?"

"Listen to me, Addie. Your doctor did what he thought was right. Though the leg appeared to have healed properly, not exercising it caused the muscles to weaken. Therefore, when you couldn't stand on it, he, like other physicians, felt that the limb was useless. During the war, I saw men regain the use of limbs simply because they wouldn't give up. They kept trying to move the injured part even though the doctors told them it would be better not to. They healed. Some even regained the full use of their limbs. Then while I was in England, I happened to meet a doctor at the men's club who believed that keeping a person down caused more harm than forcing them onto their feet as quickly as possible. He said he'd proven it on more than one occasion, but the medical profession still refused to believe what he told them."

"Surely you don't plan to force me to put weight on my..." Fear was replacing anger. "Maybe you should take a look."

"That won't be necessary. I've already seen your leg."

"It's smaller than the right one. I am deformed," she said bitterly. "I cannot walk! No matter what you do, it isn't going to change a thing! It took me a long time to accept that, but I have. Now I think it's your turn to do the same."

Guy looked toward the porthole. Her mind was set, and talking wasn't going to gain him a thing. Maybe it was better for her to believe he was being cruel. Her wrath could work to his advantage. Besides, he couldn't very well tell her that because of the months of uselessness, it was going to take even more pain and work for her to walk again. She'd feel defeated before they ever started. And there was also the possibility that his plan wouldn't work and she would indeed remain crippled.

Addie sat quietly, waiting for Guy to make his first move. Seeing his jaw muscles flex wasn't encouraging.

"Well, darling," Guy said, "starting today, we're going to find out who is right and who is wrong."

Addie scooted farther back, positioning herself so that if he came any closer, she could deliver a hard kick to his groin. "I won't be your guinea pig!"

"Yes, you will. The good doctor laid out specific guidelines that have worked for him. I would have thought you'd grasp at any opportunity that could possibly get you on your feet. Or have I been right all along? Are you nothing more than a chicken-livered coward who uses her misfortunes to hide behind?"

Adelaide was so furious she leaped from the bed. All she could think about was scratching that disgusted look off Guy's face. She landed on the floor with her right foot, and without thinking, moved the other one forward. Too late she realized her mistake. She would have fallen if Guy hadn't caught her.

"I hate you, Guymour!" She pounded his chest. "May you die in hell for what you said. You're wrong! Wrong, wrong, wrong!"

"Then prove me a liar!" He put her back on the bed, lifted the blanket from the floor and tossed it at her.

Addie quickly draped it over her lap.

"Today we're going to start working your leg, and we're going to make it strong again. Don't fight me on this, Addie. If I have to, I'll tie you down."

Addie clenched her teeth. "I want to know why you're doing all this." His ingratiating smile made Addie twice as leery.

"Because you're a Stockman now. Our family has always stuck together and taken care of one another."

"I was a Stockman before this happened, and it didn't make one bit of difference in your attitude toward me. It only made things worse."

"Oh, come, come Addie. All families have their little squabbles."

"Little squabbles?" Addie gasped. "How quickly we forget. But then you weren't on the receiving end, were you?"

Guy leaned down and took hold of her ankle. Adelaide wanted to jerk away but knew she couldn't.

"I want to see what you can and cannot do with that leg," Guy explained.

With a few simple movements, he found out she had no problem bending her knee, probably because she spent so much time sitting. However, it would only go so far when he tried straightening it out.

He began probing the calf where Addie's doctor had said the first break took place. He couldn't see or feel anything in the area that indicated it had even been damaged. "Relax, this is the easy part." He knew she was scared, but according to the doctor from Sweden, he had to find out the extent of the damage. He slid his hands on up to her thigh, probing the area where the other two breaks had occurred.

Addie tried to relax, but it wasn't possible with Guy moving his hands up her leg. She shouldn't allow him to be so familiar. It wasn't decent. Unfortunately, she'd never be able to reprimand him convincingly. She wasn't even sure she could speak. She was too engrossed in the pleasure of his touch. Without any effort, he had ignited a flame that she thought had long since been smothered. As his fingers gently probed her thigh she wanted desperately to toss the blanket aside and ask him to make love to her. He was right. She was a coward.

Addie looked at him, hoping for any sign of encouragement. Her ardor quickly faded. There wasn't a speck of interest on his chiseled features. She felt shattered. He had lied to her. He was no longer interested in her. She was repulsive to him.

She started to make a stinging comment, then thought about what Guy had said. Did she dare believe that he could really help her?

"I see no reason why we can't start exercising that leg. We'll do it every morning before you go on deck, and at night before you go to sleep."

Addie quickly pulled the blanket back into place. "You're no doctor, so why should I trust you? It was a real doctor who said I would never walk again."

"I want you to press down on my palm as hard as you can, five times. Then we'll do the same with your leg extended forward."

"Didn't you hear what I said?"

"I heard. The sooner you do what *I* say, the sooner I'll take you up on deck and you can have your breakfast. Oh, by the way, I have a gown for you."

"You what?"

"You heard me."

"Even if you had one of the sailors get it while we were stopped at that island, that was seven days ago." She yanked at the front of her shirt. "That means I didn't have to wear this for the last week!"

"You're supposed to be grateful, not angry. It's your reward for being a good girl." He grasped the sole of her foot in his hand. "Now push."

"You're worthless . . . how could you do such a thing to me?" Wanting to hurt him, Addie pushed. She wasn't even strong enough to move his hand, let alone ram it into the floor. Frustrated, she tried again. By the third time, she felt depleted and little sharp stabs of pain had started occurring.

"I can't do any more," Adelaide declared. She tried to pull her foot free, but it took no effort on Guy's part to maintain his hold.

"I said five times. You still have two to go in this position." Guy knew there was one certainty. If he gave in once, Addie would expect it again and again.

Though she wasn't happy about it, for some inexplicable reason, she did as she was told.

Guy straightened her leg out as far as it would go. "Now five in this position."

By the second push, Addie was feeling the pain of her effort and tears had formed in her eyes. How could she be so fickle? Only minutes ago she'd wanted Guy to make love to her. Now she wanted to see him lying dead on the floor! "I hate you, Guymour!" She forced her foot forward, pretending she was kicking him.

"Your words are beginning to bore me. Try to think of something different to say. How about, 'Guy, why don't we make love instead?' "

"Would it get me out of having to do this?"

"No, but it would be an interesting diversion."

"For whom? Certainly not me."

"I wouldn't count on it."

Adelaide thrust her foot again, causing a tear to run down her cheek. She remembered a long time ago when Guy had said it wasn't necessary to like someone in order to desire them. Now she understood.

When Guy finally released her, Addie swore he'd never touch her again. What she really wanted to do more than anything she could think of was to throw an absolute hitting, screaming tantrum. At least it would give her some degree of satisfaction. She gave up the idea. She was already too worn-out. "I want that gown you've kept from me. I've earned it."

Guy looked down at her. He didn't dare show sympathy. He needed her anger to get her through this. "Put your trousers on and I'll carry you out."

Adelaide picked up her britches and threw them at him. "I want my gown, or did you lie about it?"

Guy threw them back. His black eyes locked with a pair of flashing amber eyes.

Adelaide sneered. "It's too bad it wasn't a knife!"

"Stop fighting me, Addie. You won't win. Now get your trousers on or I'll leave you here until tomorrow morning. That means two more times of doing this over again and no food."

"You have no right to keep the dress from me." She brushed at a wisp of hair she'd failed to gather in her ribbon. "What are you going to do with it? Wear it yourself?"

"Act that way and I won't give it to you at all."

"You'd better not be lying."

"And if I am, what are you going to do about it?"

"You shouldn't have even told me about it. Don't think I don't know why you want me to walk. It's so your conscience will be clear."

Guy made himself comfortable on her chair. "My conscience? I must say, my dear, your thinking sometimes astounds me. Pray tell, why am I supposed to have a guilty conscience?"

"Because none of this would have happened if we hadn't used your carriage."

"Interesting theory, but it bares no validity."

"Leave the room so I can dress."

"I think not. Perhaps when the day comes that you start asking instead of ordering, I'll be more receptive to your requests."

Addie shoved the blanket aside. After everything else he'd put her through, he didn't even have the decency to look away. At least the shirt she wore came all the way to her knees.

When Addie leaned forward and adjusted the pant legs, Guy realized he hadn't given any thought to what it took for her to put the britches on. He became intrigued with the system she'd worked out. She slipped them over her feet, worked them upward to her calves, then stood on her good leg. Resting her hips on the bunk for balance, she drew the pants up higher. Her face mirrored her anguish when she momentarily pushed away from the side of the bed and tried to yank the trousers up over her hips before falling back against the bunk. She hadn't been quick enough. It took four tries before accomplishing the task.

The trousers had actually turned out to be a disguised blessing. Addie was forced to use her muscles. He was positive her right leg had been much weaker when they had started the voyage. He wondered how many times she'd fallen, then immediately admonished himself for feeling sorry for her. It was important that she learn to take care of herself. If she had continued to rely on Eleonore, she'd have wasted away.

His gaze slowly rose from soft, rounded hips to inviting breasts. The heavy breathing caused by exertion was pushing the soft mounds against the shirt material, as if wanting to be freed. It was knowing he couldn't have her that made his desire all the stronger. From the moment he'd stepped into the room and discovered she wasn't dressed, his need to spend the morning making love to her had been almost overpowering. From the first day on the ship, he'd had to force himself to be patient. But that wasn't going to last forever. He had every intention of claiming *Miss Adelaide* before they returned to San Francisco.

"When I get my gown, are you going to stand and watch me put that on, too?" Adelaide glared at him with burning, reproachful eyes.

Guy's mouth slowly spread into a smile. "Is that an invitation? From what I can see, I'm sure your breasts would be a splendid sight to behold."

Adelaide's mouth dropped opened, then snapped shut. She knew her face had to have turned every color in the rainbow. By now she should be used to his blatant comments. She should even be angry, but he had at least noticed something appealing about her. She tilted her chin. "I'm dressed. You can carry me out now."

Guy broke out laughing. "Ah, Addie, you don't give up, do you?" He swung her up in his arms. "Do you still honestly think you can order me about?"

"I just did, didn't I?"

Guy roared with laughter.

True to his word, Guy arrived the next morning with a gown draped over his arm. Addie laughed and clapped her hands, unable to contain her excitement when he held it up by the shoulder seams for her inspection. It was made of cheap material, the sleeves were nearly nonexistent, and there was virtually no shape to the gown. Even so, after nearly two weeks of wearing nothing but a boy's clothing, in Adelaide's eyes, it was beautiful. She reached out for it.

"Oh, no." Guy was tempted to say she'd have to give him a kiss first. Patience was indeed a heavy burden. "First we exercise that leg, then you get the gown." He draped it over the back of the chair. He'd deliberately bought a cheap dress to make the point that she was not going to be treated like a queen aboard ship. How wrong he'd been. Even without fine clothes the sailors treated her as if she were a goddess.

"But..." She was in too good a mood to argue. "Am I supposed to remove my trousers?"

"Ah..." Guy thought it a rather moot point. He didn't trust himself. "No, that won't be necessary. I've already examined you. Get yourself stabilized. Good." He took hold of her foot. "Push."

Addie's good humor turned into hard work. She had never experienced physical pain until the accident, and admittedly, what she had suffered then was a lot worse than what she was going through now. And though each session seemed to become more difficult, after the first day, not a single tear had formed in her eyes. Today she was even managing to curb her tongue. She wanted to make sure Guy had no reason to keep that gown out of her hands.

When they had finished, Guy gave her the bundle of cloth.

Addie lovingly caressed the calico material. Every pain had been worth it. "Where are the rest of my clothes?"

"That's it."

"But...but I need pantelets...a chemise...a corset! Why am I bothering to explain? I'm sure you're quite familiar with women's undergarments."

"I didn't have time, nor did I know the proper size. Shall I wait while you change, or do you prefer I step outside?"

"I...I can't wear this without—"

"Why not? You wear nothing under what you have on." A truth that had plucked at his ardor for some time.

"Well...of course I want you to go outside. I'll call when I'm ready." She was already anxiously unbuttoning her shirt before he'd even closed the door. Her fingers stopped moving. "Wait!"

Guy opened the door and peeked in.

"How could a gown like this be purchased on the island? None of the women were clothed like this." She could clearly remember her shock at seeing their lack of clothing. Nothing more than a piece of material covered them from the waist down.

"You said it was bought on the island, not me."

"You mean you've had it from the beginning?"

"I bought it in England." Seeing the rage leap into her amber eyes, he stepped outside and closed the door behind him.

Ten minutes later Guy continued to pace, wondering what could be taking Addie so long. All she had to do was remove her shirt and britches, then pull the gown over her head.

He knocked on the cabin door. He could barely hear Addie telling him to come in. When he entered, she was still sitting on the bed with her old clothes on, the gown resting in her lap.

Guy was totally confused. "Is something wrong?" he asked.

This time Addie didn't hold back the tears.

Guy rushed to her. "Did you hurt yourself?"

"I can't wear the gown!" She started bawling.

Guy reached out to soothe her, only to have his hand slapped away. "Damn, if it isn't one thing it's another!" He made a wide circle. "Addie, why the hell can't you wear the gown?"

"The material is much thinner than the shirt," she wailed.

"What does...?" He didn't have to finish the question. Apparently the material clung and clearly outlined her bosom. The shirt, on the other hand, was of a heavier material and billowed, leaving little to be seen. "All right, I'll take care of it."

Addie jerked her head up and brushed at her tears. "How?"

At least she's stopped her bawling! "There must be something aboard that can be used as a...vest of sorts. I'll talk to Cappy about it."

Addie's face beamed. "Do you really think it can be done?"

"I'm sure of it."

"But... how will you explain?"

"What do you mean?"

"Well, if...surely you wouldn't tell him why I need it. I mean...isn't he bound to ask why I would want something like that?" She was only digging a deeper hole for herself. "Don't just sit there staring at me. You know exactly what I'm trying to say."

Guy was convinced he'd never understand the complexities of a female. "What if I just tell him it's none of his business?"

"Oh."

"I can assure you, Adelaide, what might have been seen with the dress on was nothing compared to what you show when you wear one of those low-necked evening gowns."

Addie wiped her cheeks. He did have a point. Guy scooped her up in his arms to take her above. Having him carry her was almost worth being crippled. She had come to enjoy feeling the strength of his muscles, smelling his hair and his clean, fresh scent tinged with saltiness. At times she'd even leaned her head against his chest just to listen to his heartbeat.

"Mr. Stockman, Captain Green would like to see you in his cabin," the first mate said from above.

Guy paused before going on up the steps. It seemed apparent the first mate had been waiting for him. "Thank you. Please take Mrs. Stockman to her chair."

To Addie's shock, Guy handed her over to the first mate, then walked away! She was more than just a little embarrassed at having been handled like nothing more than a sack of grain! It would have taken Guy only a few minutes to deliver her to her chair. When the first mate placed her on her seat, she didn't even smile at him. She was glad that he quickly walked away.

"Why have ye been crying, lass?"

Addie looked up. McCregan was standing in front of her. Her fear of the big man had long since disappeared. He'd turned out to be the most considerate sailor of the lot. "How did you know I was crying?" she snapped at him.

"Your eyes be red."

"Yours would be too if you had to put up with that bully of a man."

"The first mate?"

"No. Guymour Stockman. Just wait until I get back to San Francisco. He'll rue the day he treated me like this."

McCregan glowered at her. "Mr. Stockman has been mistreating ye?"

Addie didn't hear the anger in his voice. "Did you know he has had a gown in his possession all this time, and only just now gave it to me?" She thought about all the things Guy had done to her. The accusations after Gordon died, the wager, the pain he'd put her through because he was convinced he could heal her. "He makes me push with my bad leg, claiming he's only doing it so I can walk. I don't dare say no. What if he's right? But of course he isn't right! He just wants to manipulate me. He knows I can't walk. I wish there was something I could do to make him hurt the way he's hurt me."

"I'll kill him!"

"What?" Addie came out of her musing. "No! What are you talking about?"

"I'll kill him for hurtin' ye. Don't worry about a thing. Everyone will think it was an accident."

Adelaide was tempted, but she could never live with a man's blood on her hands. Especially not Guymour's. Seeing McCregan's ugly face twisted with revenge, she realized she may have talked out of turn. Now she had to think of a way to get out of this mess without offending the big seaman. "Thank you," she said sorrowfully. She tried to squeeze out at least one tear, but nothing happened. "I know of no one who would be willing to do so much for me. But this is a matter I have to take care of myself. As I said, I want him to suffer, and that wouldn't happen if he died."

McCregan nodded. "I'll make sure he suffers."

"Oh, no. It really isn't as bad as I've made it out to be. Sometimes I get a little too carried away with myself."

McCregan raised her small hand in his big ones, and patted it. "Ye're a brave one. If'n ye change your mind—"

"I won't. Thank you again."

Addie released a heavy sigh when McCregan sauntered away. She'd have to remember not to complain aloud. On the other hand, perhaps she could use McCregan to threaten Guy? She could tell him that if he didn't do as she requested, she'd sic McCregan on him. There wasn't a man who would be foolish enough to fight the sailor. On the other hand, maybe it would be better to leave well enough alone. However, one of these days soon, she was going to make a point of telling that black-headed devil that she had held his life in the palm of her hand!

Guy had been relieved to get Addie out of his arms. Had he been carrying any other woman, he would have been certain she'd deliberately nestled closer to him. He could still feel her body heat. All of which he hadn't expected. Had he continued on with her relaxed against him, not a sailor would have been able to miss his obvious desire.

Guy knocked on the captain's cabin door.

"Enter." Seeing Guy, Captain Green stood. "Mr. Stockman, we will arrive at your island tonight."

Guy smiled. "So at last the fox has been trapped."

"I beg your pardon?"

"It was nothing. So, Captain, come tomorrow we will be leaving you for a spell. I'm sure you'll be glad to be rid of us."

That night, Adelaide was drifting to sleep when she heard the anchor being lowered. Strange, nothing had been mentioned at dinner about stopping at another island. Curious, she pulled herself up to the porthole and looked out. The moon hadn't risen yet, making it too dark to see. Something wasn't right. She could feel it in her bones.

Addie was wide-awake now. She scooted around and sat on the edge of the bunk. What was going on that she hadn't been told about? Shortly after they'd first set sail, hadn't the sailors said that this trip had been unexpected and that they didn't know their destination? Yet Guy had told her they would be at sea approximately a month before returning to San Francisco. Someone was lying, and she knew who that someone was.

Suddenly she was clutched with fear. She knew what Guy had in mind. He would put her on the island and leave, knowing she could never escape. That way he would have the Stockman fortune. He might even leave her provisions, but he was cold and uncaring. The provisions would eventually give out, and she'd have no way to get about. She would die and he'd get away with murder!

Feeling a sudden chill, she wrapped the blanket around her. She should have known lies were being told. Guy had been too secretive.

Other than a few catnaps during the night, Addie hadn't slept a wink. When the sky began turning light, she again looked out the porthole. She had been right. There was a large island straight ahead with a big, pointed mountain in the center. Lush green growth and trees were in abundance. There was also a beautiful lagoon with a long stretch of white, sandy beach. It looked inviting, but other than birds, there wasn't a sign of a living creature anywhere. She had no intention of setting one foot on the atoll. Not until they had safely reached San Francisco would she leave this ship. Guy had said she constantly stirred trouble. She had had all night to think and plan. He hadn't seen anything yet.

Chapter Seventeen

Addie tried to remain calm as she waited for Guy to come to her cabin. What with lack of sleep and worry, she was already having to cope with raw nerves. It was too bad that at some time she hadn't thought to steal a knife from her breakfast tray. At least she didn't have to dress. That had been accomplished sometime during the night.

It was still early morning when the door finally opened, and Guy strolled into the cabin.

"Have you told Cappy to make my vest?" she asked caustically.

"No."

The moment he stepped forward to pick her up, Adelaide raised her hand. "Don't come any closer. If you lay one finger on me I'll have McCregan tear you apart."

"Oh? Am I to assume that you plan to remain in your cabin?"

"I want to know why you didn't tell Cappy."

Perplexed as to what had brought on this morning wrath, Guy stood staring at her. "I didn't think it necessary."

"Well *I* did! I'm tired of you lording over me and I'm tired of being lied to."

"What are you talking about? If you awoke in a bad mood, don't go taking it out on me."

His voice was low and very still, which usually denoted anger, but Addie was past the point of caring. She had been waiting hours to have it out with him. "Why are we so close to that island? And don't tell me it's to trade cargo. There isn't a native in sight."

"Very well, I won't."

"You planned to take me there, didn't you? Did you also plan to leave me so you could collect the Stockman fortune?"

Guy rubbed the back of his neck. "We're not going to go through this again!"

"Dammit, answer my question. Did you plan to take me to that island, desert me and let me die?"

Guy was furious at her unfounded accusations. "I'm sorry to disappoint you. I don't make a habit of murdering helpless women. Not that I wouldn't have enjoyed it on more than one occasion."

Seeing the cold look on his face, icy fear knotted up in Addie's stomach. She really hadn't paid much attention to what he said until she'd heard the word *murder*. He was going to kill her right now. There was a moment of silence before she started screaming as loud as her lungs would permit.

Guy's anger tuned into a scalding rage. It took but a few steps for him to close the distance between them. Ignoring her flying fists and all the earsplitting noise she was making, he wrapped an arm around her waist and carried her out of the room like a mattress bent in half.

When he arrived on deck, Addie was still screaming and flaying him with every ounce of strength she possessed.

"McCregan! McCregan!" she yelled desperately.

"We're ready to go," Guy stated as he approached the captain, standing near the mainmast. Guy had no intention of explaining to the man what this was all about.

"No, no! Don't let him do this!" Addie screeched.

The captain looked at Addie and then at Guy in wonderment.

"Is everything ready, Captain Green?" Guy asked curtly over Addie's wailing.

"Can't you see what he's doing? Leave *him* on the island. Not me!"

"Everything is ready, sir," Captain Green acknowledged.

Guy glanced at the faces of the sailors who stood nearby. Their angry expressions warned Guy that he needed to get Addie away as quickly as possible. He quickened his steps. He still had to climb down the rope ladder to the boat waiting below. Once they had been rowed to shore he'd put an end to her caterwauling.

Guy hadn't moved fast enough. McCregan stepped between him and the railing. Trouble was staring at him in the shape of a one-eyed giant. "Stay out of this, McCregan," Guy warned. "It may not sound like it, but I'm doing this for her own good."

"Step aside, McCregan," the captain ordered, "or it will be twenty lashes."

"McCregan," Addie yelled, her breath coming in short gasps. "He's going to murder me!"

There was no question about it. Guy knew *Sweet Addie* had just sealed his fate. Several of the other sailors were already moving toward him. "Woman, you're more trouble than you're worth," Guy stated angrily before dropping her.

"How dare you?" Addie squawked upon hitting the deck. She rubbed her chin. Deciding she was all right, she sat up.

"Back with all of you!" Captain Green ordered. "There will be no fighting on this ship!"

The men paid no heed.

McCregan motioned the others away. "He's mine," he proclaimed.

Addie was pleased that someone was finally going to give Guy his comeuppance.

McCregan suddenly lunged forward, catching Guy in a bone-crushing grip. His muscles bulged as he tightened his hold around the lighter man's chest.

Addie's smile was quickly fading. McCregan showed no intention of releasing Guy, and Guy's face was getting redder by the minute. "No, no," she called, then repeated it louder. "You have to stop! I just want him thrown overboard!"

Addie scooted out of the way just as Guy fell back, taking McCregan with him. When they hit the deck, the sailor lost his hold.

Being the more agile of the two, Guy was able to get to his feet quicker. The minute McCregan raised his head, the taller man sent a crushing blow to the seaman's chin. Addie grimaced at hearing McCregan's jaw crack. She tried again. "There is no cause for this!"

Her words fell on deaf ears. The crewmen were yelling, cheering their mate on. Addie could only watch as the two continued landing one blow after another, their faces already bloodied by hard fists.

Addie cringed. Embroiled in her anger at Guy, she had again failed to consider the repercussion of her words. Why hadn't she questioned Guy about his intentions instead of jumping to her own conclusions? *Then* she would have felt justified about what was happening. No. She wouldn't blame herself! At this very moment she could have already been stranded on that confounded island!

The other crew members were forming a circle. The blows being exchanged between Guy and McCregan were vicious, and blood flew. Addie wanted to shut her eyes. If this continued, one of them was sure to end up dead.

McCregan connected with a solid blow to Guy's stomach, sending him flying a good three feet across the deck, forcing the onlookers back. McCregan made a dive for him, but Guy rolled out of the way. A heavy swoosh of air was released when the bearded giant hit the deck.

"Stop it!" Addie screamed. "Do you hear me?" If only she could stand. Everyone was too engrossed in the fight to pay her any mind. Her heart was already heavy with fear and sadness. She had never seen two men fight and she never wanted to see it again. How could they endure going at each other like this?

McCregan climbed to his feet and once again lunged at Guy. This time the tall man was expecting it and managed to step aside. As McCregan passed by, Guy grabbed him by the back of the britches and shoved him down the stairs to the officers' quarters.

Everything became deadly still. Addie looked at all the ugly, angry faces staring at Guy. "I'm all right," she uttered meekly. "Really I am."

Guy stood looking each man in the eye, waiting for anyone who wanted to try to take him on to step forward. When he realized the men were angry but stunned at the outcome of the fight, his mind started functioning again. If one came, they all would. If he was going to get out of this alive, he had only minutes to accomplish it. With one quick swoop, he snatched Addie up, then ran to the ship's railing. Without breaking stride, he grabbed a hanging piece of rigging and used it to help him leap overboard.

As she was being hoisted into the air, Addie released another scream that could be heard by everyone as she went flying through the air. Then the water came up to meet her, and the scream was suffocated as she plunged into the depths of the sea. Her lungs felt as if they were going to burst. She struggled to get back to the top, but her efforts seemed useless. Then nothing seemed to matter anymore. She knew she was about to meet her death.

As Addie came to, she not only felt rotten, there was also a vile taste in her mouth. Her skin and clothes were as grainy as the sand she was lying on. She had to be on the island. No more than a foot away were the thick green vines and dense growth she'd spied from her porthole. She was alive. Really alive!

Her jubilation quickly died when she looked to the left and saw the *Francisca* sailing away. She sat up and was about to yell and wave her arms when her throat filled with salt water. She leaned over and retched.

When Addie could finally look at the departing ship again, her heart sank. It was far out. No one would hear her. Had they thought she had drowned? She wanted to cry, but there were no tears. How could Guy have... Guy! Where was Guy? She began looking in every direction, praying she'd at least get a glimpse of him. Her breathing quickened. He couldn't have drowned. Without him, she'd die! She took several deep breaths, trying to calm down. Why was she worried? Nothing could ever get the better of Guymour Stockman, she assured herself. She suddenly realized that since the age of nine, she had honestly believed he was invincible.

As her gaze followed the shoreline to see if she could catch sight of him, she noticed the crates and barrels stacked on the beach. And if they were stacked, then someone had to have put them there. She looked out at the lagoon to see if Guy was in the water. Nothing. Fighting the panic that was threatening to take over, she became very still and listened. Perhaps she would hear a familiar sound.

"Oh, dear God," she muttered fearfully. All she could hear was birds. "I killed him! Either that or he truly has left me abandoned."

Suddenly the sun didn't seem as warm. She was becoming chilled. She looked back at the crates and barrels. Even if she could drag herself over there, how was she expected to open them? Or maybe it was Guy's punishment for all the things he suspected her of doing... and the fight with McCregan. Her teeth began chattering.

"I see you've come to."

Addie turned and watched Guy walk out from the thick growth. The look on his face wasn't friendly. She was too overwhelmed with relief to say anything. There were cuts and black-and-blue bruises on his face, especially under both eyes. Other than a pair of dry trousers with the pant legs rolled up, he was naked. Though she realized it was ridiculous, especially at a time like this, she couldn't help admiring his magnificent body.

"Your teeth are chattering."

"I . . . I thought you had abandoned me—forever."

"Abandoned? *Forever?* How do you think you managed to make it from the water to land?" Guy still hadn't forgiven her for what she'd caused aboard ship. "Oh, no. I wouldn't dream of leaving you, my pet, not after you went to so much trouble to nearly get me killed. From the day I returned from the war, you have been begging to be brought down from that pedestal you're always prancing around on. Well, darling, your time has arrived. What you've had to put up with was nothing compared to what you're going to get from here on."

"I had every right to act the way I did. I thought you were going to leave me on this island so you could get the Stockman fortune. I thought you wanted me dead."

Guy squatted on his heels. "You must have a guilty conscience or a very active imagination. Have I ever said anything to you that would imply such?"

"No, but—"

"Have I ever given you any indication that I wanted you dead?"

Addie couldn't look him in the eye. "Well—"

"Since taking you from San Francisco, have you fared well? Are you still skin and bones or are you healthier and of a better coloring? Think about it. Had I wanted to leave you abandoned, why would I bother taking you on some sea voyage when I could have had you killed right in your own bedroom!"

"I know that's true but—"

"You know? Then how could you believe I wanted you dead? Or perhaps I'm looking at this all wrong." He stood. "Perhaps it is you who wants *me* dead. As I recall, you asked Captain Green to throw me overboard and leave me stranded on the island."

Addie had to crane her neck to look up at him. "No, no. That isn't so." She pulled away the strands of hair stuck to her face. "How dare you insinuate that any of this is my fault? Who is the one who thinks I stole the Stockman fortune and killed Gordon? You! Who kidnapped me and never once said why? You! And how was I supposed to know what you were thinking? I still don't know."

"Now you're trying to twist this around so you're innocent of any wrongdoing?"

"And certainly last but not least, who was the one stupid enough to leap off a ship? We could both be dead at this very moment. I can't swim!"

"I'm not going to stand here and argue. Get your clothes off."

"I beg your pardon?"

"They're wet and chilled. Your clothes need to dry out and so do you."

"I demand to know if the ship is going to return."

Guy's mouth twisted into a nasty smirk. "Absolutely not soon enough to save you. Now get undressed. You don't have to worry about me watching. I assure you there is nothing you have that I haven't seen before."

"What if they don't return for us?"

He turned and started walking away.

"You didn't answer my question!" His steps didn't falter. "Damn you, Guymour! You are always doing this to me," she called. "It's no wonder I hate you!"

She glared at his muscled back as he disappeared into his confounded forest again! He wasn't paying any attention to her. She sighed and looked at her clothes, filthy with sand. What she had on were her only belongings. She didn't need Guy to remind her that it was her fault they were in this predicament.

She looked back at the ship. The sun shinning on the lagoon made it difficult to see, but the *Francisca* was nearly out of sight anyway. Captain Green must have regained control of his men, or the seamen would have taken her

back on board. And since Guy owned the *Francisca*, the
good captain wouldn't be about to stay away. This had to
have all been planned from the beginning, with the exception of their exit.

With Guy out of sight, Addie quickly removed her
clothes. Her teeth were chattering so badly, her neck and
shoulders ached. She held her damp clothes in front of her,
hesitant to spread them out to dry. She'd never lain naked
in her own room, let alone on a beach in broad daylight!
But if she couldn't see Guy, he certainly couldn't see her.

She spread her pants and shirt out as best she could, then
drew her knees up, trying to hide her obvious curves. Realizing her mistake, she quickly lowered them back down.
Besides, drawing them up hurt her bad leg.

The sun felt good on Addie's cold skin. Now that she had
everything figured out and knew she wouldn't be left
stranded, she allowed herself to relax. She would miss being at sea, but there was no reason she couldn't enjoy being on the atoll. And what made it even better was that Guy
had no choice but to wait on her.

Addie awoke to the delicious aroma of food being
cooked. She was about to brush the sand from her cheek
when her hand paused in midair. Most of her body had
been covered with some type of long, wide, dark green
leaves. They didn't get there by accident. Knowing she had
been lying on her stomach offered little consolation.

She shoved the leaves away before wiping the perspiration from her upper lip. There was certainly no worry about
being cold again. The weather was hot and humid.

She snatched up her britches and gave them a hard shake.
Sand went flying everywhere, including her eyes and
mouth. She spit several times to get rid of the grit, but it
accomplished nothing. Putting her clothes on made everything even worse. In an effort to pull her pants on, she
somehow managed to scoop up even more sand. And put-

ting her shirt on wasn't much better. She was convinced she could feel tiny bugs crawling on her.

"Guy?" she called. "I need water. I'm thirsty!" She waited but there was no response. "You lied to me! How dare you look at my..." She couldn't finish the sentence. "You said you were a man of your word!"

She managed to scoot forward enough to see farther down the beach. She had no idea what time it was, but he had to be nearby. There was food cooking. She licked her lips, already anticipating the meal. A bird called out, making her jump.

"Guy?" She didn't like being alone. She looked in the opposite direction. To her relief, Guy came into view. He was still some distance away, but at least his leisurely pace was moving him in her direction. How foolish. Now that she knew he was near, she'd started trembling. If she was going to tremble, she should have done it before she'd seen him!

Did Guy plan to remain half-naked during their entire time here? she wondered. Automatically she reached up to see if her hair was in some degree of order. How could she have forgotten her dip in the ocean, the sand... She dropped her hand to her side. Her hair was one thick mass of grit and grime. She would never be able to get a comb through it. Comb? She had no comb!

Addie watched the white foam from the soft breaking waves wash over Guy's feet, then recede. He stopped, leaned down, then picked something up from the wet sand. As he stood studying the object, other waves hurried forward. She was reminded of when she was a small child, also standing and letting the salt water roll over her bare feet. When the water slipped back out to sea, her feet sank deeper into the sand. She was terrified that the sand would swallow her up. A beautiful woman had picked her up and hugged her, while bestowing loving reassurances. Had it been her mother? She was consumed with excitement. That was the first memory she'd ever had of anything prior to the orphanage.

"You look rested."

Addie scratched her forearm, then reached over and lifted one of the big leaves. "You promised not to look," she said as she dropped it on the sand. "You took a most ungentlemanly advantage while I slept." Why did she seem less offended at the things he did than she used to?

Guy sat on the sand in front of her. "Trust me, my dear, had I taken advantage of you, you wouldn't have remained asleep. You're not used to lying in the sun without your clothes, and I assumed you would prefer the leaves to being burned all over your body. Of course, being the gentleman that I am, I kept my head turned while putting them in place."

Addie could see the devilment dancing in his eyes. "You're lying."

"How could you say such a thing?" He raised her foot. "It's already late afternoon, and we haven't exercised your leg."

"I slept that long?" She was pleased to see that Guy was apparently no longer upset with her.

"You certainly did. Push."

"I don't want to do that anymore. I can't stand this sand on me. I'm thirsty and starved, and whatever you're cooking is making me all the hungrier."

"The exercises we started weren't something temporary or that you could do when the mood strikes. Now, you know the rules. The exercise always comes first. And starting tomorrow, it's going to be four times a day and for longer periods of time."

Addie's expression turned to one of determination. If only she could think of a way to put a halt to all this.

"I can wait as long as you like, princess. I've already bathed and eaten once today."

Addie's stomach growled. She scratched her arm again. "All right." She gritted her teeth and pushed against his hand.

"One. Come on, Addie, you can push harder than that."

"What are you going to do when I push your hand away?"

Guy grinned. At least she was beginning to acknowledge that it could happen. It was a start. "I guess we'll cross that road when we get there. Two."

Not until they had finished and Guy stood, did Addie see the revolver shoved into the waistband of his trousers. "I have always believed that the only reason a man wears a weapon is because it makes him feel more manly. I would appreciate it if you would keep it away from me."

"I can't do that. There are javelina on the island."

"Who are they?" Addie asked. She really wasn't interested in any excuses.

"Wild boar."

"Is that all? I thought it was something dangerous."

"They're mean and have razor-sharp tusks. They have killed more than one native in these islands."

"Nonsense. You just have to know how to handle hogs."

Guy rolled his eyes. The woman was impossible. Maybe he should be grateful she couldn't walk. He'd have a hell of a time making sure she stayed out of trouble. He leaned down and picked her up.

Even as hungry as she was, Addie would have much preferred to walk. Being pressed against Guy's bare chest and feeling the short curly hairs against her cheek was too much to ask of any woman.

"It's your choice. Do you want to wash or eat first?"

"Which is the closest?"

Guy laughed. "About the same distance in opposite directions."

"Then I'd prefer to bathe before I eat. I have waited too long for this." Addie wanted to run her fingers over Guy's chest, but instead she admonished herself for being affected by his nearness. A problem she'd had since watching him step out of his tub so long ago. She was sure God was testing her to see how much temptation she could withstand.

Addie's thoughts about Guy slipped away as she became fascinated with her surroundings. There were all kinds of trees. Some short and others tall with splayed leaves way up at the top. Others had vines hanging from the limbs. The undergrowth was covered with such a variety of plants she didn't even try counting them. Gorgeous flowers of varying colors seemed to be everywhere. The island really was beautiful—and completely untamed. She became especially excited at spotting a large blue bird that actually had golden feathers.

A strange noise she'd been hearing was getting louder. "What is that sound," Addie asked worriedly. She didn't dare move for fear of creating new emotions within herself.

"A waterfall. We'll be there in a minute."

When the foliage finally cleared enough for her to see it, Addie was breathless. The water clamored over rocks high above, then cascaded into a large blue pond below. She had never seen anything as beautiful. This had to be paradise.

Guy carried her to the edge and stopped. "You've never been in sand before, have you?"

Addie remembered her revelation. "Not since I was a child." Why didn't he put her down?

"The only way to get rid of it is to completely submerge yourself in the water. I'll go in with you since you can't swim."

"No, no, that won't be necessary!" She laughed. "Of course, I can swim," she assured him. "I learned when I was a child." To her relief he sat her on a rock at the edge of the pond.

"Then why did you say you couldn't?"

"Being in the middle of the ocean is a lot different than being in a pool." Addie was able to work her way down the rocks until the water was shoulder deep. It felt wonderfully cool against her heated skin. More importantly, because of the buoyancy, she could actually stand on her own. It had been a long time since she'd done that.

Addie proceeded to scrub her body, but the task was impossible with her clothes still on. She was going to have to undress. She glanced at Guy, who sat leaning back on his elbows with his eyes closed. Dare she take her clothes off? Why should she worry? He couldn't see anything even if he wasn't sleeping. She was covered with water. Feeling deliciously wicked, she removed her shirt. After several rinses to rid it of sand, she reached up and placed it on a dry rock. Removing the pants was more difficult. But the water was allowing her to do things she could never do on land. Before scrubbing the britches, she again glanced at Guy. He looked as if he were asleep.

After the britches had been cleaned and placed near the shirt, Addie was ready to tackle her hair. She dipped down. As she came back up, she saw her britches floating by. They must have slipped from the rock. She reached out to retrieve them. Too late she realized her mistake. She had stepped off the rock ledge and was sinking down into the depths of the pond. She began thrashing her arms, desperately trying to reach the top again.

Knowing Adelaide wouldn't disrobe if he watched, Guy had pretended to be asleep. From the way Addie was cleaning herself, it was apparent she didn't realize that the clear water allowed him an ample view. Her long legs, tiny waist and high, firm breasts were a pleasurable sight for his weary eyes. He looked away, aggravated at himself. Had he now reached the point of peeking at women? A grin tickled the corner of his mouth. If William knew what Addie had put him through, he would have said he deserved it. Then his cousin would have laughed himself to tears.

Guy glanced back to check on Addie's progress. He thought she was washing her hair when she disappeared beneath the water. It wasn't until she surfaced, waving her arms and gasping for breath, that he knew she was in trouble. He should have listened to what she'd said the first time. She *didn't* know how to swim.

Guy pulled his gun from his waistband, tossed it onto the ground and dove cleanly into the water. It took but a minute to grab Addie and draw her up to the surface. "Dammit, woman, I have never met anyone who can get into as much trouble as you!"

Addie was still sputtering, but that was her least concern. How could she breathe normally when she was naked and Guy was holding her? She was already extremely conscious of his virile appeal. How many nights had she lain awake, trying to visualize what it would be like to have him possess her? Now she had the opportunity to find out. The possibility already had her heart beating at twice the normal speed.

Guy stood her back on the rock ledge beneath the water, then he treaded water. At least she hadn't tried to drown him. "Once you get out of a house, you are dangerous. And you lied to me again! What if I had walked away?"

"Make love to me," Addie whispered. Her breathing became uneven as she waited for his reply. Would he laugh at her?

The request came as a complete surprise to Guy. But the way she was staring at him with those soulful eyes told him her desire was real. He damn well wasn't about to refuse the invitation. He had been teased, tempted and badgered by this woman, but this time there would be no turning away.

Addie's heart soared when his arms encircled her, his breath warm and moist against her face. His lips joined hers as he pressed their bodies together. She gloried in the feel of his touch.

His kiss was hungry and demanding and, following his example, Addie returned the fire he'd lit. She knew that the moment she'd dreamed of all these years was at last going to happen. Never had she wanted anything as much as she wanted Guy to make love to her. It pounded in her head and throbbed between her legs. His hands already had her body begging for more, but when his tongue toyed with her sensitive breast, she knew she would die from the pleasure.

Guy carried Adelaide out of the water and gently laid her on the soft bank. He was shocked at her brazen request, but he was delighted that her passion appeared to be every bit as strong as his. He quickly removed his trousers, then lowered himself on her. He had no problem getting her to spread her legs for him. Her eager hands and wild kisses had created so powerful a need that he couldn't have waited much longer. He entered her with a hard thrust.

Too late Guy realized his mistake. Even if her body hadn't stiffened, or she hadn't made faint groans of pain, he would have still known he had taken her virginity. It took every ounce of willpower to keep from gaining his own satisfaction.

Guy remained motionless, trying to collect himself.

"Please, Guy, don't stop," Adelaide begged, her voice raspy. "I wanted this. Don't leave me disappointed."

What was done was done and there was nothing Guy could do to change it. But he could make it pleasurable for her instead of leaving her to believe that coupling meant nothing but discomfort, or that the man was the only one to receive satisfaction.

Slowly he began moving his hips again. "Does that hurt?"

"Oh, no." Strange, wonderful sensations had started to build. "Don't stop."

"You feel so good," he whispered before kissing her neck. "Your body is perfect. It would drive any man to desperation."

"How can you say that when..." It was becoming difficult to speak.

"Touch me like you did when we were in the water, and think about the pleasure we can share."

Addie couldn't think of anything else. His movements, his lips, tongue and hands quickly erased the sharp pain she'd felt. No one had ever made her feel like this. She couldn't seem to get enough of him. She began moving her hips, encouraging him, wanting him. Something was about to erupt and though she had no idea what to expect, she eagerly strove toward making it happen. As if sensing her need, Guy's movements had increased and he slid deeper inside her. Her aggression grew from a sense of urgency that drove her on. She had become a woman possessed.

Then everything exploded, and Addie was filled with wave after wave of inexplicable bliss. Somewhere in the recess of her mind, she felt Guy quiver and lie down on her, but she was too enraptured to feel his weight. Guy had been wrong. She hadn't been a fool to wait so long, because only he could have taken her to such grand heights of pleasure.

"Are you all right?" Guy asked as he rolled onto his side.

Addie quite liked the concern she heard in his voice. Was it possible that by letting him make love to her she'd gained an advantage? "Yes," she said softly.

Guy chuckled. "I think this was something we should have done a long time ago." He moved onto his back.

Though she could now acknowledge to herself that she was madly... irreversibly in love, Addie wasn't foolish enough to believe Guy felt the same way. But given enough time, who knew what could happen?

Without even turning her head, Adelaide could feel Guy studying her. Addie suspected she was probably being a ninny, but even after his hands had covered every inch of her, her bravado had disappeared. Letting him see her naked was going to take some getting used to. She sat up and reached for her shirt. It was too far away. Had she lost her britches?

Addie couldn't stand it another minute. There was one question she had to ask. "Was I ... I mean ... was I disappointing?" she blurted.

Guy smiled. "Quite the contrary."

Addie shrugged. "I only asked because it has been a while since I've been with a man." What was she going to do about her britches?

Guy sat up. "Tell me, Adelaide, do you ever tell the truth?"

"Of course I do! And don't bring up truth to me. You said we were going to take a short voyage and return to San Francisco."

"Are you sorry we didn't?"

"No," she admitted truthfully. Her gaze drifted downward, and all she wanted to do was die. The evidence of her promiscuousness was smeared down her legs. It seemed as if she'd been told a long time ago that sort of thing happened. Did it always happen when men and women coupled?

"Within an hour, you've already told two lies. You said you could swim and now you're trying to make me believe that other men have enjoyed your pleasure." He stood and picked her up.

"Not men," she said, trying to hide her chagrin. "Only one. You know your grandfather and I were married." She was relieved when he took them both into the water.

Once in the water, Guy turned her back to him and began washing it, something she would never have expected him to do. It occurred to her that she really knew nothing about this man. Their time together had never been spent getting to know each other.

"I don't usually act in such a fashion when making love," she said, trying to make excuses for the animal way she'd acted. "I just became a little carried away this time."

Guy chuckled. "And here I thought I might have had something to do with it."

"Oh. Well, I'm sure you did—"

Guy raised an arm and scrubbed it. "You can stop right there. Until we coupled, you were a virgin."

"That's not so!"

"I know when I've bedded a virgin, my dear, and the blood from your maidenhead only serves to prove it."

"That doesn't happen every time?"

Guy was astounded at how truly uninformed Addie was. "No, only the first time." He removed a leaf from her hair and let it fall into the water.

"Is my hair dirty again?" she asked.

"No. It smells delightfully of fresh fern. You have very beautiful hair. I like it when it hangs loose."

His hands trailed down the flat of her stomach, then slipped between her legs. She unsuccessfully tried to prevent a quiver of excitement.

"Are you feeling embarrassed about what we shared, Addie?"

She nodded. His finger was creating wonders of bliss.

"You needn't be. Loving is eternal." He gently tugged at her earlobe with his teeth. "Do you still think I didn't create those wild feelings?"

Addie forced herself to pull away. She had experienced the sharing between a man and a woman, and now the lovemaking had to end. She couldn't afford to have Guy discover her newly found secret. He was a clever man, and if he was aware of her love, he'd find a way to use it against her.

Addie turned and faced him. "What we did was wrong. I trust you, as a gentleman, to see that it never happens again. I think I've lost my britches. I need you to dive down for them." There was that smile again. She knew she wasn't going to like his answer.

"It's a big area. They could be anywhere."

"You aren't even going to try, are you? I can't very well go around without anything on."

"Your shirttail comes practically to your knees."

"Yes, but . . ." Addie could see by the look on his face that he wasn't going to budge on the matter.

"Are you sure you don't want me to lose my shirt, as well?" she asked sarcastically.

"That's a superb idea." He laughed. "Then I could look at you when I want instead of having to use my imagination. You have beautiful breasts and should be proud of them."

"Then perhaps that's the way I should be dressed when the ship returns to pick us up," she said angrily. She refused to draw back even after seeing the angry look on his face.

"And perhaps you could bed each sailor," he snapped back at her.

Guy's biting words were Addie's delight. Was he jealous? She couldn't resist pushing it further. "Perhaps I could. You're a good teacher, but they might show me things you don't know about."

"They know nothing!" Guy suddenly laughed. "Why you little minx. You're deliberately goading me."

Addie reached up and grabbed her shirt. "Won't the food burn? Shouldn't we go eat?"

"It won't burn."

Still embarrassed about Guy seeing her naked, Addie tried to put her shirt on underwater. She had little success.

"Let me do it for you," Guy offered. Without waiting for her reply, he took the shirt from her hands and draped it over her shoulders. "Hold your arm out."

Addie started to do what he said, but changed her mind when the effort caused his chest to rub against her sensitive breasts. She moved away. "You're supposed to keep us from touching!"

"I never agreed to that. How could I when I can think of nothing I want more at this minute than to hold you in my arms and feel you pressed against me?"

"I . . ."

He reached out and pulled her to him. Addie wanted to protest, but she became lost in the warmth of his eyes. His hand slid down and cupped her buttocks, fitting her against him. Her lips parted as he lowered his head. He traced the outline of her lip as his hand again slipped between her legs, probing, teasing. "Tell me to stop," he said, his lips lightly touching hers.

"I can't."

"Then what do you want me to do?"

Not letting him have his way was a silly notion to begin with. She was only cutting her own throat. She closed her eyes and allowed her desire freedom. "I want you to continue on with what you've been doing."

Chapter Eighteen

Sated and content at being carried in the arms of the man she loved, Addie paid little attention to their surroundings until they came into a clearing.

"Surely this isn't where we will be staying?" Adelaide gasped.

Guy laughed. "What else do we need? The beach is on one side and running water on the other."

His positive attitude didn't alleviate Addie's concerns about residing in such primitive conditions. The only thing in the clearing was a thatched structure with sides and a roof, and two wooden chairs sitting outside, looking completely out of place. Nearby was a round, hollowed-out area that held a big pot sitting on a thick bed of hot coals. The delicious aroma of food reminded her again how hungry she was. "Where did the food come from?"

Addie forgot the question the minute a native girl of approximately eighteen years came from behind the hut. Addie's eyes widened. The girl's only attire was a colorful cloth that had been secured around her swaying hips. Her top half was bare.

Adelaide was immediately devoured by jealousy. The girl was not only lovely, but her long silken black hair hung to her buttocks and she proudly displayed a very ripe figure. She even had shapely legs to walk with. Was she here to keep Guy's bed warm?

"You didn't tell me there were others on the island," Adelaide said contemptuously. "Does everyone here go about half-naked? How can you let her walk around like that? It's sinful!"

Guy smiled. "The natives have dressed this way for centuries. It's not my place to change their customs."

"Why is she here?" she asked suspiciously.

"She's here to do the cooking and look after you."

"And what about you? Is she here to look after you, as well?" As soon as the words slipped from her mouth, she regretted saying them.

Guy placed her in one of the chairs. "Are you jealous?"

"No...of course not," she lied. "But you could have had the courtesy to tell me ahead of time."

"I didn't think of it." He grinned. "However, you can smooth your feathers. I have no desire for a harem, my dear."

Addie knew she had been imprudent, but he'd made love to her only minutes ago, and she didn't like the way he'd looked at the girl. Why couldn't he put his shirt on? "You might at least have her cover herself."

"She would take it as an insult. She's very proud of her figure."

"I have better breasts," Addie muttered beneath her breath. If the woman wasn't embarrassed, Addie was embarrassed for her. What was she supposed to do? The girl and Guy appeared to be quite content going about half-naked! Realizing she wasn't wearing much more herself, she reached down to be sure the bottom of her shirt was as far down as it could go.

"If something were to happen to me, the girl would keep you safe. Her name is Mailu. She doesn't understand English, but you can indicate what you want with your hands."

While Guy had been talking, Mailu had dipped the contents from the large kettle into a bowl. She smiled broadly and handed it to Adelaide. It smelled wonderful and looked terrible.

"What is in it?" Addie asked.

"It's fish stew," he replied.

"Bouillabaisse?"

Guy chuckled. "Not hardly." He sat on the other chair and accepted the bowl that was handed to him.

Addie's appetite had diminished considerably. She looked down at the thick concoction for several seconds waiting to see if anything started swimming around.

"There is nothing in it that will harm you," Guy assured her.

Addie raised the bowl to her lips as Guy had done, and sipped the contents. It was quite tasty. The large bites of what she assumed to be fish were very delicious. "Where did the chairs, pots and the other items come from?" Addie asked. She watched the native woman dish food for herself.

"I've sailed here quite a few times since my return from the war. Each time I've brought something back that I particularly wanted. Like these chairs. The natives live quite comfortably by using what the island has provided for them. I still like an armchair to sit on."

"How did you know about the island?"

The girl was now sitting on the ground beside her chair.

"My parents used to bring me here." He started to say the lagoon was where his father had been attacked by a shark, but thought better of it. It was the only time he'd heard of a shark crossing the reef. However, he'd never be able to convince Addie of that.

It wasn't hard for Addie to understand why Guy's parents had enjoyed coming here. The island was enchanted. "How long do you plan to keep me here? And don't take me for a fool. Everything was too well thought out."

"We still have work to do on your leg."

"But I . . . I'd assumed that after what happened at the pond—"

"The exercises would stop?"

"I wish you'd cease using that word. I'm not a horse."

"If you can think of a better one, let me know."

Addie wasn't about to drop the subject. "To answer your question, yes. I had thought that you would at least be more considerate of my situation."

"Now I know why you were so willing to sacrifice your virginity." Guy's grin was deadly. "Believe me, though the offering was most appreciated, it gained you nothing. Maybe now you will finally come to realize just how serious I am about this venture."

Addie wasn't going to let him think he had the upper hand. "I wouldn't call it a sacrifice. I wanted you to make love to me. Before I married Gordon, I remembered you saying I had remained a virgin entirely too long. I decided you were right. It certainly wasn't difficult to seduce you."

Guy released a hoot of laughter.

"Aren't you going to say anything?" Addie asked.

"What's there to say? We both got what we wanted."

Addie winced, but other than that, she was able to hide how much his words hurt.

"Apparently I haven't clearly defined your situation. You will not leave this island until you can walk."

Addie's bowl slipped from her hands. "You can't mean that!"

Mailu jumped to her feet and started scraping up the mess.

"I mean every word."

"Surely you won't continue to torture me. Not after what we shared."

"Sweetheart, we haven't even started yet. Torture? You can hardly call a few strains and pains torture."

"How would you know? You're not the one that's had to suffer!" Addie was so irate that the only thing she could think to do was eat her food, but she no longer had any food. Guy had turned their lovemaking into something soiled.

Addie waved her hand at him. "Why is it so difficult for you to accept that I will never walk again? Nothing you do makes any sense. Whoever heard of pain helping someone get well? It's over. You can't make me do any more."

"I'm willing to admit that I can't do it without your co-operation."

"Good. I'm glad you finally see my side. At last it's finished."

"Yes, I see your side very clearly. Over the weeks, I've come to know you bite out when you're frightened, you adjust surprisingly well to unfamiliar conditions, you're stubborn, and contrary to the woman you used to be, you are only going to do as little as you can to get by with. I've also learned what I had to do to force you to work with me. I never said it was finished. By putting you on this island, I've left you with no alternative, my dear."

"I doubt that."

"We're going to stay right here until you are so sick of this island you'll do anything to get off it. This place may appear to be a paradise, but before too long, the isolation will wear on you. There's nowhere to go. And since you can't walk, it's going to be even harder. It won't take long before you'll be desperate to leave."

"You think you've thought of everything."

"I know I have."

"As you said, I adjust well. And now that truths are being told, perhaps you'll be kind enough to finally say why you're doing all this."

Mailu offered Addie another bowl of soup, but she shook her head.

"Eat the food, Addie," Guy ordered. His eyes had become as black as onyx. "I'll not put up with you trying to starve yourself."

"You can't force me!"

"Haven't you learned yet that a challenge makes me all the more determined?"

Addie shifted uneasily in her chair. Maybe she'd be wise to give in just this once. Seeing the concerned look on the native girl's face, Addie smiled and accepted the food. She glanced at Guy. "Well? Are you going to answer the question?"

Guy stood and walked to the edge of the clearing. He thought for a minute before facing Adelaide. "The one quality I have always admired in you was your determination not to let anyone get the better of you. Because of that, it never occurred to me that you would allow yourself to become useless. Well, I chose not to let you get away with it. Who knows? Maybe I even cared about what happened to you."

"I'll never believe that. Not after all the ways you've mistreated me."

Guy released a throaty chuckle. "There's a chamber pot in the hut if you need it." He walked only a couple of feet before disappearing into the thick bush.

Addie finished her stew with a vengeance. She was glad Guy had left! Being around him was becoming increasingly difficult on her nerves. She should never have let him make love to her. Now she could add acting like a trollop to all the other reactions he seemed to bring out in her!

After handing the empty bowl to Mailu, Adelaide released a heavy sigh and leaned back in the chair. She was tired of constantly butting heads with Guy. She glanced at the girl sitting silently, finishing her meal. Addie sneered. How was she supposed to think with a set of big breasts constantly staring her in the face?

For the remainder of the morning, Addie remained in her chair with nothing to do. Mailu cleaned the bowls and pot, then disappeared for nearly an hour. When she returned she seemed exceptionally happy. Maybe Guy wanted a harem after all. She's probably been with him, Addie thought painfully. Had he also taken her to the pond? And wasn't the woman supposed to be watching after her instead of running off to her lover?

Mailu handed Addie a hard, brown, round thing that looked as if it were dead and had small vines growing on the outside of the shell. The girl made it clear that Addie was to drink from it. Addie refused, positive that the tawny woman wanted to poison her. When Mailu offered water, Addie accepted.

Then, to Addie's delight, Mailu produced a beautiful shell comb. Addie's surly disposition improved considerably. And when the girl insisted on doing the combing, she relented. It was apparent that Mailu had never seen blond hair before. Getting the knots out of the thick hair proved to be a long, arduous task. But when Mailu had finished, the lustrous mane fell in waves way below Addie's shoulders.

Addie napped off and on during the afternoon. When awake she thought about how much she loved Guy, and relived their time together at the pool. The rest of the time she considered her plight. Guy had been right. She would indeed quickly tire of the island if she was expected to do nothing but sit in a chair. It wouldn't have hurt him to stay and visit with her. He could have even shown her around the island. Guy had no intention of making it easy for her.

Guy didn't return until supper time, then to Adelaide's aggravation, he chose to talk to Mailu instead of her. She wished she understood the language so she'd know what they were talking about.

During their meal, Addie found out what the brown thing was that Mailu had tried to get her to drink from. Guy called it a coconut and insisted she try it. After discovering how good the milk and meat were, she was sorry she hadn't accepted Mailu's offer earlier. She also learned about the rats in the coconut palms who also feasted on the fruit. Something she would have preferred not to know about.

Worn-out, Addie soon informed Guy that she wanted to go to bed. He said something to Mailu, who ran inside the hut. When she reappeared, she proudly held up Addie's nightgown.

"How did you get it?" Addie asked excitedly.

Guy had to admit that there was nothing that could equal Addie's smile when she was happy. "Captain Green made sure your personal items were brought here with the supplies."

Mailu came forward and started to unbutton Addie's shirt.

Addie shook her head and stopped the girl. "No, no. I can do that myself."

Guy repeated to the girl what Addie had said. Mailu smiled, nodded her understanding and stepped back, waiting patiently.

"If this is for my benefit, Addie, I've already seen everything, darling."

He explained the situation to Mailu. She was giggling when she and Guy respectfully turned their backs.

Addie quickly changed. "I'm finished," she announced when she was ready. She yawned. After not getting any sleep last night, and with all that had happened today, she was exhausted.

When Guy swooped her up, Addie gratefully settled into his strong arms. Would he kiss her good-night or ask to make love to her again? Would she ever stop fantasizing? "You also have my dress, don't you?" she asked.

"You certainly are the suspicious one."

"Well, don't you?"

Guy looked down at her with a half-cocked grin. "I have both of them."

"There are two?" Oh, how wonderful it would feel to wear a gown again.

"That's right."

"But you're not going to give me either one, are you?"

He started toward the hut. "Only good girls get rewards."

"I'm not a child! But I can play your game. You're not going to win, you know."

When they entered the small hut, the room was already lit by a candle. Addie was shocked to see nothing but an old chest of drawers, matting on the ground, and canvas and rope stretched from one post to another. "Am I expected to sleep on the floor?"

"What kind of a monster do you take me for? If you slept on the floor you'd have to put up with rats and other varmints crawling about."

Addie knew he was only trying to scare her.

Guy pointed to the canvas. "That hammock is your bed."

"Where will you sleep?"

"In the other one on the other side."

It was in the shadows and Addie had missed it. Knowing he wouldn't be sleeping with Mailu was almost as good as a good-night kiss.

Lying in a hammock proved to be more difficult than Addie had imagined. Each time she moved, the blasted thing tipped. Three times Guy managed to catch her before she hit the ground. When she did get settled, she was afraid to move. Guy blew out the candle and she heard him settling himself in his own swinging bed. Even as exhausted as she was, it took some time for Addie to fall asleep.

Addie opened her eyes at hearing a scratching noise. She lay very still and listened. It was above her head. She looked up. On the rope attached to the canvas was a huge rat, watching her. Its eyes shone like two red rubies. She screamed, but it didn't move. She struggled to free herself from her confines.

"Addie, wake up. You're dreaming."

Addie awoke cradled protectively in Guy's arms. She was still shaken from the dream.

"Are you all right?" Guy asked.

Addie clung to him, letting the heat of his body warm hers. "I thought a huge rat was looking down at me."

"Did he get you?" he teased.

Addie grinned. "I didn't stay asleep long enough to find out." She sighed. "Thank you for coming to my rescue. You can put me back."

"You feel so good," he whispered into her hair. "Are you sure you want me to put you back?"

She looked up, and his lips claimed hers, his kiss drawing her deeper and deeper into his world of pleasure. She didn't have to give him her answer.

Guy eased Addie gently down onto the floor, and when he lay beside her, her love was like sweet nectar. His hand slipped beneath the bottom of her nightgown, then moved up her inner thigh. "I'll take my gown off," Addie offered.

"Let me do it for you," Guy said against the smoothness of her cheek. As he slowly pulled her gown over her head, his hands trailed up the inside of her arms and his tongue toyed with an already hardened nipple. Then he drew the dark bud into his mouth, sucking, causing a moan of pleasure to escape from her parted lips.

"We have all the time in the world." He traced the outline of her lips with his tongue. "I want to explore every inch of your body. I want to show you what it truly feels like to be made love to. I want to see you come alive with need of me."

Time and place disappeared, and all Addie was aware of was Guy and the erotic ecstasy he created. His hands and mouth took her to heights of unrestrained passion, and still he teased and tempted until her ardor knew no bounds. She gladly did whatever he asked of her, and her pleasure was returned twofold.

Guy deliberately drove Addie to the point of wild abandon. Not until she pleaded for him to enter her did he finally do so. Her divine body was covered with perspiration and she writhed beneath him, her need for fulfillment as savage and ancient as time itself. Her eyes flew open and he covered her mouth with his. He swallowed her scream of ultimate joy and he joined her in the wild dance of lovers.

Even though Guy could still feel Addie throbbing against him, he had no intention of leaving it at that. He began slowly moving his hips again. As he had suspected, in only minutes he had Addie's breathing coming in gasps. Her eyes were already clouded with desire. He chuckled with delight. Like him, Addie wanted more. They were an insatiable pair. He caressed a full, desirable breast. The once-caustic housekeeper was now his—body and soul.

For the next two weeks, Addie and Guy spent most of their time making love. Whether it was on the flat surface of a black rock, in the pond, or in the lagoon made no difference. Addie's love continued to deepen. Having Guy at her side was like a dream come true.

They laughed and teased, and Guy talked about school in England. He also ignited Addie's interest in learning how to swim, and then he was teaching her in the lagoon. Though she wasn't aware of it, he was determined more than ever to get her up on her feet. When they would come out of the water, they'd lie naked on the pristine beach, resting and enjoying the feel of the sun's rays. Their skin had already turned a dark, golden brown and Addie's hair had lighter streaks running through it.

Mailu brought Addie a colorful cloth, which she proudly tied around her hips. But though she was no longer embarrassed to be naked and felt more like a native, she continued to wear her shirt. Guy and Mailu enjoyed teasing her about it.

After making love in the thick, green bush, Addie lay beside Guy, looking up at a single white cloud that had blocked the sun. The smoldering flame she had come to recognize in Guy's eyes was exciting, but never once had he said anything about love. She didn't dare bring up the subject for fear for driving a thorn in their happiness. She knew their utopia couldn't last and that she had no choice but to settle for what she could get. No man as handsome and virile as Guy would want to spend the rest of his life carrying a cripple around. But if she could walk—

"You were wrong, you know," Addie said as she folded her arms beneath her head.

Guy grinned but didn't bother to open his eyes. "About what?"

"You said I'd get tired of this island."

"I've made it too easy for you. But you're still going to get bored."

"Guy, I want you to be honest with me. Do you truly think I can walk again?"

"Yes, but I don't know to what degree. You may have to use a cane, but at least you would be able to do things for yourself."

Did she dare let herself believe that could happen? The disappointment would be too great. But maybe with Guy as support, the truth wouldn't be as devastating as it had been before.

For the first time, Addie forced herself to think about what she would be as facing, and the things Guy had said to her. He certainly had nothing to gain by helping her try to walk, and he could have given up at any time. Especially after all the trouble and anger she'd caused. Yet his determination had never faltered. Even now, he was just waiting until she gave in and agreed to start the exercises again. And he didn't have to bring her to the island. When McCregan had given her his hat, she had thought it was the most unselfish thing anyone had ever done for her. Never once had she stopped to realize that the most unselfish person she knew was Guy. The very man she had fought, hated, wanted and loved since she was twelve years old.

"Will it be terribly painful?"

"I'll not say that it's going to be easy."

Addie realized he must have been thinking about her leg, also.

"For over half a year you've done nothing. Yet since we left San Francisco, your good leg is twice as strong and you can push much harder with the bad one. The chances of you walking are good. But that can't be accomplished unless you make up your mind to exercise regularly. And what if you have to use a wheelchair? You'd still be able to get up and down. That's a lot better than what you settled for before.''

''I don't know if I can afford to take the chance. I wanted to die when I found out I was a cripple.''

''You can't afford *not* to try. Think about it for a couple of days.'' Guy sat up. Addie's leg wasn't the only reason he'd brought her here. He could no longer deny the question that had been gnawing in the back of his head. ''When you married Grandfather, did you know there would be no sex in the marriage?''

''That's a strange question.'' She sat up beside him. ''Yes, I knew. Gordon had told me the wedding was to be platonic.''

''And you were willing to settle for that?''

''Yes, I could never have thought of Gordon as a lover. He was more like a father. I had great respect for him, and in my own way, I loved him.''

Guy brushed sand from his arm. He really couldn't blame her for marrying his grandfather. The old man had always been capable of talking almost anyone into doing what he wanted. Since he'd come to know Adelaide better, he no longer believed she had tricked the old gentleman.

''Adelaide, I think you should know that your wreck was no accident.''

Adelaide's face mirrored her shock. ''What are you talking about?''

Guy recounted Will's tale. ''Do you know of anyone who would have wanted you or Jason dead?''

''No.'' Adelaide was thoroughly shaken. Who could possibly want her dead?

''Of course, they could have been after me. It was my vehicle.''

"Oh, Guy, that means we could be in danger when we return."

"Unless Will has come up with the culprit. It's nothing to worry about now. Do you have any idea what motivated Grandfather to marry you?"

"Indeed I do. It was Penelope's visit. Gordon and I were both upset over William's lack of attention to her condition."

It was starting to get dark. They dressed, and Guy carried Adelaide back to camp. That night, Addie told Guy she wanted to walk again. "If you believe, I'll believe. I'm not going to say I'll always be at my best, but I'll honestly try."

Guy hugged her to him and kissed the top of her head. "I'm proud of you, my love. I know it wasn't an easy decision."

Addie was ecstatic. Guy had never call her "my love" before. Was it true? Was he trying to tell her he loved her? She prayed she had made the right decision about trying to walk, but in Guy's arms she felt as if anything were possible. What did she have to lose other than a lot of pain and discomfort? She groaned, already anticipating what was to come. Though she had said nothing more about it, Addie was deeply concerned about the wreck not being an accident. If someone had tried to kill her or Guy, they would try again. She couldn't bear the thought of losing the man she loved.

Addie's life became a bustle of activity. Even Mailu pitched in to help. She massaged Addie's legs and wrapped the bad one with warmed leaves every afternoon to help heal and strengthen it.

Guy was ungiving when it came to her exercises. At times she felt she could do no more, and she'd balk, refusing to move again. At other times, especially when she was tired and frustrated, she rained vicious words at him, wanting to get into an argument. But no matter what she said or did, Guy managed to coax her into continuing, then to her aggravation, he'd push her all the harder. She didn't mind swimming each morning and night in the lagoon until he started lengthening the distance. Each time she left the water she was exhausted. At the same time, she felt a keen sense of accomplishment.

Before long, Addie started seeing the results of her labor. The leg had begun to fill out, and it was getting stronger. The happiest day of her life was when she stood alone.

Guy made her a crutch, which she used to start putting weight on her leg. But instead of a small end, he'd attached crate slats to the bottom so the crutch wouldn't sink into the ground or sand. She no longer had to be carried, and she was already missing the joyful feeling of spending so much time in Guy's arms.

Though they still made love, everything now was centered on getting Adelaide on her feet. Her determination had become as strong as Guy's. Guy had made her believe, and nothing was going to prevent her from walking again.

Chapter Nineteen

Eleonore took one last glance around the parlor to be sure there wasn't something else of value she could steal. The new housekeeper, Ivy, had become too suspicious and was keeping a close eye on her.

Though disinclined to do so, she knew she had to leave right away. She had already dallied too long. It was doubtful that Adelaide had discovered what she had been up to, but she couldn't afford to gamble on the possibility of it happening. The bitch could very well expect answers when she returned.

"Are you looking for something?"

Eleonore spun around and discovered William Stockman standing in the doorway. "Yes," she replied. She smiled seductively. "I thought I had dropped my handkerchief in here. It is very important. Miss Adelaide gave it to me. Apparently I was wrong. I'll go to my room and search again."

"Please be seated, Eleonore."

The petite redhead sat primly on the sofa and patted the cushion beside her. "You will join me?"

"No, I prefer to stand," Will replied coldly. He pursed his lips. She was indeed an enticing bit of fluff.

"Have you heard anything about Miss Adelaide? I have been so worried about her. She was in such poor condition when your hateful cousin took off with her."

"I've heard nothing from either of them. I have, however, received some disturbing information. It seems you've been accused of pilfering."

"Pilfering? What is that?"

"Continuously stealing."

"Aha! It's that housekeeper!" She stood, her fists knotted to express her anger. "She's jealous because men look at me, not her." Eleonore moved her shoulders back so William couldn't help noticing her full breasts hidden beneath the pink gown. "It is she you should be talking to. I have seen her take things from this house with my very eyes. I confronted her, saying I would report all of this to you. Ivy said no one would take my word over hers. So I have been waiting for Miss Adelaide to return."

"And does Mrs. Stockman pay you such a wage that you can afford expensive dresses such as you are wearing now?"

She turned away and walked to the window. With there never being any visitors at the house, she had started wearing some of Adelaide's old clothes. Hems and tucks could do wonders. Nevertheless, she had become unforgivably careless. She'd forgotten she had the gown on. "It is one of Miss Adelaide's gowns. I didn't think she would mind if I wore it." It was better to use as few lies as possible, otherwise, they became hard to remember. "If I'm to be blamed for anything, it would be this." She made a dramatic turn and faced him. "But she has let me wear her old clothes before." She looked at him with total innocence.

"Perhaps that is so, but for the time being, I think you should move elsewhere. With Mrs. Stockman gone, there is no need for your services."

"But it was Miss Adelaide that hired me and she should be the one to fire me!"

"I will expect you to be packed and out of the house by this afternoon."

"But... but where will I go?" Eleonore could see that Will was single-minded on the issue. She was going to leave anyway, but perhaps she could turn this to her advantage.

"This is so sudden. I have no money. And what about my letter of recommendation?"

"That will have to come from Mrs. Stockman. If you leave your name and address at my office, I'll see that she receives it as soon as she returns. As for the money, I shall give you a small purse to tide you over. I'm sure it will be adequate."

Eleonore was quite pleased with the outcome of her performance.

"I'll have my carriage at your disposal at exactly three o'clock."

Though she would have liked to spit in his face, Eleonore maintained a look of coyness.

Promptly at three, Eleonore left the Stockman mansion. Not wanting anyone to be able to find her, she had William's driver take her to Union Square on Powell Street. It took some talking before she finally convinced the man that she would be fine.

As soon as he was out of sight, she caught a cab and went north. At Green Street the cab headed east and came to a halt at a boardinghouse Rupert had told her about. It was inexpensive but respectable. She would rejoin the theater and wait for Adelaide's return.

As Guy watched Addie glide through the salty water with smooth, firm strokes, he was feeling a strong sense of pride. Addie had come a long way. Though a small degree of effort was still needed, she was walking now. He didn't even have to push her anymore, nor did she fight him the way she used to. He chuckled. The woman also put as much vigor into her lovemaking as she did learning to walk again. Anyone who had known the sedate housekeeper would never believe the naked woman in the water was one and the same.

Addie stopped swimming and smiled. He waved back but shook his head when she motioned for him to join her. Once she had made up her mind, her progress had been unbelievable. The time had come for him to start thinking about returning home.

Seeing her smile before she continued on reminded him of a day when they were young. He and Will seldom talked Addie into anything. They couldn't even convince her that no one would notice if she skipped an occasional chore. Young Adelaide would invariably give them that same smile, listen attentively to whatever they were proposing, then continue on her way doing exactly what she'd set out to do in the first place. Even more frustrating was their inability to hardly ever catch her in a trap.

He remembered one particular antic they had tried to pull. He and Will secretly had followed Addie for five days to determine if she always did the same chores at the same time. To their delight, their efforts had proven fruitful. Every morning, at precisely nine o'clock, Addie entered their grandfather's chambers to clean.

At eight-thirty the following morning, he and Will ran a cord up one side, across the top and down the other side of their grandfather's doorframe. Climbing on a chair, Guy had reached up and placed three raw eggs in front of the cord. This way they were certain at least one was sure to hit Addie. The chair was put back in place.

Guy could still picture the two of them, each holding his end of the string. With Will on one side of the doorway and him on the other, they pressed their backs to the wall so no one approaching could see them. They had been so pleased with their ingenuity that they'd had to place hands over their mouths to prevent their giggles from being heard.

It seemed as if they had waited forever before hearing the muffled sounds of Addie talking to someone. Then they heard her approaching footsteps. Anticipation was about to kill both of them. At just the right moment, the cord was pulled. Unfortunately, they couldn't sit for several days after that. Addie had turned and gone down the hall and their grandfather had been the recipient of all three eggs.

Guy chuckled. How uncomplicated life had been back then. Unfortunately, that was not the case now. When they returned to San Francisco, Jason's killer would still be at large. Guy unthinkingly drew a question mark in the sand with his finger. It was the not knowing that made the situation so damn hard to handle. Not knowing who the killer had been after, and not knowing who the killer was. Now he was left with no choice but to wait until the beast struck again. To date, he hadn't a clue as to who was behind all this. He'd mentally checked out friends and acquaintances, only to come up empty-handed. He'd even tried blaming it on Prince Rupert Stalinsky II. But it made no sense that Prince Rupert would do such a thing. He needed Adelaide alive, not dead.

Guy grinned. A sea gull had just dived down to check what was going on across the water. At first Guy had thought the gull was going to peck Addie on her bare fanny, but it flew away.

Although he had never asked, he was certain Addie thought she loved him. The island had a way of making people romantic. But things changed once they returned to civilization. He had seen the difference in how his parents had acted toward one another. Except for when she was on the island, his mother tended to be of a cold nature. No one ever suspected there were problems in the marriage. His father had once told him never to wed a woman who wasn't eager to hop in bed.

Since staying on the island, he'd actually felt like his old self. He cared for Addie and probably even loved her, but how long would that last? He had become a cold-blooded bastard. Was he capable of being the kind of husband Addie deserved? He sighed. There was only one way to find out. They needed time apart—away from the tropical Eden—to be completely sure of their feelings. When they returned to San Francisco he'd make sure they went their separate ways. Addie and Rupert would have a chance to decide their future, as well. Hell, who was he trying to fool?

He wasn't about to let Rupert put a hand on Addie. He'd make damn sure the prince was escorted out of San Francisco right away. He didn't like anyone messing with anything he considered his.

As Adelaide pushed herself across the lagoon, her thoughts were on the crime. If the perpetrator had been after Jason, then neither she nor Guy had anything to worry about, other than that the man should pay for what he had done. And if someone was after her, why hadn't they tried again? Even though she'd remained in the house since her accident, surely someone could have sneaked in. Her biggest concern was that it might be Guy the man was after. If so, he would surely be waiting for Guy's return. She didn't even want to contemplate what the consequences could be.

Guy saw Addie motion to him again, but this time she was ready to come out of the water. He stood, then waded in to meet her. Occasionally she still had trouble moving against the light undertow caused by the receding waves.

When Guy reached her, Addie was out of breath from her swim. He leaned down and swung her up in his arms.

Delighted, Addie asked, "What's this? Am I being spoiled? Not that I mind, but you usually make me walk." She laughed. "I always loved being carried." She snuggled against him.

"And what about me?"

"What do you mean?"

"Do you love me as much as you love being carried?" he asked.

Addie looked up, stunned by the question. There was an intensity in his lean, dark-skinned face she'd never seen before. She couldn't lie this time. He'd come to know her too well. "I've loved you since you were fourteen and gave me my first kiss." She could see by his expression that he was surprised at her reply. "Are you going to tell me you didn't know?" she asked nervously.

"I knew, I just didn't realize it had been since child-hood." His lips spread into an ornery grin. "Had I known sooner, I would have won my racing stallion before you left."

Addie laughed with relief. The truth hadn't changed anything between them. She kissed his wet, naked chest. Would she be pushing her luck too far if she told him she hadn't had a monthly period since leaving San Francisco? Remembering Will's attitude toward Penelope, she decided not to.

"Guy, I don't want you to think I expect anything in return," she said, trying to be act magnanimous. "I know you don't feel the same about me, but I'm content with what I have. I will always cherish the memories and know that every step I take is because of you."

Guy placed her on one of the long leaves they now used to keep the sand from caking on their wet skins. The salt and sand from the water glistened on Addie's brown, naked flesh. He was still amazed at her lack of embarrassment. Yes, the lady had changed a great deal since she'd first arrived, and he wasn't just talking about her walking. Her firm body was like an aphrodisiac. It aroused his passion with minimal effort. After this long he usually tired of a woman and was ready to move on. But it wasn't happening this time, and he had already started worrying about it.

But for now, enjoying a lusty romp wasn't one of his priorities. He was angry as hell at Addie's willingness to release him so easily. Hadn't she just said she loved him? "Will you let me go freely?" he asked irritably.

Addie ached to tell him she'd never let him go, but she was too indebted to him to do such a thing. "Yes." She looked down the beach so he couldn't tell how much it hurt to say that.

"Is that so you'll also be free and you can run to your prince?"

"Rupert? Why would you ask such a question?"

"While we're discussing freedom, I suppose we should explore all the possibilities. If I stay with you, would you let me have other women? How about Mailu? Is there any reason you can't start sharing me with her?"

Hurt and furious, Addie swung her arm around, hitting him solidly on the chest. The unexpected blow knocked Guy back onto the sand. "How dare you ask such a question?" Adelaide scrambled to her feet. "The answer to your question is an unequivocal yes! I do mind! If you want to bed Mailu, there is nothing I can do to stop it. But don't you ever, *ever* touch me again!"

Addie turned to leave, tears already streaming down her cheeks. But she didn't move fast enough. Guy grabbed hold of her ankle, knocking her back down on the sand.

"I'm sorry," Guy said, trying to catch her arms. She was too incensed to listen to him.

"How could you say such things to me when I'd just finished telling you I loved you?" Addie demanded. She began bombarding him with her fists.

Guy managed to catch a wrist. Feeling lower than the scum on the Barbary Coast, he rolled her onto her back and lay on top of her. He felt even more the guilty cad when he realized she was crying.

"I'm sorry," he repeated tenderly. "I should never have said such things."

"Then why did you?" Addie asked between sobs.

Guy rolled off her and sat up. "I don't know why I did it. I guess I was angry because one minute you said you loved me, and the next minute you were practically bidding me goodbye." He combed his hair back with his fingers. "You might have at least asked what my thoughts were on the matter."

Addie tried brushing her cheeks but only managed to get more sand on her face. Had she heard right? Was Guy saying he wanted them to stay together, or did he say it because his pride was smarting? She sat up and looked out at the lagoon. She wasn't sure what she should say. "You have never mentioned anything about love or caring." She picked up a handful of sand and watched it drain back out of the end of her closed fist. "I know you brought me to the island to help me walk again. I owe you everything, and I was trying to tell you that I would never stand in your way if you wanted to end our relationship when we return to San Francisco. I'd understand." She threw away the sand that was left in her hand, not caring that it flew back in their faces. "Actually, I thought I was being quite considerate!" she said angrily.

Was her love nothing more than gratitude? Guy reached out and pulled her onto his lap. "I'm sorry I hurt you, but I'm not ready to be put on a sacrificial altar." He brushed her nose off and kissed it. "Why don't we just wait and see what happens? The tropical heat, sand and way of life are illusions of an Eden that everyone searches for. Things will change when we return home and confinements are returned to our lives."

"You sound as if you're talking from experience."

He looked down at her and smiled. "I am, but I'm also repeating what my father told me many years ago. He was right. The native girl that I had thought I could never live without drifted into nothing but a memory. A pleasant memory, but still a memory."

"But you had to have been very young. There's a lot of difference between—"

"No, nothing has changed. It doesn't matter whether you're young or old, the effect is the same."

Addie wondered whether it was his feelings he was concerned about, or hers. "Would it be improper to ask how you feel about me in Eden?"

Guy grinned. "I can't get enough of you."

Addie climbed off his lap and stood. "Well, it's a start." Feeling alive again, she gave him a look that was every bit as ornery as his. "I'm going back to camp. Are you coming along?" She tied the cloth Mailu had given her around her hips. She'd given up the shirt. It was too hot.

Guy laughed as she strolled away, deliberately swinging her hips from side to side. He shook his head, enjoying the view. Who would have ever believed? he thought humorously. He took off after his blond goddess.

After Mailu had finished massaging Addie's legs, Addie and Guy sat comfortably relaxed in their chairs, both lost in their own thoughts.

Though loath to do so, Guy knew the time had come for them to leave the island. Adelaide's declaration of love had bothered him more than he had shown. It wasn't that he hadn't been aware of it, he'd just refused to acknowledge it. He didn't want to hurt Addie, but as with other women he'd known, it was time for him to walk away. It was time to return home, while Adelaide still expected their relationship to end once they reached San Francisco. As long as she wasn't deluding herself as to his feelings, the parting would be easier.

"Why don't we go wash off," Guy suggested.

Adelaide smiled. She'd be willing to wager a coconut that wasn't all he had on his mind.

As they strolled down the path toward the pond, Adelaide listened for the sound of the waterfall. When she finally heard the water cascading from above, she became excited. It was the same each time. It was like discovering it all over again.

When the waterfall came into view, Adelaide's excitement escalated. For the first time, there was a misty haze over the pool. It looked mysterious and very inviting. She dropped her sarong and jumped into the water. When she came back up to the surface, all she could see was the haze that surrounded her.

"Guy?" she called.

He came up beside her.

Addie laughed. "Isn't this wonderful?" When he didn't reply, she turned and looked at him. There was no humor in his lean face. Adelaide sensed trouble. In the next instant she knew why he had brought her here, but she wanted to hear him say it. She didn't have long to wait.

"Addie, it's time to go home."

It was such a simple statement. And it wasn't that she hadn't been expecting it now that she could walk. She just hadn't expected it so soon. "How are we going to do that?"

"Smoke from a fire will signal to the other island that we're ready to leave. I have a ship waiting there."

Adelaide smiled benevolently, hiding the pain that yanked at her very soul. The time of separation would soon be at hand. "So escape has been available all along. Captain Green has been waiting all these weeks?"

"No. Before we left San Francisco, I made arrangements for the *Sea Lady* to set sail for here after she berthed in San Francisco. We'll leave tomorrow for home."

Strange how she could feel Guy already withdrawing from her. He tried putting his arms around her waist, but she pushed them away. "I'd as soon you don't touch me. At least not now."

"Addie," he said softly, "you knew we'd eventually leave. Sweetheart, we'll be together on the ship."

How easily sweet words fall from his lips. "Guy, do you plan to marry me?"

"Let's just give it time."

She moved away so she would be hidden by the fog. "Then I will want separate accommodations aboard ship. Let's try to make our separation as uncomplicated as possible. When will it arrive?"

"Tonight. I'll go now and light the fire."

Adelaide heard him climbing out of the water.

"I'll see you in camp. Be sure and come straight back."

She hated the sound of concern in his voice, even though she knew it was sincere. Guy might not love her, but he cared. And maybe she should even be grateful that he was so honest. He had never pretended that their relationship was anything more than that. But it was the warm, caring, loving things that he did and said that had been her undoing. She swam to the edge of the water and pulled herself out and onto the rock. She suddenly remembered something she'd once read. Something about enjoying the good things that come into our lives as opposed to remembering the sadness of things lost.

Adelaide pulled her hair over her shoulder and twisted out the water. Loving Guy had never been easy, but what wonderful memories she would always have.

After tying on her sarong, Adelaide looked to her left at the path leading back to their camp. Disinclined to return, she glanced to her right, then straight ahead. Guy had warned her about some pigs, but apparently his nervousness stemmed from never having been around them. Other than walks along the beach for exercise, she had seen very little of the island. With their departure set for tomorrow, this would be her last opportunity to do any exploring.

Ignoring Guy's warning, Adelaide began walking. She didn't stop to question why the shrubs became denser the farther she went. She finally started making her own trail. Not being in any rush, she stopped to admire flowers and, at times, paused and looked up at the coconuts so high in the trees. Guy had explained that rats lived in the trees and ate the fruit. That was the reason so many could be found on the ground with big holes in them. Realizing she wasn't standing in the best of places, she moved on. If a coconut landed on her head ... well, she wouldn't think about it.

Occasionally Addie saw lizards of varying sizes and colors, something she would probably never have noticed if Guy hadn't pointed them out earlier. While admiring a tree she hadn't seen before, she noticed a trail of smoke coming from inside the volcano. She had seen the same thing from the ship's porthole over three months ago. It made her feel squeamish, especially after Guy had explained the eruptions. It was time to return to the camp.

Ten minutes later, Addie was busy trying to determine her whereabouts. Everything looked the same, and her position in regard to the mountain didn't seem to have changed. She could still see the smoke. Guy had said this was a small island, so she couldn't be too lost. Eventually she had to reach the ocean. Unless she had been going around in circles.

"Adelaide!"

Addie breathed a sigh of relief at hearing Guy calling her. "I'm here," she hollered back. Seeing a clearing ahead, she hurried toward it. Guy's voice was coming from that direction. "I'm here!" She waved her hand. "In the clearing!"

"Don't move! I can see you."

Addie wasn't about to move. She had just spotted a boar lying beneath a tree some twenty or thirty feet away. It looked bigger than their hut and meaner than anything she'd ever encountered before. Even its brown, wiry hair was intimidating. Possibly she had been wrong about not having to worry about them.

The beast's beady eyes never left her as he scrambled to his feet. He snorted his warning while digging ruts in the dirt with his long, curved tusks and tossing it into the air. Addie was petrified. The creature was going to charge, yet her fear was so strong she couldn't move. Then he was coming at her. She couldn't even manage a scream. At the last minute Addie snapped out of her trance and leaped to the side. The swine's fangs missed her by inches.

A hand suddenly landed on Addie's shoulder. She was shoved back, and Guy was standing where she'd been seconds ago. He was between her and the javelina. Knowing he was about to be killed, she tried shoving him away, but she only ended up being knocked to the ground. Then she saw the gun in Guy's hand. He fired a shot just as the huge animal swung around. The bullet hit him, shoving the boar to the side. He squealed in protest, straightened up and charged again. Addie stuck fingers into her ears and squeezed her eyes shut. Two shots followed before everything became quiet. When she opened her eyes, the boar lay on the ground not more than two feet from Guy.

Guy cautiously went over and gave the swine a shove with his foot. Satisfied that it was dead, he turned to Addie. "What the hell did you think you were doing?" Guy demanded.

Addie puffed out her chest. To say Guy was angry would be putting it mildly. "There's no reason for you to yell at me!"

"Do you have any idea how close you came to being killed? You were supposed to go straight back to camp," Guy reminded her. He groaned, then walked over and pulled her into his arms. "Are you all right?" he asked, his anger quickly subsiding.

"I'm fine. I'm sorry, Guy. I just wanted to see more of the island before we left."

He kissed her sweet lips. "What am I ever going to do with you? It would be a full-time job just to keep you out of trouble." He kissed her again before turning her loose. How could he stay angry at a woman with such a magnificent figure and who had the good sense to wear only a cloth around her hips? Maybe Addie had learned a lesson from this, at least until she found something else to get into. He glanced at Mailu, who was waiting on the other side of the clearing.

"Come along, sweetheart," he said to Addie. "We'd better get out of here before that big fellow's friends decide to join us."

Addie couldn't move fast enough. She knew she had made a terrible mistake that could have been fatal, and she couldn't blame Guy for having been angry at her. But hadn't he been magnificent? He had calmly stood with his gun aimed while the boar had thundered toward him. She had never witnessed such bravado.

That evening, when the captain of the *Sea Lady* and his first mate came ashore, Addie was proudly wearing one of the gowns Guy had bought in England. The lack of underclothing no longer seemed significant. And though she said nothing, the starch in the material made her skin itch. Would she ever again be comfortable wearing proper clothes?

As the men talked and Mailu prepared their meal, Addie's mind drifted back to when she'd first seen the native girl, and how shocked she had been at the woman's lack of clothing. She smiled. Earlier this evening, she'd asked Guy what was to become of Mailu. He'd said she would be picked up in the morning and taken back to her people on the main island.

Tomorrow morning, she and Guy would be taken out to the ship. Would she ever return? She looked across at her handsome lover. The three men were having a conversation about ships, but she wasn't listening. Instead, she was wondering if Guy was anxious to return home. For a short time, he had been her life. She knew as surely as she was sitting there, she would never love again. But she was certain she had something of his that he didn't know about. There was little doubt that she was with child.

Chapter Twenty

Adelaide returned to her cabin. Sharing meals with the captain of the *Sea Lady* at least broke the monotony of the trip. Guy hadn't joined them tonight. She had the impression he didn't like the way Captain Blake flirted with her. She could only cross her fingers and pray that she wasn't just fantasizing.

As she opened the door and entered her cabin, Adelaide noticed how brown the back of her hands were. Of course the light was dim, nevertheless, Eleonore was undoubtedly going to give her a lecture about how a woman's skin was supposed to be the color of alabaster. Adelaide laughed. Just wait until Eleonore discovered the color was the same from head to toe.

Wide-awake, Adelaide turned up the lantern, made herself comfortable on the bunk and picked up the book she had been reading. She missed having Guy beside her, she missed their conversations, and she especially missed their lovemaking. Keeping him at arm's distance was maddening. Hardly a night had passed that she hadn't been unable to sleep for the need of him. Why hadn't anyone ever told her that love could create such hell? Still, she firmly believed that she was doing the right thing by refusing to let him make love to her. But she wasn't playing the sacrificial lamb. Not at all. The night before they had boarded the ship, she had made up her mind that she wasn't going to give up Guy without a fight. It was a gamble, but she was not only trying to make him jealous, she was hoping that his need for her was every bit as strong as her own. Though he refused to admit it, she was convinced he loved her. He just had to acknowledge it.

She looked down at the pages and tried reading. The word *blood* suddenly glared up at her and a vision flashed through her mind. She became very still. Every nerve in her body was sending warning signals. The vision had to do with Penelope's death. Instantly she realized things had happened that she had forgotten. Penelope had collapsed to the floor, and Eleonore was kneeling beside her, trying desperately to stop the bleeding. When Penelope pulled out the knife and let it fall to the floor, Eleonore had raised her bloodstained face to look at Adelaide. There was such a look of hatred that Adelaide had been stunned. Eleonore's lips had moved, though what she'd said hadn't been loud enough to be heard. But Adelaide had had no trouble deciphering it. Her lips had formed the word *bitch*.

The book dropped from Adelaide's hand and fell to the floor. She had forgotten the incident, because at that moment she'd heard Gordon's groans and ran to help him. Other things came to mind. Just before the fight, Eleonore had yelled to Penelope, "You can't do this! We made a bargain!" What had she meant by that? And hadn't Gordon told her that Penelope had demanded a personal maid of her own choosing? That would indicate that she had wanted to bring along a friend. Yet she and Eleonore appeared to hardly know each other. Was it all an act?

Adelaide rose to her feet and paced the small cabin. What if Eleonore had been a relative instead of a friend? Maybe a sister. No, no. That was stretching it too far. They didn't even look alike.

Try as she may, Adelaide couldn't think of anything that would indicate Eleonore hated her enough to want her dead. Quite the contrary. The redhead could never do enough for her. And what possible reason would she have to want Jason or Guy dead?

Adelaide stopped and looked at the floor where the satchel she'd brought with her few things rested. She went over and opened it. Inside was a cracked mirror she'd found in the room. She raised it and took a long, hard look at herself. She ran her fingers over the scar just below her hairline, the thin one that partially divided her left eyebrow, the one on her cheek, and finally the one at the chin. That one was the deepest, but now even it was hardly noticeable. None of the scars detracted from her looks. She thought they gave her character. As a matter of fact, she could never remember looking healthier or prettier!

A hard laugh circled around the room. She had been so wrapped up in feeling sorry for herself that she'd forgotten how Guy's scar seemed to have disappeared with time. Yes, it was still visible, but it had never made him any less attractive. Her scars were much smaller. No wonder he never gave her any sympathy. There was nothing for her to have been concerned about.

Adelaide returned the mirror to the satchel. When she had last looked at herself in the mirror, it had been less than a week after the accident. The bruising and swelling hadn't had time to go away, nor had the healing begun. How long had it taken for her face to start looking normal again? Adelaide suddenly knew the answers to all her questions. Now that she could see the truth, it all seemed so simple. Her mistake had been to trust the wrong person. She knew who had caused the accident and why.

The discovery made her nauseous. She needed fresh air. She grabbed the blanket from the bed, tossed it around her shoulders and left the cabin.

As she stood by the railing, Adelaide was heartbroken over the deception she'd been so blind to. She had trusted Eleonore. She had thought of her as a friend. But she realized now that the feeling hadn't been returned.

Adelaide knew she hadn't been pretty to look at after the accident, but at some time, her face had to have started healing. So when did the healing process start erasing bruises, small cuts and swelling? Eleonore never once acknowledged the changes. Instead, she'd say, "You're smart to stay home instead of giving those wealthy people about town a chance to laugh and point behind your back." Or, "It's not so bad that you'll never walk again. I'll take care of you."

Adelaide slowly shook her head. She had been so vulnerable at that time. She had blessed Eleonore for being so supportive, when all the time the redhead was deliberately undermining her confidence.

Adelaide turned her face to the breeze. Her hair blew out of control, but she didn't care. From the first day, Eleonore couldn't say enough about Rupert. And after the wreck, she'd constantly nagged Adelaide to see him. When Addie had finally submitted due to loneliness, Eleonore had praised Rupert, and insisted that he was the only one who really cared about what happened to her. No one else cared enough to even inquire about her health. On the ship going to the island, Guy had told her Mary came by constantly and Eleonore had turned her away. Even then, she had believed Eleonore's tale, not Guy's. Eleonore had even insisted that Adelaide give serious consideration to Rupert's proposal. "He loves you, and he doesn't care about how you look." Adelaide shivered. How naive she had been. A duck sitting on a pond, just waiting to be shot. Poor Jason. She was pretty sure he had been killed just to get out of Rupert's way.

"You're going to get sick standing out here in the cold air."

Adelaide turned, and was immediately overwhelmed with love. Guy was standing near the rail behind her. It would be so easy to give in to him and put a stop to her misery, but it would solve nothing. Eventually she would end up right back where she already was. No, she had to stick to her plan. She had to keep her distance. "You're right. I guess I should go back to my cabin." She hesitated. "We missed you at supper tonight."

"I wasn't hungry. Food was brought to my cabin later."

Addie thought to tell him about Eleonore but changed her mind. She wanted him to worry about her. "Captain Blake said we'll be docking in San Francisco in three days. I'll miss the island."

Guy nodded.

"What will you do when we return?"

"I'm sure there will be plenty of work waiting. Especially after being gone so long." He looked out at the long streak of light that the moon cast over the sea. The water seemed so calm, which was more than he could say about himself. Every instinct told him to swoop her up in his arms and reclaim what had been his, but he made no effort to do so. Addie had been right. It was better to end it like this and go on with their lives.

"Guy, I've never thanked you for what you have done for me," Adelaide said softly. "I'm thanking you now. Had it not been for you, I would never have walked again. I will always love you for it." She turned and walked away.

Guy continued looking out at the sea. He caught sight of several dolphins who seemed to be following the ship. Did Adelaide really love him, or was it nothing more than gratitude? It didn't matter. As he'd told her on the island, everything would change once they had returned home. And it wasn't as if they'd never see each other again. They were related, and they were bound to run into each other on social occasions.

Thirty minutes after the boat had docked, Guy hailed a cab, then paid the driver to take Adelaide home.

"I'll send someone by in a week or so to be sure you're getting along all right."

Adelaide tried to smile and act as if their parting was unimportant, but she knew she wasn't fooling him for a minute. Was this it? "Goodbye," she whispered.

Guy helped her into the buggy. "Goodbye, Addie. I'm sorry, but I guess the time wasn't right for us." He closed the door behind her.

Guy felt a strange sadness as he watched the cab move away. This was the first time in months that Adelaide wouldn't be within reach. Had he been a fool to let her go? He hailed another cab. He'd feel differently when he arrived at his offices at the shipping line. Knowing Will's propensity for women, it was doubtful he'd be alone, or even at home. He'd wait until later to inform his cousin of their return.

When Adelaide arrived at the mansion, she was surprised at how good it felt to be home. She hadn't realized she'd missed the place. When she walked into the entry, it looked huge. Even after spending almost her entire life in this house, everything seemed strange...different than she remembered. She straightened her shoulders. There was no reason to put off what had to be done. She would tell Eleonore that she knew everything.

Adelaide hadn't taken two steps before Roger appeared. The butler's normally stoic face immediately lit up with delight. "Miss Adelaide! You've returned. You're walking!"

Within minutes, practically every servant in the house had gathered about their mistress, excited, and all talking at the same time. When Adelaide was finally able to ask Ivy where Eleonore was, she found out the lady's maid had left.

During the following week, Adelaide visited Will and Mary, enjoying their look of astonishment at seeing her walking. She also went to see the doctor. She wanted him to see that he'd been wrong, but she also needed to talk about her pregnancy. She couldn't understand why her stomach wasn't getting any larger. When she left his office, she had a hard time coming to terms with her disappointment. She wasn't pregnant. He'd said her lack of monthly periods had undoubtedly been due to the tropical climate she'd been in, something quite common with women.

Knowing she wasn't pregnant, combined with her concern that Guy hadn't come to see her, Adelaide put all her energy into finding Eleonore. For the next two weeks she had her driver take her all over San Francisco, on the chance that she might see Eleonore walking down the street. She sent servants to the finer homes in town, asking if they, or any other families they might know, had hired the petite redhead. Finally she hired detectives. But Eleonore was not to be found. It was as if she had crawled into some hole and buried herself. But Adelaide had been with Eleonore long enough to know that once the woman set her mind to something, she wouldn't quit until it had been accomplished. If Eleonore had meant her harm, they would undoubtedly meet again.

At night, Adelaide went over and over what had taken place on the island. She was even more convinced Guy loved her. She just had to figure out a way to make him acknowledge it. She had thought to go confront him with accusations of cowardice when it came to making a commitment, but there was always that little nagging voice in the back of her head that asked, what if I'm wrong? She decided to try a different approach. Perhaps Will could help her catch Eleonore, as well as Guy. She sent a message, inviting him to supper.

William sat in his office staring at the folded piece of paper in his hand. Adelaide had invited him to a private supper. The day after her return, she had stopped by to let him know she was back, and that she felt wonderful. Will could never remember having seen such a transformation. He hadn't thought it possible for her to be any more beautiful than she already was, but the woman who had stood firmly on two feet in front of him that day looked absolutely vivacious. Even her darkened skin and sun-streaked blond hair seemed to enhance her beauty. He had wondered what Guymour could possibly have done during their absence that not only had Adelaide back on her feet, but had also turned her into a self-assured, passionate woman. And when they talked, there was a warmth about her he'd never seen before. Without saying so, he knew there was no longer any hard feeling between them. They were at peace with each other.

He'd seen Guy only briefly. His cousin had also changed, but not for the better. He was serious about everything and appeared to be quite tense. He had excused himself by saying he had returned to all kinds of business problems, and he'd had little sleep. Guy had some of the top men in the shipping business working for him, and they were quite capable of handling everything. His other investments were in equally good hands, so how could there have been such serious problems? It had taken him approximately a week to figure out that Guy's problem wasn't business. He had nearly choked with laughter when he realized Guy's problem was Adelaide. For the first time in his life, Guymour Stockman was in love, and he was fighting it like hell.

Grinning, William scribbled a note. A few minutes later, he handed it to his secretary and told the man to see that it was delivered to Mrs. Stockman's house.

As Eleonore sat in the cab headed for the boarding-house where she had been living, her lips were curved into a cold smile. A wealthy lover had informed her that Adelaide Stockman had returned. He'd gone on to say that he would like to have known what she and Guymour had been up to all that time they had been gone. Especially when everyone in San Francisco knew of the gentleman's reputation with women.

The carriage stopped, and Eleonore climbed out. When Adelaide died, she wanted the bitch to know it was she who had done the killing. She'd have to think of a way to make that happen. She hurried into the boardinghouse. She had to get to the theater for tonight's play.

"As always, my dear, the meal was excellent," William complimented as he escorted Adelaide to the parlor for port. "It's too bad you never took me up on my offer of marriage. We would have made a magnificent couple."

Adelaide laughed. It had been a wonderful evening. "You never loved me, Will."

"Of course I did, but I must admit it was a bit shallow."

Adelaide sat on the love seat while William poured their drinks. "And how many women would I have had to share you with?"

"Too many," he replied lightheartedly. He handed Adelaide her drink then relaxed on the chair across from her. "Now, let's talk about why you invited me tonight."

Adelaide smiled. When had they all grown up? "I needed a confidant." She told him of her suspicions about Eleonore, and her reasoning. "Do you have any suggestions?"

Will took a deep breath then slowly let it out. "It might be wise if you move, Addie. At least for a few years, or until she can be located. Right now, you can't have her jailed, you have no proof. At the same time, your life could be in serious jeopardy. Your prince hasn't been seen, either."

"A few years? I can't do that!"

"I'm concerned about you, Addie. Perhaps I should hire protection for you. What does Guymour say about all this?"

Adelaide rolled the glass between her hands. "I haven't told him."

"Why? He has more contacts than either of us."

"Eleonore isn't the only reason I had you come tonight. I also need your help on another matter."

William finished his port and stood. "Addie, what could be more important than your safety? If you're not going to

tell Guymour, I am. Maybe he can convince you to move."
He poured himself another drink. "I don't think you're
seeing what could happen."

"Oh, come, come, William. I'm very aware of the consequences." She tugged at the neck of her green gown. She
still hadn't gotten used to wearing so many clothes. "And
I would even be willing to move if I could convince myself
that Guy doesn't love me."

Will spun around and stared at her. "You want to use me
to make him jealous," Will exclaimed.

"Why...what a wonderful idea." Adelaide tried to look
as innocent as possible.

Will quite liked the idea of getting the better of his
cousin.

"Of course, you're probably not willing. After all, the
two of you have always been as close as thieves. However,
after losing so fine a stallion because of the wager on me,
I'd think you'd jump at an opportunity to get back at him."

Will sat back down and smiled. "I've already had him
delivered to Guy's stable. What is it you have in mind?"

"I want him to think that you have replaced him in my
bed."

"It's not going to be easy. He's buried himself in work.
He hasn't been going anywhere. Would you mind telling me
the purpose of all this?"

Adelaide placed her glass on the end table, her port
barely touched. Like Guy, Will hadn't lost that Stockman
orneriness. "I love him," she said simply, "and I believe he
loves me. Will, I want to be his wife."

Will's mouth spread into a wide grin, and he gave her a
big wink. "If we start appearing at balls and dinners together, he's going to hear about it."

"Yes, yes, yes." Adelaide clapped her hands together. "I
knew you would help me."

"I just can't think of anything I would enjoy more than
to see Guy married and settled down. Maybe I should move
in here. That would make it even more convincing."

"Oh, no. I don't trust you that much."

"Maybe you're right." Will stood. "Had you planned on going to the Masterson ball to celebrate Mary's engagement?"

"Of course."

"I'll be here promptly at nine. How the tongues are going to wag." He started toward the arch doorway, stopped and turned. "Addie," he said soberly, "make sure this house is secure and all the servants know to watch for Eleonore or anything that might seem strange. I'm serious about this. I'm going to hire someone to watch the grounds, and I'll see what I can do to find Eleonore. Keep yourself safe, Addie."

Adelaide nodded. "I will, and thank you."

Two weeks later, Guy barged into the expensive waiting room graced with small gilded tables and richly colored tapestry chairs, past the clerk, down the cherry-wood-paneled hall and into the large office where Will sat talking to a client.

Seeing the thunderous look on Guy's face, William stood. "Mrs. Kelly," he said to the elderly woman as he rounded the desk, "I'll look into the case and contact you within a week." He took her by the arm and practically lifted her from the chair. "Now if you'll excuse me—" he escorted her to the door "—I have a very important meeting to attend to." He closed the door behind his client and looked at Guy, who was standing in the center of the room. "Guy. How nice of you to pay me a visit."

"What the hell do you think you are doing?"

"Me?" William asked. "I haven't any idea what you are talking about."

"Addie. Do you think you can walk into her life and take over?"

"Why should you care? You are finished with her, now it's my turn."

"The hell it is!" His word were distinct and his voice quiet and deadly. "You listen to me, Will, I want you to stop having anything to do with Adelaide, or once again we're going to get into a fight over a woman."

"Addie has told me all about what happened on the island. It was finished between the two of you. As I recall, you were the one who chose to end the relationship."

"It is because of what happened on the island that I feel responsible for her. You don't love her."

"Neither did you."

"Have you taken her to your bed?"

"Perhaps you would like to explain what this is all about. Do you plan to chase away every man she comes in contact with? I intend to marry her."

Guy walked to the door and placed his hand on the knob. "You told me that before, and nothing came of it. This time I won't allow it to happen. I'll marry her before I'd let you do it."

"Or any other man? You don't own her, Guy. You should know that she is quite capable of making up her own mind. If I didn't know better—"

Guy had left the room. Will chuckled as he rubbed the back of his neck, a gesture he'd seen his grandfather do many times. He dropped his hand to his side. His and Addie's scheme was working even faster than he'd anticipated. Guymour had looked like hell. He hoped his cousin had been suffering. He had never seen the man react in such a manner toward any woman. After all these years, Will now knew for certain that Guy had never loved Olivia. She really had lied about everything. What a fool he'd been to marry her. Now if he could only locate Eleonore, everything would be just fine.

Will collapsed in the chair his client had been sitting in. Other than the opening of the Alhambra Theater on Bush Street and the baseball game he'd actually seen played inside, 1868 had proven quite boring. Until Adelaide had stepped back into his life.

Chapter Twenty-One

"Miss Adelaide, a message was left for you."

"Thank you, Roger." Adelaide set her book of poems down and accepted the paper. "Wait a minute while I see if there will be a reply."

Dear Mrs. Stockman,
I believe I have a vase that previously resided in your home. When I purchased the piece, I thought it strange that a vase of such value would be sold in my humble shop. Only recently did a customer come in who claimed he had seen the vase in your house. I would appreciate you verifying that it is indeed yours, and naturally I would expect to be compensated for the money I gave in good faith. The vase is Chinese with hand-painted flowers. Yours truly,

Ling Woo
The House of The Dragon

"Roger, have my carriage brought around front. I have to go to a shop in Chinatown."

"I'll accompany you."

"No, no, I can go by myself."

"But Miss Adelaide, Mr. William said you shouldn't leave the house without someone to protect you."

Adelaide swallowed her laughter. It was doubtful he could whip a child. "Never mind what Mr. William said. I'll be just fine. Now go send Rita to my room. I'll want to leave as soon as I've changed my dress."

Adelaide hurried out of the room. She had discovered a good many things missing from the house since her return, including the vase that had always been in the entry. Eleonore had been very busy while she was gone. Gordon had personally brought the vase from China, and it was one of his favorite possessions. She couldn't possibly reject an opportunity to get it back.

As always, the streets of Chinatown seemed to be covered with people busily moving from place to place, carts, and shops. It took several stops before Adelaide's driver found out the location of the House of The Dragon. The entrance was in the alley, and Adelaide had to leave her carriage and walk to it.

The further Adelaide walked down the narrow alley, the more uncomfortable she became. There were less people, and many were staring. Strange odors wafted through the air, people wearing ragged clothes lay sleeping on the dirt next to walls—at least she assumed they were asleep—and she passed a deformed child begging. Since this was obviously not the safest of places to be, her steps quickened.

At last she found the shop she was looking for. As she stepped inside, she was startled when a bell attached to the door jingled. No one appeared to be inside. She nervously glanced about. The shop was cluttered with everything from copper masks to paper kites. It was difficult to move about, and the smell of incense was overwhelming.

"Hello," Addie called. No reply. She moved forward. "I'm Mrs. Stockman. Is anyone here? I've come to see the vase."

Hearing a noise, Addie turned. She was astounded to see Eleonore step from behind a curtain. She looked like a beautiful petite doll, ever innocent of any wrongdoing. "You sent the note to get me here," she gasped. She had been a fool. Roger had been right. She shouldn't have come alone.

"And it worked." Eleonore showed the knife she had been holding behind her back. "I thought it proper that you should die the same way you killed Penelope."

"What are you talking about? It was an accident. You tripped on the pillow and knocked me into her. You were there. You saw it!"

Eleonore started walking forward. "I saw you thrust the knife into her stomach!"

Adelaide moved backward and bumped into a heavy old chair. Trying to keep an eye on Eleonore, she moved around the object. There was a strange, glassy look in Eleonore's eyes that frightened her. "Why did you want me dead?" She was trying to stall until she could make it back to the door, but things kept getting in her way and Eleonore was steadily advancing.

"She was my sister. We were going to share everything. The money the old man gave her, the money we stole, your jewelry I took that you never missed—we were going to be wealthy. But Penelope decided she wanted it all. She told me no one knew her in France and she could start a new life. Especially with the large amount of funds we'd accumulated. Then, just before you came into the room, she told me she had given it all to the man she planned to marry. I was left with nothing."

Adelaide was making no progress whatsoever. Moving backward was impossible. She was bumping into everything. "But that wasn't my fault."

"Not your fault? Everything was your fault. You didn't even marry Rupert!"

Adelaide saw the big chair she'd bumped into minutes ago. She had been going in a circle! She quickly glanced about, trying to locate the door.

"You can't escape, Adelaide," Eleonore said sweetly. "I locked it."

"Why did you kill poor Jason? He couldn't have done you any harm."

"It left one less person in Rupert's way." Eleonore stopped and raised a vase. "See, I didn't lie. I've had it all along." She set it back down. "Had you married Rupert, I would have been wealthy. But you kept putting him off."

Adelaide found the door. Eleonore had told the truth about that, also. It was locked. She was becoming frantic. Eleonore had no intention of letting her leave alive. There had to be a door behind the curtain where the redhead had appeared. The knife Eleonore was carrying was still hanging to her side, so she didn't plan to attack immediately.

"Do you have any idea how much money it cost me to dress Rupert, supply a coach and pay for your outings? Then, just like Penelope, he deserted me. He took a train East and said he would never return. It's too bad you never knew what it was like to have to wait hand and foot on a woman you detest."

Adelaide stopped. Eleonore had blocked her path to the curtain. "Was Rupert your lover?" She had been left with no choice. She had to get the knife away from Eleonore.

"He was my brother." With a deep guttural growl, Eleonore charged forward, knife finally raised.

Adelaide stepped aside at the last moment, just as she had seen Guy do on the ship when he fought McCregan. With the agility of a cat, Eleonore spun around and slashed out with the knife, laughing all the time. Adelaide grabbed the hand holding the razor-sharp weapon, but Eleonore was a lot stronger than one would expect. She wrenched free.

"Now you will die, Mrs. Stockman. Maybe your lover will be so saddened I'll have to console him. Wouldn't that be ironic if I ended up with your money after all?'

Adelaide felt something cold. She wrapped her hand around it, and as Eleonore came forward, she threw it. Again she ran. She had almost reached the curtain when she heard a rumbling sound. She came to an abrupt halt. The noise was louder. Things were clattering. Then everything started moving. Adelaide tried grabbing hold of something to help stabilize her. Objects were falling in every direction. The floor was shaking so badly, she could hardly stand. She glimpsed at Eleonore, who lay on the floor. She wasn't moving.

Something crashed down beside Adelaide, barely missing her head. Knowing she was caught in an earthquake, panic gave her the strength to push forward.

Adelaide wasn't sure when the earth stopped shaking, or when she'd finally left the shop. But as her mind cleared she realized she had to have been wandering for some time. She wasn't even in Chinatown. The sight around her was unbelievable. There was destruction everywhere. Buildings had collapsed, people were on the ground moaning, while others passed by, calling someone's name. Addie fell to her knees in the middle of the cluttered road, placed her face in her hands and wept.

Having left his carriage to search on foot, Guy climbed over bricks and parts of crumpled buildings as he made his way down the narrow alley. He was furious with himself for not taking advantage of what he'd had all along. It shouldn't have taken a damn earthquake to make him realize what a fool he'd been. Why had it been so difficult to accept how much he loved Addie? Paying little attention to his hands, bleeding from a fall, he finally reached what was once the Chinese shop where Addie had gone to see about the vase. As quickly as possible, he searched through the rubble, raising small beams, tossing them to the side, praying he would find Adelaide alive. Then he saw a bloody leg. Heartsick, he uncovered the face. His worry was only momentarily alleviated when he discovered he was looking down at the body of Eleonore. Where was Addie?

After determining Adelaide was not in the immediate area, Guy hurried off to search for her. She couldn't be dead. Not now that he had come to realize she was his life.

For the first few hours, Guy refused to believe he had lost Addie forever. But as he made his way down one street after another, his fear grew in intensity. She had to be alive!

If anything had happened to Addie, it was his fault. After several days of mentally picturing Will in Addie's bed, Guy had been crazed with jealousy. He'd gone to the mansion to demand Adelaide never see his cousin again. It was Roger who had told him where the lady had gone, along with a few other things about Eleonore. Guy had been furious that no one—especially William—had informed him of what Eleonore had done. Angry and worried for Adelaide's safety, he had been on his way to Chinatown when the earthquake had struck.

Guy moved on to yet another street. Exhausted, but determined to continue his search, he looked down the way at the street strewn with rubble. Suddenly his eyes focused on a blond-haired woman slumped over. He started moving toward her, slowly at first, afraid he might be wrong. But as he drew closer, his feet moved faster. Then the woman turned and looked at him. He had found Adelaide! He ran to her.

"Are you all right?" Guy asked worriedly as he raised his beloved to her feet. "Thank the good Lord you weren't with Eleonore." He brushed aside the hair hanging in her face. "Beautiful," he whispered. He drew her quivering body into the protection of his arms and kissed the top of her head.

Adelaide clung to him.

"I was so afraid I had lost you," Guy murmured into her thick tresses.

Adelaide wasn't sure she had heard correctly. Had he said . . . her heart started beating erratically. She stepped back and looked up at him. "At least you wouldn't have had to put up with me anymore had I died." She waited anxiously to hear his reply.

"Don't ever say that," he snapped at her.

Adelaide was suddenly feeling very giddy. The worry in his eyes, the stubble from lack of shaving, and even the rent and dirt on his normally meticulous clothes mirrored the torture he had been suffering. He loved her! He truly loved her. At this moment, he was vulnerable. She had never seen him like this before and she may well never see him like this again, and she had every intention of taking advantage of it. "Have you been looking for me long?"

Seeing that Addie had regained her composure, Guy dropped his hands to his sides. "It seems like a lifetime."

"Were you worried?"

"Hell, yes, I was worried!" he stated angrily.

"Why? Because you love me?"

Guy broke out laughing, more out of relief than humor. "I think you know me too well." He wrapped his arm around her slender shoulders and started leading her away from the devastation.

"Well?"

"Well, what?"

Adelaide drew to a halt. "Are you going to say it or not?" His face grew serious, but she could see the corner of his mouth twitching with humor. He swooped her up in his arms and kissed her, a glorious kiss that she had waited so long for.

"I love you more than I ever thought possible, Miss Adelaide." Guy smiled down at her. How could any woman look such a mess and still be so beautiful? He started walking, wanting to get her away from there as quickly as possible. "I believe we should marry right away, before everyone in San Francisco starts talking about us. I can't think of a thing I'd rather do than to spend the next year in bed with you." He looked back down at her. "I've missed you," he said seriously.

"I've missed you, too," Adelaide whispered before snuggling against his hard chest, absorbing the warmth of his body and loving the feel of his arms around her. Had it been so very long ago that he'd left for England and had asked her to wait for him? Not even in her most fanciful dreams could she have ever imagined how much everything would change once Guy stepped back into her life.

Adelaide looked up at him. "Tell me again."

Guy smiled. "I love you, dirty face."

"What are you talking about?"

"You'll see when you look in a mirror." He tightened his hold on her, vowing to never let her out of his sight again.

Epilogue

There wasn't an empty pew in the cathedral as Adelaide started down the isle, her arm tucked safely beneath Mc-Cregan's. Mary's two daughters were leading the way and tossing red rose petals to the floor as they went. Her white wedding gown was a work of art. The dress and ten-foot train were covered with hand-sewn seed pearls, and received oohs and aahs from admirers as she passed by.

Adelaide would have sworn she heard Gordon laughing with delight. She looked ahead at the best man. William cut a dashing figure, but no one in the church could compare to the man standing next to him. She could still feel the thrill when her beloved had swept her up in his arms, and had covered her with sweet, wonderful kisses. He had sworn that their time apart had been nothing but hell for him, and never again would he leave her side.

Sean McCregan stepped aside and Guy took his place. Adelaide was warmed by the feel of him standing next to her. No man or woman had ever shared a greater love.

Guy leaned over and whispered in Adelaide's ear, "You're beautiful. I never knew I could love as deeply as I love you."

Addie suddenly wondered if Gordon had planned this all along. Of course not. Here she was, fantasizing again. She

thanked God for the bountiful blessing he had bestowed on
her. Guy squeezed her hand, and the preacher began the
ceremony that would make them man and wife for all eternity.

*   *   *   *   *

Harlequin® Historical

What do A.E. Maxwell, Miranda Jarrett, Merline Lovelace and Cassandra Austin have in common?

They are all part of Harlequin Historical's efforts to bring you longer books by some of your favorite authors. Pick up one of these upcoming titles today and see what a difference an historical from Harlequin can make!

REDWOOD EMPIRE—A.E. Maxwell Don't miss the reissue of this exciting saga from award-winning authors Ann and Evan Maxwell, coming in May 1995.

SPARHAWK'S LADY—Miranda Jarrett From this popular author comes another sweeping Sparhawk adventure full of passion and emotion in June 1995.

HIS LADY'S RANSOM—Merline Lovelace A gripping Medieval tale from the talented author of the Destiny's Women series that is sure to delight, coming in July 1995.

TRUSTING SARAH—Cassandra Austin And in August 1995, the long-awaited new Western by the author whose *Wait for the Sunrise* touched readers' hearts.

Watch for them this spring and summer wherever Harlequin Historicals are sold.

WOMEN OF THE WEST

Exciting stories of the old West and the women whose dreams
and passions shaped a new land!

Join Harlequin Historicals every month as we bring you
these unforgettable tales.

Don't miss any of our **Women of the West!**

If you enjoyed this book by

DELORAS SCOTT

Here's your chance to order more stories by one of Harlequin's great authors:

FLYAWAY VACATION SWEEPSTAKES!

This month's destination:
Glamorous LAS VEGAS!

Are you the lucky person who will win a free trip to Las Vegas? Think how much fun it would be to visit world-famous casinos... to see star-studded shows...to enjoy round-the-clock action in the city that never sleeps!

The facing page contains two Official Entry Coupons, as does each of the other books you received this shipment. Complete and return all the entry coupons— **the more times you enter, the better your chances of winning!**

Then keep your fingers crossed, because you'll find out by August 15, 1995 if you're the winner! If you are, here's what you'll get:

- Round-trip airfare for two to exciting Las Vegas!
- 4 days/3 nights at a fabulous first-class hotel!
- $500.00 pocket money for meals and entertainment!

Remember: The more times you enter, the better your chances of winning!*

*NO PURCHASE OR OBLIGATION TO CONTINUE BEING A SUBSCRIBER NECESSARY TO ENTER. SEE REVERSE SIDE OF ANY ENTRY COUPON FOR ALTERNATIVE MEANS OF ENTRY.

VLV KAL

FLYAWAY VACATION
SWEEPSTAKES
OFFICIAL ENTRY COUPON

This entry must be received by: JULY 30, 1995
This month's winner will be notified by: AUGUST 15, 1995
Trip must be taken between: SEPTEMBER 30, 1995-SEPTEMBER 30, 1996

YES, I want to win a vacation for two in Las Vegas. I understand the prize includes round-trip airfare, first-class hotel and $500.00 spending money. Please let me know if I'm the winner!

Name_____

Address _____ Apt. _____

| City | State/Prov. | Zip/Postal Code |

Account #_____

Return entry with invoice in reply envelope.

© 1995 HARLEQUIN ENTERPRISES LTD.   CLV KAL

FLYAWAY VACATION
SWEEPSTAKES
OFFICIAL ENTRY COUPON

This entry must be received by: JULY 30, 1995
This month's winner will be notified by: AUGUST 15, 1995
Trip must be taken between: SEPTEMBER 30, 1995-SEPTEMBER 30, 1996

YES, I want to win a vacation for two in Las Vegas. I understand the prize includes round-trip airfare, first-class hotel and $500.00 spending money. Please let me know if I'm the winner!

Name_____

Address _____ Apt. _____

| City | State/Prov. | Zip/Postal Code |

Account #_____

Return entry with invoice in reply envelope.

© 1995 HARLEQUIN ENTERPRISES LTD.   CLV KAL

OFFICIAL RULES
FLYAWAY VACATION SWEEPSTAKES 3449
NO PURCHASE OR OBLIGATION NECESSARY

Three Harlequin Reader Service 1995 shipments will contain respectively, coupons for entry into three different prize drawings, one for a trip for two to San Francisco, another for a trip for two to Las Vegas and the third for a trip for two to Orlando, Florida. To enter any drawing using an Entry Coupon, simply complete and mail according to directions.

There is no obligation to continue using the Reader Service to enter and be eligible for any prize drawing. You may also enter any drawing by hand printing the words "Flyaway Vacation," your name and address on a 3"x5" card and the destination of the prize you wish that entry to be considered for (i.e., San Francisco trip, Las Vegas trip or Orlando trip). Send your 3"x5" entries via first-class mail (limit: one entry per envelope) to: Flyaway Vacation Sweepstakes 3449, c/o Prize Destination you wish that entry to be considered for, P.O. Box 1315, Buffalo, NY 14269-1315, USA or P.O. Box 610, Fort Erie, Ontario L2A 5X3, Canada.

To be eligible for the San Francisco trip, entries must be received by 5/30/95; for the Las Vegas trip, 7/30/95; and for the Orlando trip, 9/30/95.

Winners will be determined in random drawings conducted under the supervision of D.L. Blair, Inc., an independent judging organization whose decisions are final, from among all eligible entries received for that drawing. San Francisco trip prize includes round-trip airfare for two, 4-day/3-night weekend accommodations at a first-class hotel, and $500 in cash (trip must be taken between 7/30/95—7/30/96, approximate prize value—$3,500); Las Vegas trip includes round-trip airfare for two, 4-day/3-night weekend accommodations at a first-class hotel, and $500 in cash (trip must be taken between 9/30/95—9/30/96, approximate prize value—$3,500); Orlando trip includes round-trip airfare for two, 4-day/3-night weekend accommodations at a first-class hotel, and $500 in cash (trip must be taken between 11/30/95—11/30/96, approximate prize value—$3,500). All travelers must sign and return a Release of Liability prior to travel. Hotel accommodations and flights are subject to accommodation and schedule availability. Sweepstakes open to residents of the U.S. (except Puerto Rico) and Canada, 18 years of age or older. Employees and immediate family members of Harlequin Enterprises, Ltd., D.L. Blair, Inc., their affiliates, subsidiaries and all other agencies, entities and persons connected with the use, marketing or conduct of this sweepstakes are not eligible. Odds of winning a prize are dependent upon the number of eligible entries received for that drawing. Prize drawing and winner notification for each drawing will occur no later than 15 days after deadline for entry eligibility for that drawing. Limit: one prize to an individual, family or organization. All applicable laws and regulations apply. Sweepstakes offer void wherever prohibited by law. Any litigation within the province of Quebec respecting the conduct and awarding of the prizes in this sweepstakes must be submitted to the Regies des loteries et Courses du Quebec. In order to win a prize, residents of Canada will be required to correctly answer a time-limited arithmetical skill-testing question. Value of prizes are in U.S. currency.

Winners will be obligated to sign and return an Affidavit of Eligibility within 30 days of notification. In the event of noncompliance within this time period, prize may not be awarded. If any prize or prize notification is returned as undeliverable, that prize will not be awarded. By acceptance of a prize, winner consents to use of his/her name, photograph or other likeness for purposes of advertising, trade and promotion on behalf of Harlequin Enterprises, Ltd., without further compensation, unless prohibited by law.

For the names of prizewinners (available after 12/31/95), send a self-addressed, stamped envelope to: Flyaway Vacation Sweepstakes 3449 Winners, P.O. Box 4200, Blair, NE 68009.

RVC KAL